I0784467

The Ancient Book of Magic Secrets

An exploration into being human

Rohn Bayes

First Edition

Cover photo of the White Shaman Mural generously provided by Robert E. Mace.

Thanks to Marisol Cortez, Vic Shayne and Katie Nickas for help in editing this book

Spanish translation in chapter 14 by Edith Gonzalez, contact: earthangel_2711@yahoo.com

Spring Water Press

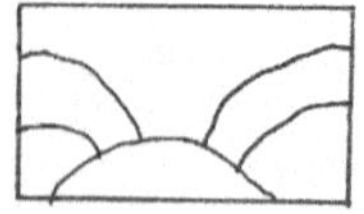

Contents

For the humans

Preface

Humans have lived on this planet for three million years, according to the paleontologists. They were our ancestors, that's where we came from. Talk about a family tree.

Homo sapiens, the species that we belong to, has been around for 300,000 years. We branched off.

In just the last six or eight thousand years, we have come up with civilization, the lifestyle that we all practice now — virtually all of us; there might be a few hunters and gatherers out there somewhere in some remote corner of the world.

Our species is venerable and ancient. We hold the wisdom of ages. We have distilled it and stored it in our cultures, we have recorded it in our poetry and our scriptures, our songs and our dances.

All this wisdom — and yet we have taken such a destructive attitude towards nature, towards our home planet. Looting the resources and having wars. Good lord!

It's like we have forgotten our wisdom. Our ancient book of magic secrets has fallen to the floor, lost in the dust. We've created technology to make us wise but we're *not* wise. How could this have happened? Let's investigate.

A brief history of humans

The first members of our hunting and gathering club appeared in Africa. They were still sleeping in the trees, judging by their long ape-like arms, but also making tools and walking around on the ground, standing upright. We call these folks Homo habilis which means 'handy man' because of the stone tools found nearby — basically chipped stones.

They also, at some point, developed the ability to create symbolic representations of things (art), to encode a mental image into vocalizations (language) and then transfer it to another person. This was not only the beginning of our stories and our sophisticated social structures but also of our strategic planning. It was this strategic planning ability that enabled us to journey forth from Africa and conquer new lands and have amazing adventures. What's over the next hill and what are the possibilities? Now we can ponder those questions.

Conquering new lands was certainly a big deal for our ancient ancestors, but having amazing adventures was also important. The adrenalin rush, the endorphin high, having something to tell a story about back at the campfire — those things were a big part of life back then. All the stories of great heroes and awesome adventures, all the sculptures of goddesses and kings, all the paintings of powerful beasts being pursued by brave, nimble hunters attest to that.

And so, we wandered out of Africa, leaving behind some of our mates on the old savannas, and traveled up to the Levant and to the Fertile

Crescent. That's where we invented agriculture and "jobs" — you know, as in something you have to do every day whether you like it or not. Then we journeyed on and discovered the great Indus River flood plain and planted the seeds of the great Indian Civilization. Then on to the fertile Yellow River in China where we founded the Shang Dynasty, the mother culture of all Asia.

Some of us turned right and moved on to Australia, learning how to sail a boat in the process. Another branch turned left and headed towards Europe and took up cave painting, while another hardy band, or many hardy bands, followed the wooly mammoths across the Bering Straits from Siberia and straight into America. Their descendants migrated all the way down the coast to Tierra del Fuego.

All the while we encountered different climates and strange foods and weird animals (some of whom wanted to eat us) and found a way of adapting to all of it. What a species!

Our cultures also adapted. The characters in our stories and the gods we believed in and the adventures they had, morphed to fit the environment we found ourselves in.

All gods and heroes have super powers. Thor has his thunder hammer, Zeus his lightening bolt, Hanuman, the monkey god, could lift mountains and leap across oceans. They all have super powers but they all have to make a sacrifice. Ask old King Gilgamesh about that, he had to walk across the desert wearing nothing but animal skins and then cross the boundless ocean. The Norse have Odin, the god who had to hang upside down on a tree until he was almost dead before he could bring the knowledge to humans in the form of the Runes. The Indigenous people of the Lower Pecos region of North America tell the story of the sacred deer who leads the ancient ancestors out of the underworld and into the first sunrise so there can be light and then is sacrificed by an arrow from the sun and becomes the morning star. Then there's Christ. Same play, different players.

This amazing cast of characters and their wild variety of expressions (that we invented), this uncanny ability we have to adapt and overcome any eventuality, this big brain that has allowed us to develop language and talk it over, turns out to be humanity's greatest strength and also its worst enemy. Now that we have conquered the whole world the question is: can we survive in the world we have conquered? Now that we have explored everyplace else the question becomes: have we explored ourselves?

Overview

The Ancient Book of Magic Secrets is comprised of eight non-fiction essays plus eight chapters of fictional narrative. My intention is to tell the story of being human from two different perspectives. It seems entirely appropriate to me, since humans are composed of two different elements — dirt and spirit. And so, the fictional account of Han and Hannah appears concurrently with the essays, or they may be a little off center. I guess that too would be appropriate for a book about humans.

Han and Hannah are on their journey. We are all on our journey. That's one thing that makes us human.

Synopsis

We begin our exploration of humans with an examination of the **City** in Chapter One. It happens to be the city where I live but it could be any city. They all start off in a similar way — a valuable resource like a river or a harbor is recognized by the ancient people, it's a divine gift from the gods in fact. They set up camp, the interlopers come, conquer the place, enslave the natives and bring civilization.

Next we dig deeper into the human experience and go inside our own body to visit the **Little People** and learn how they communicate and interact with us. Friendly bacteria have colonized our digestive tract since millions of years ago and have learned how to live symbiotically with us. They should be good at it by now.

Then we explore how all of nature communicates using the language of **Symbiosis**. Couldn't be simpler.

Thousands of years ago, before alphabetized language showed up and 1,2,3, we had pseudo-languages, marks on caves, lines and symbols designating different things. Thousands of years before that we developed spoken language. What exactly have we been talking about and who exactly have we been talking to? We peer into the mirror in this essay called **Communicating with the Gods**.

In North America, some cultures recorded their wisdom in the form of cave paintings. These were their books, their libraries and the caves were their temples. In the Lower Pecos region of west Texas and south of the border in the Mexican state of Coahuila, there are over 300 cave paintings from a culture that was alive between 2,000 and 4,000 years ago. The artists who painted these symbols, layered them with meaning, with information and with a sense of narrative (like any good artist) and many of them can still be seen today in their original colors, like the one on the cover of this book. What do they have to say?   What kind of wisdom is contained in these **Ancient Books of Magic Secrets**?

Next we examine **Money**. It may be the root of all evil but we sure are in love with it. Ever since its invention long, long ago in some city-state of old Sumer, we have certified it as the highest good and the means for attaining the highest pleasure. Well maybe not in church on Sunday morning, but in reality. It's the matrix through which so many of our activities, energies, aspirations and desires are focused.

Old King **Gilgamesh**, they say, found some wisdom and the secret to immortality. Well he got famous at least, he's in all the anthologies. As the curtain rises on this play we see the awesome walled city of Uruk where young King Gilgamesh rules with impetuous and unbridled desire.

Last but not least (because this is where it all started), is **The Nature Pool**. This one was the easiest to write because it happened in my own backyard.   Besides the frogs implored me repeatedly to tell their story as they sat half submerged in the thick watercress at night. *Trreekk ur trreekk ur do wow wow do wow wow.*

Chapter 1

The City

Our story begins where we have ended up —
in the city. For most of our history, 99.7% of it,
we lived in small groups, highly mobile, and
with little infrastructure. Now most people live
in a city. Our roaming areas of old have been
replaced with the "metropolitan area".
"Metropolitan" from the Greek *mētr-* 'mother' +
polis "city" — "mother city". We have come
home to our mother, then, and it is the city.

A brief history of cities

The first cities appeared in the Middle East
6,000 years ago. The invention of farming in the
fertile alluvial soils of the great Tigris/Euphrates
river basin provided for more and more
sophisticated living arrangements. If you didn't
have to build a new house every 2 months or
live in a cave you could really get into some
architecture. Build something that lasts, bake
bricks out of clay and stack them up like they'll
never fall down.

Hunters and gatherers were limited to small
groups because they had to be mobile enough to
move around to wherever the food was but if

one person could grow enough food for 10 people then 10 people could have other careers — merchants and priests and kings and warriors to protect the storehouses full of wheat and barley from the other kings.

At around the same time, cities started popping up along the Indus River valley at the border of present day India and Pakistan. There people had been developing an advanced culture for quite some time. Mohenjo-daro and Harappa are their names. Later, small farming communities along the Yellow River in China grew up into urban centers. The region became known as the Shang Dynasty. Later still, in the "New World" people built fantastic stone cities in the mountains that run along South America's west coast — the Inca. They terraced the mountains and grew potatoes, quinoa and corn. On the high central basin of Mexico, surrounded by volcanoes, the ancient Mexicans planted their corn and built their cities.

The urban experience flowered in human history as if it were a flower whose seeds had gestated in the rich mud of human pre-history just waiting for its chance to bloom, as if it were the great coming back together after the great dispersal of the tribes out of Africa and into every distant land.

The city: a description

And if your perspective is that the purpose of "city" is to concentrate energy and resources in a small area to facilitate human commerce, then you would be affirmed by the booming success of our cities. You can do a lot of business in a modern city, way more than you can do out there in the countryside, or in a small town or, God forbid, the empty wastelands of the desert or the snow covered mountains where no one would want to live anyway unless you were in a monastery. No, we build our cities in nice places and they are beautiful. Towers and decorated arches and elaborate edifices of all kinds line the streets and the streets themselves are painted with symbols and signs to denote the presence of some kind of central planning.

The downtown area of any healthy city, the urban core, the heart of the metropolis is thick with human commerce. Ideas and money rain down and flow like honey. Cars and people move about in a casually frantic but semi-orchestrated manner. The signs tell us what to do, traffic lights tell us when to move, parking signs tell us where to stop, lane markings remind us not to touch each other. Everything runs smoothly when you obey the rules. No questions asked. And when all the desirable land is occupied in a city we start building vertically. It's sort of like living in the trees again.

The city is a modern day forest with its tall buildings and hidden nooks (aka alleyways) populated by gnomes and dwarves (aka street people). It satisfies our primal need to be with the trees. It is from the ancient spooky woods that we derived our folk tales and the trickster; city is the birthplace of our modern day superheroes and the joker.

Cities create their own ecology and their own weather. In the canyons of the downtown, the prevailing wind is funneled into counter currents, blowing in different directions, forming eddies at the intersections and throwing the street trash around in crazy patterns. The detritus of our lifestyle, Starbucks cups, plastic bags, torn bits of cardboard and discarded Jehovah's Witness tracts become the wind trackers for the street savvy.

The canyons divert the light and create their own reflective patterns on the pavement. Written on the walls of the canyons are the names of our heroes: First National Trust and the First Baptist Church and City Hall and Hyatt Radisson.

In the urban lakes and streams there are ducks, fish and turtles. Snakes still live in the vacant lots and in undisturbed areas under the bridges. At night foxes, skunks, possums and owls come out to forage and hunt in the city. During the day pigeons and squirrels do well, as do hawks. Pigeons eat the city's garbage and hawks eat the pigeons. Raccoons roam the river banks and eat the baby ducks. Bats roost in the highway underpasses by the thousands and emerge at night to eat the bugs attracted to the street lamps. It's a biosphere.

A preface to a story

Parks are laid out too so that people don't go completely insane living without trees or the color green in their day. Here in San Antonio, Texas where I live, Travis Park is located pretty close to the heart of downtown. It features a large circular planter, twenty five feet across, right smack in the middle where the statue of a Confederate War hero used to stand until one night the city lifted it off its pedestal with a crane and hauled it away. Now there are petunias growing there and zinnias and salvia, all doing quite well in the dark soil; some green from the potato vines falling over the planter wall adds to the color scheme.

Outside the circumference of the planter is a plaza laid out with tile and brick in the shape of circles and arcs and a few metal tables with chairs and sun shades attached. Farther out are other rings marked by walkways and surrounded by trees with grassy spaces beneath them. Large oaks they are. Powerful sentinels they appear to me. Huge, biding their time quietly, supporting the sky and the four directions if you believe the old ones, the ones who were here before us. And all around, the park is squared with streets and intersections and beyond that the city's buildings rise up. When there is no more land available you build up.

Long, long ago before we could even imagine a city we lived in a city of trees in Africa and the trees were our home and our friends, offering protection and support and something to eat. We loved our tree city but we stepped out and started exploring new realms. We wanted to see what else there was to eat and what was over the next hill and if there was something better than what we already had. We left our tree houses and started traveling through the world, hunting and gathering all along the way.

So anyways, there still are hunter/gatherers among us — the street people. They are a peculiar and unique tribe who thrive in the urban habitat; they are found nowhere else. The downtown area of San Antonio used to be a rich alluvial valley lying between two spring fed rivers — the San Antonio and the San Pedro. At this point, where Travis Park sits, the two are only a quarter mile apart and this is where a lush forest grew. Fruits and nuts fell out of the trees, animals large and small found their groovy nooks and hiding spots and a gentle sloping meadow led down to the gurgling stream. The river was wide enough to harbor all sorts of aquatic life, but not so wide that you couldn't cross it easily. The old ones knew this place as Yanaguana, the 'peaceful waters'. It was a place where the hunting and gathering was good.

A story

Across the street and kitty-corner from Travis park is the Travis Park Methodist Church with its baroque old stone staircase that serves as a bed some nights for the street people. Its steeple rises into the sky with a graceful, hopeful arc and almost makes it above the parking garage across the way. It has no hope of topping St. Anthony's hotel on the right. It's from this direction that the local foot traffic comes into the park.

At one of the metal tables with chairs and sun shade attached I have stationed myself and notice a mother with two small children entering the park and walking across the grassy area. They sit down at a nearby table. She has firm control of the kids, no running around. On the other side a group of skaters congregate at the bus stop, slouched over with their boards leaning against the bench. A squadron of bike cops rolls down the street, passes them, turns off into the park and circles back around. They start talking to the skaters. Two more cops walk down the sidewalk and join in. One cop seems to be the boss, she steps back and confers with a colleague. A police car pulls up with its lights on.

What on earth is going on over there? I think to myself. There seems to be no movement or plot, no significant changes in stance amongst the central cast, nobody in handcuffs.

Around the plaza there are only two other people that I can see, one guy partly hidden by a low brick wall. He pops his head up from time to time and looks around. He is, I assume, supine. The other one is on the far side of the plaza and lost to interpretation, standing next to a table with the sun shade attached.

I notice a guy coming down the sidewalk whistling and walking with great gusto. He's smiling and looking around, he seems to be talking to the zinnias as he passes by. He strolls right through the center of the plaza and into the grassy area on the other side underneath the trees, still whistling, waving his arms. A man pulling a small piece of luggage on wheels walks by.

Hmm, wonder where he's going? Maybe to the cheap motels on lower Broadway.

I notice a woman sitting nearby, about 20 feet away, glancing from side to side. I've seen her before, on the steps of the Travis Park Methodist Church. She looked directly into my face as I walked by. Here she is again, sitting on the curb of the planter, with the zinnias and the petunias and the potato vines, one leg dangling over the edge. She has some bags on a table nearby, stuffed with personal belongings. The whistling guy is in the grassy area, the skaters are having a conversation with about 8 or 9 cops. The lady with the little kids has disappeared and I have forgotten my reading glasses. Can't really dive into my book or do much writing which is what I came to the park for, so I decide to leave.

Should I stop and talk to the lady by the planter? I ask myself, *If I don't I'll never know who she is,* I answer, *what kind of a tribe she belongs to.*

So I wheel by next to her on my bike and say, "Hi, beautiful evening, huh?"

She looks at me and says something, which I cannot now recall for the life of me, it's like it went right through my brain and out the other side, but her appearance I remember perfectly. It was composed and reserved and when her eyes settled on me I felt like she was seeing right through me somehow, like I was transparent.

"I was just sitting here noticing everything," I continued, "the trees and the sky and the lights from the building, trying to write about it."

"Are you a writer?"

"Yeah, I write."

"Have you written a book? I like books."

I see a couple of books sticking out of her bag on the table. "Yes, I've written a book." I reply, not telling her that it was self-published poetry. "What's your name?"

"Kalisa."

"How is that?" I could not believe what I had just heard. The sounds didn't join up to make anything recognizable in my mind.

"Kalisa."

"How do you spell that?"

15

"Anyway your heart desires." she says, and
looks at me. I feel like I'm staring into the face
of an idol, a mythic beauty, someone who
escaped from the movie Avatar, or appeared
magically from another kingdom somehow
somewhere very far away.
"My name's Rohn."
"Hi Rohn."
Her face is adorned like Jezebel herself, like
Shamat the temple priestess who was
commissioned by Ishtar to seduce the wild man
and bring him out of the wilderness in the epic
of Gilgamesh. Her hair was braided and coiled
like it was springing out of her head, gushing out
like water from a spring, flowing out like jungle
foliage dark and thick and hidden inside there
was her face, half lit. Her lips were slightly
parted, and painted right at the center, was a
narrow strip of iridescent pink, as if were you to
kiss her you might become enchanted and
transform into . . . something . . . who knows
what, maybe something that could feel the love
coming out of the trees and the stars above.
The light was changing and shadows were
starting to appear. I asked her if I could sit
down. She bid me welcome. We started talking.
"What are you reading?" I asked, pointing to
the books.
"Books." she said.
"Ah. Where'd you find the books?" thinking
maybe she got them off the street somewhere.
"In the library."
"Well that makes sense."
So she reads books, she looks like the Nubian
Queen of Egypt, she's all recalcitrant and
mysterious, hmm, and she's sitting here alone in

the park, apparently a street person. I was just trying to calibrate. There's a crazy guy marching around in the green space nearby, remonstrating, gesticulating, acting out. It's kind of weird. I can hear him but not really see who it is.

"What is a city anyways?" I asked gesturing at the urban landscape. She stares at me in disbelief. "Yeah, I mean look around." I scanned the surroundings with my eye, glanced up at the trees. "What is it? It's so many things. This space and those buildings and the trees in between and the towers and the skyline and how it interacts with the sky and how it makes its own weather. Did you know that? Yeah, it influences the weather, creates its own weather because of the tall buildings and all of the asphalt."

"I don't know about that."

The crazy guy seems to be getting closer or at least louder and more persistent, like he was trying to harass her. She seems to be uncomfortable about it, shifting in her seat and glancing the other way.

I told her that the trees are our friends. "Look we're surrounded by a circle of trees. Would you like to hear a poem?" I offered hopefully.

"Yes," she replied.

I pulled out my tree poem and began right in with the trees, cheers, symbiotic creatures and all that. When I got to the part about the scary monsters in the forest, a look of horror came over her face and she physically shrank away from me.

"Trees are our ancient companions but they also harbor our scariest monsters." I reassured her. "The dark spooky forest is where all our fairy tales came from. The trees and their shadows and their branches evoked shapes and faces in the minds of our ancient ancestors and they became the fairy tales and monsters and wizards and witches."

"What does 'evoke' mean?"

"That means something that causes pictures to arise in your mind."

"Like drugs?"

"No, not like drugs. Like a movie, or you read something and you imagine a character in your mind. Do you know the story of Cinderella?"

"No."

"You know about fairy tales, right?" She just looks at me.

"You don't know about fairy tales?"

"Not really," she responds quietly.

The crazy guy is marching back and forth, yelling things, like he's possessed, like he has a demon inside him, like he's trying to get inside this lady and possess her too. She's distracted. I feel embarrassed and stop talking. She puts her head down in a pose of benediction. When she raises her face a few moments later she looks directly into mine.

"That guy?" I say.

"Yes."

"Who is he?"

"I don't know."

There is a long pause in our conversation as I consider all the possible ramifications of this situation, all the potential consequences of any particular course of action. What she may be considering is not clear to me. The crazy guy seems to be out of his mind and getting closer.

"Look, I'm in kind of a bind right now, can you help me out?"

Oh, my mind says to me, *she's just trying to get some cash, working the streets.*

"Five dollars would be good."

I leave the mythic realms of Lilith and Lolita and Layla and come back to the reality of a simple panhandler working the park. I give her a dollar. She looks at it intently as if she had never seen such a thing before or maybe she was staring at the eagle and the pyramid trying to discover a deeper meaning, a connection between the two, some hidden wisdom that would give her power and ensure her safety living on the streets of the city. Who knows what she was seeing, but it was at that moment that I realized I had been released from the spell, that I was free to go on my merry way and at the same time I was disappointed that I was no longer enchanted. I rolled off.

Starbucks is open late and has a patio, so I parked my bike there and took a table, thought about what had just happened. I thought about Kalisa, that she had appeared to be in great danger and I had just left her there, abandoned her basically, took care of my own needs, maintained my own comfort zone while hers were being threatened. I couldn't stop thinking about her, that she had in fact been asking for my help, and more than just one dollar. I began to feel sad, like once again I missed my calling, didn't understand what was being asked of me. Once again I had been unable to respond, blew my chance, was too reluctant, too diffident.

I left my table at Starbucks, got on my bike and circled back around. The night was complete now; street lamps were turned on, nighthawks were on the wing, the whole menagerie of downtown characters had emerged with the darkness. I turned the corner and went past the grassy area where the crazy guy had been, but there was no sound and no crazy guy; there was no queen of the night in danger either. She was gone.

In the morning I found myself still thinking about the woman in the park, the enchantment and the eerie scene with the devil man. How did she pass the night? Where did she sleep? Is she safe? Is she still alive? My feeling of guilt for abandoning her in the face of clear and present danger had not abated. If anything it had grown more acute, but what was I to do, offer her shelter in my home, buy her a hotel room?

I got up on my bicycle and rolled downtown before the sun could get high enough to break up the clouds and beat on my head. I was working hard, pedaling down Broadway and suddenly I had the feeling that maybe last night in the park under the stars and the watchful eyes of the trees was all a Shakespeare's play, a Midsummer Night's Dream, a ruse. I remembered the look of horror on her face when I mentioned the scary monsters, how she had seemed so surprised, like she was playing the ingenue. When I gave her the dollar bill, she just stared at it like she had never seen one before. Maybe the whistling angel guy and the holy terror harasser guy were one and the same, playing both parts in a beautifully orchestrated two person ensemble and she was the simple maiden, dazed and amazed, the divine apparition, the maiden in distress. She said she had never heard a fairy tale before, is that possible? Maybe the play was all for me and my own edification and entertainment under the starry sky in the open park. The whole scene replays in my mind as I ride.

When I reach the park she's not there, of course. Now it feels whole. In the light of day I can see the stage that she sat upon and the offstage where the demon raged. I really should have given her more than one dollar.

A few words about my fair city, San Antonio

A hundred million years ago this place was underwater, as was most of Texas. It was covered by a giant inland sea that stretched from what is now the Gulf of Mexico to what is now Canada. In its waters marine life proliferated. Air breathing mosasaurs that looked like modern day dolphins leaped about, fish that looked like giant tarpons with fangs cruised stealthily through the waters, shellfish seven feet in diameter (the ammonites) lived here, and sharks and rays and giant marine reptiles. They all frolicked and fed and found their niche in this warm shallow sea.

On land, Tyrannosaurus rex ruled, one of the largest and swiftest of all the predacious dinosaurs. Giant flying lizards (pterosaurs) with their 36 foot wing spans swept through the air. It was the Cretaceous Period, the halcyon days of ferns and cycads and conifers. Leafy trees and grasses appeared, along with flowers and bees. It was warm and wet and life was blooming all over the planet.

Then the land began to shift (as it always does), the Rocky Mountains rose up in the northwest and the inland sea drained away. The shoreline formed across what is now Texas. For millions of years the animals that had thrived in the warm nutrient rich waters, deposited their calcified skeletons on the ocean floor when they died. From these deposits, limestone formed as the pressure of the water slowly hardened and compressed them. The shoreline oscillated back and forth due to the seismic activity, covering and uncovering the limestone and during periods of exposure, the limestone weathered and became full of holes. Sediment from the mountains to the north buried them and the sea returned, adding more layers of limestone until ultimately there were hundreds of feet of porous limestone separated by several layers of impermeable sediment, kind of like a layered birthday cake. All this was pushed underground and became broken and tilted. Fault lines and fractures became entrances into the birthday cake and it began to function as a huge underground reservoir, As rainwater entered from the higher elevations the pressure caused the water to emerge from fissures in the lower elevations — artesian springs. These springs are the sites, not surprisingly, of the earliest human habitation in this region.

The first people to find the spring that would eventually become San Antonio were nomads. They were following the game animals and the seasons in pursuit of food and a comfortable lifestyle. It was not surprising, then, that the mastodons or the bison or whatever giant herbivore they were hunting, would lead them here. And when they saw the spring for the first time — beautiful, clear water gushing out of the earth, forming a pleasant river and a gentle river valley with groovy nooks and niches for all kinds of plants and animals to live in — they were certainly impressed — *'wow this is the best place ever!'*   Friendly trees growing along its banks with fruit hanging down from the branches. Reeds growing in the shallow water to weave baskets and mats.   Fish, frogs and turtles. Alligators. Water birds. Snakes. Fig trees. It was a virtual 'Garden of Eden' where everything that was needed was provided. Food, fuel, shelter, wood, flint to make stone tools, everything was there, just pick it up and use it.

It's not hard to imagine the enchantment that this place had on those first people. It's not hard to imagine where the idea of the Garden of Eden came from, it's in almost all the cultures after all.   Of course the natives didn't call it the Garden of Eden, they called it Yanaguana — 'peaceful waters', at least that's the Spanish pronunciation of it. Originally it was closer to Ya Gna Wena, meaning 'place where I rest' and was applied to the entire region of springs and streams in this area.

The Spanish, of course, changed everything, not only the language but the culture. Native words were replaced with Spanish words, the native culture was replaced with the Spanish culture and slowly the memory of those ancient days was erased. Except in the minds of the descendants of those people (who still live around here) and a few notations in the history books, it's as if that time never existed.

For these early humans living in a direct intimate connection with nature — appreciation and reciprocity would have been a natural response to what they felt and observed around them: Father Sky feeding Mother Earth with the beautiful rain and Mother Earth feeding all the creatures here below with her beautiful spring water. This was the simplest and the first religion: Father Sky above and Mother Earth below 'and in between the people living with their friends the trees.

And when all was in balance in their gentle river valley, when there was an abundance of food, when they were blessed by Father Sky and Mother Earth then Yanaguana was filled with gifts from the gods. They knew it too and received it well; they would tell their stories of the creation of the world and of the first people — their revered ancestors, those who came from before and showed the way. They would tell the stories of their adventures and what they had learned about how to live.

This went on for about 20,000 years, more or less, according to my reckoning. There were good times and there were bad times, there was drought, there was flood, there was sickness, there was occasional conflict, but the tradition was that whenever you came to the spring, you laid down your weapons and entered with an attitude of appreciation for Mother Earth and her life-giving waters.

By the time the Spanish explorers showed up, a thousand generations had lived and died here, leaving virtually no mark to show that they had ever existed except for the stories they told their kids growing up around the campfire. But the

Spaniards saw this world very differently. These were no gifts from the gods, these were resources to be used. And they did use them, they built an outpost to guard their empire's far flung frontier right in the middle of Yanagua. As an added bonus there were lots of friendly, pagan savages around to enslave (and save). Somebody's got to dig these limestone blocks out of the ground and pile them up to make a church and a fort. Somebody's got to dig the irrigation ditches and hoe the fields.

So, that's how it started — the city I mean. Once "civilization" was established, most of the native people wandered away or intermarried into the new status quo and it became a Spanish colonial town. No gold or silver was discovered but at least they got to name everything after Catholic saints and build stuff for the king of Spain and save the lost pagan souls for the glory of God and the pope who also had an interest in the affair.

And so the central plaza was laid out and the church was built and the center of the city was created as was the Spanish custom and decree. Now we have a gathering place, now we have a heart of the city. Geographically, architecturally and spiritually the town grew from the central plaza like a flower opening up, in every direction and in every manner.

San Antonio became a meshing place and a crossroads. Immigrants arrived, Germans and Poles and Italians. People from the Canary Islands were among the first to come; they built the first residential area (la villita) with houses for normal people, not just soldiers and missionaries. There were ex-slaves, lots of

Mexicans (well at least there were a lot of Mexicans after there was a Mexico in 1810), some half breeds who no one knew exactly what they were, the enterprising American immigrants, the frontiersmen who showed up in town to re-provision, the farmers to buy seed, the ranchers to sell horses. El Camino Real "The king's highway" passed through here on its way to Natchitoches, carrying the ox carts and wagons from Mexico City.

The low water crossings, where people met and had conversation, became energy nodes. Houses sprang up, neighborhoods, markets, restaurants, bars — they were building a city. Out along San Pedro Creek where some of those neighborhoods appeared, an inscription has been chiseled into the rock wall bordering the creek: "*De Todos Caminos Somos Todos Uno*". It literally means "*From all roads we are all one*".

Today, from the central plaza, now called Main Plaza, you can see the history of the whole town displayed in a chronological sequence that goes way back to 1731. First they built the Cathedral and it was the largest building in town. People prayed there and put their fate in the hands of God. Then they put up the courthouse, larger still, and here the judges were appointed and adjudicated the affairs of the day, determined right from wrong and who owned what and who owned whom. Then they built City Hall, larger still, to demonstrate who had the real power — the politicians. Then they put up the bank which financed everything and gave credit where credit was due. Then the hotels showed up, which are bigger still, dozens of stories high, dotting the downtown, displaying their pre-eminence as the primary economic and cultural engine of the city.

From our origins in the deep Paleolithic past, when people came as pilgrims to visit Mother Nature at the springs, to the present day with the famous River Walk and Henry B. Gonzalez Convention Center, the pilgrims still come. They come to sell steel pipe to municipalities at the business fair and then sit by the peaceful river and drink the medicine waters (now called a margarita). Same as it ever was.

The first cities

The story of San Antonio is essentially the story of all the cities that arose in all the other lands throughout history.

For the people of the Middle East 6,000 years ago, the fertile alluvial soils of the great Tigris Euphrates river basin were a blessing from Enki, the water god, and they responded by inventing farming. Being able to plant and harvest food in the same place enabled more sophistication in their living arrangements. If you didn't have to rebuild your house every 2 months or live in a cave you could really get into some architecture, build something that lasts, bake bricks made out of clay and stack them up like they'll never fall down.

In the beginning people lived in small towns, farming communities really, and had pretty much everything they needed — regular crops coming in, clay pots to store it in (which they never had before, new innovation) woven clothes, bronze knives, domesticated animals which they could use for milk, wool, meat or transportation — multipurpose.   What could possibly be missing in their lives?

The urban experience is what was missing. The sense of excitement that people felt when encountering the new and the unknown. Meeting strange people from exotic places, the throngs, the fairs, the temples, the wares, the news, the entertainment, unbelievable economic opportunity — that's what the city offered.

Uruk and Ur, Eridu and Kish and Nippur and Larsa were the names of those first cities in the Fertile Crescent and their politics, like all the early cities, were about a king and a priest or more likely a priest/king ruling with a mandate from heaven. The temple was at the center of the city and whichever god or goddess it was that gave benefaction to the king was worshipped there, next to the king's palace. There was no separation of church and state, they were concomitant. In fact this tradition endured all the way through medieval Europe — pope and king ruled the world.

The role of the king/priest was common all over the ancient world, and the urban equivalent of the ancient shamanic traditions of the tribe. There was always that person who could bring the message from the gods. The shaman was a proto-king, in that sense, for he offered practical advice for the hunters and for the gatherers and they revered him for it. Eventually, as things got urbanized, and he or she (don't mean to be gender specific here), got a little more respect and a little more power, they ended up becoming what we know today as a king or a queen. Totally my theory but it's possible.

Not long after Uruk and Ur got started, the Indus river civilization arose, possibly a spin off. It sponsored two major urban centers, archaeologists call them Harappa and Mohenjo-daro. **Sitting astride the great flood plain of** the Indus River and its tributaries and the now dry Ghaggar-Hakra, the area of urbanization of these two cities and the others that sprang up was far larger than the Mesopotamian region. To the west, the Sulaiman mountains rose up, to the east the vast Thar Desert and to the north the mighty Himalayas that gave birth to the Indus river that flowed down through the cities to the Arabian sea. Nestled within this idyllic region the great culture of India was born along with the Hindu religion. Harappa and Mohenjo-daro, each, contained as many as 100,000 people, the surrounding cities and settlements an estimated 4-6 million more people. It flourished between 2600 BC and 1300 BC, then declined and disappeared. No one is quite sure why. Things like that happen.

The ancient ancestors of the Chinese started growing rice in the Yellow River valley and its tributaries as far back as 6,000 BC. According to the official myth of the Shang Dynasty this is how it happened. The Emperor's wife, Jiandi, swallowed an egg dropped by a black bird and subsequently gave birth to Xie, who, along with his pal, Yu the Great, battled the massive flood that swallowed up the entire Yellow River valley for two generations. In return for their heroics, they were granted the skills of agriculture and irrigation, and farming began in the rich soils of the Yellow River valley. By 1700 BC they were building cities and having dynasties, writing poetry on turtle shells and growing lots of rice in the raised beds and irrigated fields, just like Xie and Yu showed them.

In the "New World" farming was invented much later. Potatoes, beans, cacao, cotton and corn began to be farmed in ancient Peru. Agricultural communities emerged in the Andean highlands and on the Pacific coast around 2,000 BC. The most successful farming communities started becoming cities and by the time the Christian era rolled around (not BC anymore) true cities like El Paraiso along the Pacific coast and La Galgada and Kotosh up in the Andean mountains appeared. In the high plains, the Bolivian altiplano, Tiwanaku, the ceremonial center was built, with a temple complex where 30,000 devout adherents worshipped Viracocha the creator deity.

In the well watered coastal valleys of Mexico, twenty five hundred miles to the northwest, crops like corn, squash, beans and chilis were being farmed by 2500 BC and by 1200 BC the first cities were built there by the Olmecs: Tres Zapotes and La Venta on the Gulf coast. Then came Monte Alban built by the Zapotecs in the valley of Oaxaca on the other side of the mountains, and then Tula, the home of Quetzalcoatl, Teotihuacan, the City of the Gods with its huge pyramid and equally huge population, around 150,000 people and finally Tenochitlan, the capital of the Aztecs, built on the islands of Lake Texcoco where the eagle landed on the cactus and ate the snake (as portrayed on the Mexican flag).

All these cities sprang up in different parts of the world, on different continents, with different climates and different landscapes, different religions and different cultures. They were separated by vast distances and didn't know of each other's existence, except for the Fertile Crescent people and the Indus River people who traded with each other, and the Andean people and the people of the central valleys of Mexico who shared knowledge with each other but otherwise they were isolated and developed independently. Even so they created a common experience, the urban experience, as if the scattered tribes wanted to join back together again after their dispersal from Africa and form a more perfect union.

And come together they did, they formed a great many clever if not perfect unions that accommodated many thousands of people, not just a few dozen. They built cities and lived the urban life style.

In that sense the city is a celebration, a natural exuberance, a collaboration and a confirmation. *'Yes! This is how we do it. We plant wheat and barely on the muddy flood plain of the river valley and it's sure to grow. Wheat and barley for everybody! We can make bread. We can make beer, we can live here all year!'*

That's how it was in the old Fertile Crescent. They were very successful with it. Now cities are everywhere and most people are city dwellers. It's not just the exuberance and energy, the rush of city life, it's also the pride we feel in our huge buildings soaring above us and in our vaulted expressways arching through the sky, buzzing with cars moving at a high rate of speed. But wait a minute — the faster we travel, the farther we have to go, so . . . hmm, we don't get there any faster than we did when we were riding a horse.

Well, that's the subject for another time. Right now let me introduce you to Han and Hannah. They live in the city.

Chapter 2

Han and Hannah

It's dawn. Han awakens to the sound of birds chirping vociferously overhead, a car whooshing by in the distance. He opens his eyes and looks up into the branches of a tree. The sky, broken into a hundred jagged pieces by the tangled branches, reminds him of a puzzle, something you have to put together.

Water is splashing nearby and he turns his head. There is a waterfall and a garden and a pool.

He closes his eyes and replays the dream he just woke up from, the one that has come to him so many times before . . *running through the forest hunched over . . . I'm carrying something . . . I'm wounded . . . they're chasing me . . . two maybe three, maybe more . . . they're close . . . I can hear their feet pounding, the forest is thick . . . I'm running as fast as I can . . . stumbling over vines crashing through bushes . . . I don't know where I am, I don't know where they are . . . I'm afraid . . . the clearing . . . the pond . . . dive in . . .*

Han blinks and opens his eyes as wide as he can . . . *I need coffee* . . . parts the mosquito net and emerges into the world, stands upright, still blinking.

"God. I need coffee." He walks over to the pool and dives in. The sudden rush of cold water narrows the capillaries of his circulatory system shunting blood flow from his extremities to the core functions — heart, lungs, brain, A primal awareness takes over, his memory function purges. His recurring dream, along with all the other recent events, are released from temporary memory storage into the ebbs and tides of the synaptic flow. The only thing remaining in his mind is the feeling of the water flowing over his body.

When he surfaces, he floats on his back and looks at the sky, grayish-blue. From somewhere above the clouds there is the sound of an airplane passing over . . . *full of people . . . looking out the window at the clouds . . . wondering what's down there . . .* The space between himself and the people in the plane is a thing, it seems to him, a tangible thing with dimensions and qualities. In his mind he sends out a filament of awareness to the people in the plane and climbs out of the water.

It's still warm enough to dry off in the air, although signs of autumn are starting to appear. Arms outstretched like a cormorant drying his wings in the sun, he notices the leaves curling on the branches of the big pecan tree standing in front of him . . . *the winds have shifted . . . the air smells different . . .* He has been monitoring wind direction and speed all summer. The changes had been unremarkable, but now they are apparent and he can sense the shift.

The backyard where he's standing is enclosed by a grey cedar fence and the back porch of a house.   He climbs the steps of the porch and enters a small, sparsely appointed kitchen. Melon colored walls greet him; painted that color when he moved in.   His therapist at the time told him it was a calming color.

. . . . three tablespoons of dark Guatemalan grind . . . heat the water . . . The coming winter enters his mind and those who lived here before all the people and houses arrived.

. . . poor varmints . . . opossums, raccoons, snakes, hawks, coyotes . . . the ones that survived . . . why do we have to extirpate everything that was here before we showed up? . . .

When the water starts to boil he lifts the kettle and pours the steaming water over the coffee grounds and down through the filter into the cup *. . . like lawn mowing . . . like lawn mowing is genocide for the bug people . . . nowhere to live . . . everything chopped down . . .* and carries it outside with a bowl of granola he has filled with almond milk.

The waterfall spills into the pool from where it comes out of the garden.   The garden is filled with watercress growing in profusion.   Han bows as he approaches and inspects the small green leaves.

"It's a goodun, it's a goodun." he says and sits down at a plastic patio table under the Pecan tree and begins to partake of his breakfast.   Han is pretty much at home under the Pecan tree in the backyard; this is where he camps out if the weather permits.   This is where he spends his nights and much of his days.

The camp is composed of one plastic patio table, three plastic patio chairs and a futon under the mosquito netting beneath the pecan tree. A few wooden crates with books and journals jammed into them sit nearby. A bike is leaning against the pecan tree. It's a fast looking bike with lots of gears on it and panniers for carrying stuff.

When the granola is finished and most of the coffee, he leans back in the plastic patio chair to grab his guitar. For an instant he can see the sky through the branches of the pecan tree . . . *why do people invade and conquer other people? . . . why don't they just stay home, chill out? . . . that would be nice . . .* He leans forward with guitar in hand and starts to strum, different chords one after the other. When he finds the right one, the one that calms his mind, he plays it over and over again. Below the waterfall, he can see fish moving in the dark water.

✳✳✳✳✳✳✳✳✳✳✳

Hannah is putting on her makeup, a little mascara, a hint of eyeliner, a light touch of 'Rouge Effete' lipstick by Maybelline. Her costume for the day is an orange and black kimono with a long skirted dress underneath.

. . . I'm still pretty . . . is the thought that goes through her mind as she fits the top of the lipstick back on the tube and places it on the shelf . . . *I'm cute . . .* She turns and exits the bathroom.

Her one bedroom apartment is shared with Chrissy who sleeps on the couch and stuffs her bedding behind it each morning so it looks like an actual living room during the day. That was one of the requirements Hannah had insisted on

36

when she moved in, that and labeling the food.
The truth is, she needed help with the rent and
Chrissy was the least possibly disastrous
roommate she could find.   Screwing on the
toothpaste would just have to wait until another
phase of life.

That's the way she sees it, life as phases that
come and go. . . . *things happen, they bring
whatever they bring and then their time passes
and they move on, another phase begins . . . it's
always been like that . . .* she thinks to herself
and grabs her purse,

"Chrissie, I'm leaving. Hope you have a great
day."

"Hey girl. You too. Do you know what time it
is?"

"Six."

"In the morning?"

Hannah laughs. . . . *at least she's funny . . .*
"You're funny."

"I know I am."

"Bye."

"Peace and love. Turn out the light."

She gets in her car, a 12 year old Volvo which
she bought because it had an excellent safety
rating and she thought it might be good in
crashes, starts the engine, turns on the radio and
lights a joint.   Downtempo psy-chill comes
pouring out of the speakers, she leans back in
the seat and closes her eyes, inhales deeply.
When she opens them again, she sees the
parking lot of the Tanglewood Apartments with
each car in its allotted space and it appears to her
as something romantic; all those cars spending
time with each other in adjoining slots.   She
pulls out of the parking lot and turns west

towards downtown with a smile on her face. The music touches her soul and soothes her spirit. The general angst of modern society dulls and dims in her brain. Some traffic lights are red and some are green.

Tuesdays through Saturdays she arrives before 7 am to set the machine in motion. She knows in her heart of hearts that if she doesn't wind it up, it won't go. . . . *it's always been like that . . .* she thinks, unlocking the front door of the Green Coconut and stepping inside. She flicks on the lights and goes straight to the computer. It boots up and she loads Spotify; 1940's dance music fills the restaurant: Bing Crosby and Dean Martin singing love songs.

The routine begins: first grinding coffee for the Daily Joe and then moving to the prep area, setting it up. She pulls the bakery items out of the fridge and loads them into the glass display case by the register, taking inventory at the same time: twelve blue berry muffins, five peanut butter cookies, two ginger snaps, one remaining piece of coconut chocolate cake, the Green Coconut's signature dessert as advertised on the top of the menu — "Chococo". Suzanne makes it twice a week in her oven at home.

Next stop and her favorite part of the business, the fresh veggies consigned from local gardeners. There are radishes, okra, sweet corn, string beans and some home made honey on display. There are baskets of squash and pumpkins sitting on the shelves decorated with straw and a doll-like stuffed scarecrow. A refrigerated case with large glass doors holds yogurt and kombucha and two different kinds of sprouts. It's her genius idea to create a farmer's market inside the restaurant. By quarter to 8 she's got the place organized and ready for Suzanne and Anand to arrive. The only thing unsettled is her mind, vague worries pass over her like clouds on a stormy night. . . . *fuck! the payroll . . . when am I going to do that . . . and the taxes, oh god . . . the engine light, how bad can it be . . . Jesus . . . Jesus . . .*

****

"It's a food desert — no food for the butterflies, the birds, the bugs." Han mutters as he washes out his coffee cup and bowl at the sink.
"Everyone wants a lawn that looks like they're living in merry old England or a golf course. Gees. Where can the poor little bugs go?"
He returns to the backyard with a pair of scissors in hand and starts topping the watercress and stuffing the small succulent leaves into plastic bags. After each one is filled, he seals it and lays it on the rim of the bog garden. After he's filled six bags he stops and looks at them. "Hey you guys are beautiful."
Sometimes he tells people that his bike was a Comanche war pony in a previous life. It's just a joke, but in a strange way he kind of believes it. He goes on adventures around town with his bike and imagines the Comanches on their raiding parties back in the 19th century. He has revelations while he's riding his bike, the angel whispers in his ear and tells him things. The angel told him about the changing and how to read the sky, but that part of the story has yet to be told.

39

He loads the watercress into the panniers, straps on his helmet, slips on his sunglasses and gets up on his bike . . . *economic development justifies everything, even war . . . gees . . .* finds the toe clip, takes a stroke, finds the other toe clip, brakes down the driveway and into the road. The sky is one huge cloud broken by a few dull blue streaks. Stroke stroke, corner, stroke stroke . . . *what we need is to be reminded . . . of everything we've forgotten . . . we've forgotten everything . . .* and he's gone.

Once on Broadway the traffic picks up and things get serious fast, he brings his focus in. Breathing and listening for cars occupies his mind. He hammers down on the pedals, picking up speed, picking the lanes where the traffic is clear. His brain is processing the visual data, scan and compute, no extraneous thoughts. He lines up the next move, setting the approach, scoping out the intersection and moving through it with a minimal amount of braking. He re-checks the scanner: angle of the sun, light wind from the northeast, traffic medium, no cop cars . . . *free and clear . . .*

Everything looks fairly normal from long range but when the motorists get closer they begin to notice anomalies, the head scarf flying from his bike helmet like a flag, the open shirt flapping in the wind like a superman's cape, the 8 day old beard, the head lowered and into the wind, looking around with quick short movements like a heron hunting for minnows.

"Whoop! Whoop!" exclaims Han . . . *it's not illegal to yell, it is a good thing . . .*

The motorists don't hear him. In fact in a few blocks they will have resumed their familiar thought patterns and the familiar scene of cars in the road will have replaced the sight of the lone bicycle rider with the waving flags racing down the street. By the time they reach their destination and get out of their car only remnants of the memory will remain, a subliminal image casting a shadow onto the next conversation, perhaps, or the next encounter or the next explanation. Han is equally unaware of the motorists or their thoughts. He's getting off on his endorphin high.

He turns onto a side street. Manicured shade trees, lawns and respectable houses with ranch style roof lines sit beside the road. A squirrel, darts into the middle of the street and stops there, staring at him. It shows no intention of moving, so he cuts behind it at the last instant, the squirrel sprints to the other side. . . . *animals live close to the edge, every day . . . could be a hawk, could be a car, could be an owl . . . could be a bike . . .*

A couple of turns and the road becomes wider, lined with shops serving the neighborhood. He brakes, exits the street onto the sidewalk, dismounts and locks his bike to a street sign at the entrance to the Green Coconut.

Inside the shop, the Saturday morning brunch rush is starting up. People are milling around the front counter holding their menus. A few people are seated at a long table, talking and gesturing with their plates of food and lattes at hand, plastic tumblers with orange juice for the kids. The table is made out of pieces of mesquite wood milled down and sanded, spliced together and arranged in a continuous slab down past the open grill, almost to the backroom where more tables and chairs are gathered. That was Suzanne's boyfriend's project. Behind the counter Suzanne is gesturing to a young couple ordering brunch. Behind the grill, the aproned Ananda is scooping and frying, her wing-mates, Daniel and Sophie are filling orders, grabbing tags, they got a system. The brick walls and the open beamed ceiling lend a feeling of good old American ingenuity and the efficient flow of labor lends a feeling of good old American entrepreneurism.

"Number 12." announces a woman with a pixie cut and wearing a brightly colored kimono. She's tall and seemingly in charge of the place; her eyes are on the whole crowd, the flow of people. She moves out into the dining room and Han makes his way into position to intercept her.

"Hullo are you the manager?"

"Yes I believe so." responds Hannah.

"My name is Han, Han Solo and I grow these bountiful organic aquaponic water cress and I thought maybe you'd like to feature some in your premium salad entree here." She looks at him quizzically.

"Local is very popular with diners as you well know." he adds with a smile. "It shows that you support your local community and are into high quality organic produce."

"Yeah, well we're not quite organic around here you know."

"Oh I know."

"So, these have been on your bike?"

"Oh yes. Fresh air and sunshine that's all they've ever known all their lives. They're very high in vitamins A and C and foliacal acid.

"How much?" she picks up one of the bags.

"Free for you m'lady. Here isn't it four?" hands her three more bags. "It's good for mental energy and mental clarity." points to his head. "See you tonight?" She looks at him with a bemused expression. He leaves.

****

Massive buildings surround him and tower over him. . . . *it creates a force field, an aura,. . . energy message . . . massage . . . it radiates . . . am i ok, are you ok? . . . the radiation exposure to so many transmitters creates a peculiar signature in the human brain . . . the urban experience . . . So* goes Han's soliloquy as he rides through the downtown, observing and reflecting. It is for this reason that he takes the long way to Joe Joe's.

He sees a street person sitting alone at a bus stop in quiet repose, collecting messages perhaps from their familiar spirits. Around the corner the Witnesses display their religious tracts: "God has a purpose for your life, would you like to know?" says the sign. Business is slow. The buildings rise into the sky like giant trees.

"Street people are not homeless, where they sleep at night is their home, under a bridge or on some cardboard." says Han in a declarative voice. He bypasses the congestion at the intersection, jumps the sidewalk, cuts through the alley and crosses the street, rolls through the park. "The natural world, as natural as it gets here in the park. Right here in the park. Downtown urban center. The variety of species. Humans of course ubiquitous. Share the space with oaks and grasses and flowers and birds and

43

squirrels.   We have created an artificial
symbiotic system . . . humans create trash,
pigeons eat the trash, hawks eat the pigeons."
Han has stopped in the middle of the park and is
shooting video with his camera phone, panning
the downtown scene while adding his
commentary.

****

Joe Joe's Cafe sits at the corner of Jones and
Avenue B.   It has two monkeys on the roof.
They're made out of plywood and seem to be
conjoined or engaged in a mutual project,
something not made clear by the sign.
Speculation about the nature of the project fuels
part of the myth behind Joe Joe's.
Han enters carrying the last two bags of home
grown watercress.   It's warm and smells like
coffee.
"Omar, my brother." calls out Han.
"I'm almost out." responds Omar.
"Be it so." he replies and hands him the last
two bags of watercress.
"Wow. Nice."
"Yes. It is."
"I am amazed at the size of this watercress."
"It's a secret process."
"No doubt."
"Can I take your order?" says the barista tilting
her head as she moves into position behind the
register.
"Could I order something?"
"Anything."
"I would like to order world peace and
cooperation. Share everything, nobody owns the

44

world.   Everything together like in the Coke commercials And a machalatta."

"What's that?" asks the barista raising her eyebrows.

"A chai latte with a machatta."

"Oh, ok." she responds with a puzzled smile and runs his card.

Omar laughs.

"You always got to do that."

"Omar my friend." Han grabs his shoulder, "When are we going to start the revolution?"

"I think we already started it the minute you walked in the door."

"So be it. My kingdom is not of this world. It is of another realm. Thereupon which I cannot tell you much because I don't know yet. Oh sorry I was prophesying for a minute there. Where am I? Ah Joe Joe's." he looks around "Omar!"

Omar laughs.

Han raves on, "People need to wake up. We live on a planet. It's a big round ball. It's suspended in cold dark empty endless space. We're part of the human race" He says in a slightly too loud of a voice for a public space. "We're part of the biosphere and we came from here." he concludes with an exaggerated gesture.

"I agree with you." says Omar and glances at Han as he works on an order behind the bar.

"Thank you." Han wanders over to the middle of the cafe and sits down at a table, opens his belly pouch. The diffuse light falling through the large glass windows that make up the entire eastern wall of the cafe, illuminates his face without leaving a shadow.   Inside, lots of shadows play back and forth.

. . . everybody is cautious . . . wearing their daytime costume . . . they want to be seen but they don't want you to know who they are . . . he thinks as he searches his belly pouch. *. . . it's all fake . . . fake identities, fake jewelry . . . only the light is real . . . bouncing off everyone . . . shining on everyone . . . some wear striped shirts and blue jeans . . . some are button down . . . look at that skirt it's whatever you feel . . . the flowy robe guy . . . right . . . nobody knows who they really are . . . we're all just getting dressed up . . .*

His 'machalatta' arrives, a drink that is not on the menu and exists only in his creative imagination of the moment and of the barista. She smiles as she hands it to him.

"Thank you so much." Han accepts the cup and looks at it reverently. *. . . the first hit is always the best . . .* and hits it, caffeine *. . . she's coming over tonight . . . i think . . .*

****

Hannah is looking at herself in the wall mirror and dusting some rouge on her cheeks. *. . . hmm this is interesting, he doesn't know who he is but who does? . . . could be fun . . . I want to know what he knows, what he wants to know . . . what does he want to know? what I know? . . . lipstick or no lipstick? no, gees look at my hair, who cares, he doesn't even comb his . . . scruffy guy . . . hmm . . .*

"Chrissy, what do you think about this?" she primps for her roommate, denim jacket, flowered blouse, black tights, puma running shoes.

46

"Acceptable."

"What?" she purses her lips and pouts.

"Depends on what you're trying to do."

"Trying to figure it out."

"Then go with that."

"Thanks."

Jacket billowing and legs wrapped tightly around her bike, she cruises through the suburban streets. The sky is dimming and she switches on her light. She slows, curls up the driveway, steps off her bike and walks it into the backyard.

"Hi Han Han." she says and lays down her bike. She goes over to him and gives him a kiss on the lips.

"Hi Hannah."

"Here check this out. I made a pipe." She shrugs off her backpack and opens it.

"Cool. How'd you do that?"

"Easy I just drilled it out with my handy dandy drill bit, reamed it out with my little reamer tool, sanded it off with some sandpaper. Voila. Oak."

"Hmm, how does it work?"

"Like this." She loads it up with ground up herb from a pouch.

"Yeah but won't it burn up?"

"Nope." She lights it up. "Taste it." she hands it to Han. "It's not marijuana."

"What is it?"

"It's not marijuana, it's a smoking mixture a friend made. Supposed to calm you down."

"I'm calm."

"Look at this."

"A flute."

"Yeah." she trills it for him.

"It sounds . . . like a flute."

"And? It looks like a flute."

"So you made these?"

Hannah shakes her head affirmatively, "I sell them on ebay. The flute's for you. I made it for you."

"Really? Are you sure?"

"For sure."

"An entrepreneur."

"For sure."

That's what attracts him, she's quirky and she's an entrepreneur. And she's cute.

"Thank you." Han has his arm around her, attempting a kiss. They topple over onto the futon. Her legs entangle his. Non locality becomes intimacy. They wrestle and fight with each other and their demons for half the night and end up mostly naked and totally lost in the innocence of the morning light as it comes down from the sky above and embraces them both, each half embraced by the other's embrace. The sun is rising, it's a new day.

They tremble, their eyes open and when they find each other they laugh.

"Too much. I cannot believe you are in my arms." he kisses her.

"Han." she murmurs.

"C'mon." he says. They jump in the pool.

Chapter 3

The Little People

There is a city inside of us, many cities really, nations, empires.   They have trillions of inhabitants called microbes. All together they're called the microbiome and they live in our body and on our body. They're in our gut, on our skin, in our mouth, our nose, and our lungs. There are communities living on the inside of our eye lids, at the base of our hair follicles, in the birth canal (which is how newborns establish their own colony) and in many more nooks and crannies of our body.

Each of these regions has their own unique variety of microbes, they like to form communities (very family oriented) and work together.   Our mouth, for example, contains different populations at the back of the mouth, the cheeks, the top and the bottom of the tongue and in the gingival crevice, where the teeth descend into the gums.

These different unique communities of microbes are the source of our different distinct smells, obviously our arm pits but also morning breath that comes from our mouth.   Our gastrointestinal tract makes some pretty interesting smells.

In our gut, most of the microbes, or little people as I like to call them, are bacteria, around 90%, but there are also fungi, viruses, protists, and archaea. If you don't know what archaea are, go google it like I did. No just kidding, archaea are ancient single-celled organisms that look a lot like bacteria but do different things, like have sex. Protists are tiny, microscopic, multi-cellular organisms that are neither animal nor plant nor fungus but are eukaryotic. Kinda like Sponge Bob Square Pants they can take different shapes. Quite a collection. There are hundreds of different species, all with their own lifestyles, their own behaviors and their own unique ways of relating to the host. We're the host. When they're out of proportion or stressed they contribute to the dis-ease of the host. We are the host. We are the field of action for this massive operation — somewhere upwards of 100-200 trillion individual little people.

Yes they're primitive, or simple if you like, but they're alive and they have their own genetics, their own metabolism and their own way of communicating with each other.

Since we are the habitation zone, the home planet, if you will, maybe we should come up with a better name for our body: animated host mechanism, inhabited planetary ecosystem, inter-species communications network, alien invasion event horizon.

The amazing thing is that the microbes are so symbiotic and not bent on our destruction, or even our domination. Nature, as it turns out, uses symbiosis as a survival strategy and has done so since the beginning of life. It's built into the DNA of all cells. "Disease", as pointed out by Lewis Thomas in his brilliant book 'The Lives of the Cell'. "usually results from inconclusive negotiations for symbiosis." More on that later.

Communications network

The little people have a nifty communications network, they talk to each other, and to our own cells, using chemical signals — 'messenger molecules'. They manufacture these molecules as part of their metabolism (metabolites) and send them out, broadcast them if you will, as coded information to other microbes, or receive them from someone else's broadcast.

And, believe it or not, they communicate with our brain. They do this through the 'second brain' 500 million neurons that surround our gastrointestinal tract and are connected to the vagus nerve which ends (or starts) at the base of our brain — the medulla oblongata.

The microbes in our gut are talking to our brain? Yes, they are. They stimulate the production of neurotransmitters in gut cells which in turn stimulate the vagus nerve. This much is known, but how much nuance goes into that communication is yet to be discovered.

Microbes and the immune system

Among all the microbes that are found in our gastrointestinal tract there are bound to be some bad actors that have to be identified and singled out, countermanded and terminated. Our digestive system is a massive interface between the microbes from the exterior world and the

51

microbes on the interior world. About 60 tons of food passes through a person's gut in a typical lifetime, and this is the place (plus our lungs) where we make intimate contact with the outside world and with the microbes that live there. They could be friendly, benign or dangerous and the immune system is standing by, ready to identify and protect, assisted by the little people.

They do this by alerting the immune system of any undesirables in the neighborhood so it can activate its patented multi-prong immune response. They also do this by out-competing the pathogens for resources, taking over the available space so they have nowhere to live. And sometimes they kill them off in direct hand to hand microbial combat using their own special antibiotic secretions.

The symbiosis of the microbes

As already mentioned, most of the little people live in a state of symbiosis with us — benefiting our body and being benefited, or at least hanging out and being neutral, not bothering nobody. They go to great lengths to maintain this harmonious state of affairs (called homeostasis) where the host is healthy and the microbes are in complimentary proportions and well balanced. The little people have a long standing tradition of maintaining homeostasis not only in our body but in all the other organisms they have colonized and interacted with. That includes pretty much everything. It's postulated that all animals from jellyfish to elephants have symbiotic microbes living in them as essential parts of their biology.

The microbes built this place. The biosphere on planet Earth that we share with all the other species of life was built on the foundation of what the little people accomplished way back in the day; way back when they were photo-synthesizing and being creative in the primordial oceans, back when they were learning how to get along with each other, learning about the benefits of being generous. Bless me, bless you. "Do unto others as you would have them do unto you", is how we've enshrined it in our moral code. It's the Golden Rule. They invented that.

One could also think of the little people as colonizers, opportunistic invaders, because that's who they are too. Their intervention goes back millions of years and was part of the evolutionary adventure of life on earth. It's an established pattern in nature: get up close and personal with your fellow creatures, pair up and help out if possible, let them know if you need anything.

The microbial world

Long, long ago when life first sparked up on this planet, there were only single-celled microbes floating around in the primordial oceans, and not too many of those. But for the next 3 billion years they had the place to themselves and millions of different species evolved, trillions of individuals, skadzillions, multiplying at will, developing their style, experimenting with speciation (through spontaneous changes to their genetic code), producing different behaviors, experimenting with different ways of procreating, experimenting with different ways of talking to each other by synthesizing different chemicals. They were learning how to get along, how to survive and thrive in the vast watery ancient microbial world.

It's hard to overstate the rich cultural implications of that era as the first organisms devised the first strategies for survival. They learned by experimenting and discovering what worked. They had the time and there was so much to learn. One microorganism's waste became another microorganism's food. That's clever.

There was barely any oxygen in the atmosphere and no food chain at all so the very first organisms had to eat chemicals like hydrogen sulphide and carbon monoxide. Some of the microbes ended up inventing photosynthesis and started eating sunlight. Others went in for customization and incorporated smaller cells into themselves (endosymbiosis), and became more than themselves, super cells or what we call today eukaryotic cells — cells with a purpose (and a nucleus). That's what we are. We're animals composed of many, many eukaryotic cells (estimates range from 15 to 100 trillion).

Indeed, inside our eukaryotic cells are organelles that once were their own separate organisms until they got incorporated. They still have their own genome and operate semi-autonomously although in a highly coordinated manner with our own cells. Mitochondria is one of those adopted organisms. They produce little energy packets, ATP, through the process of respiration that power virtually all the body's functions. Then there are other organelles that don't have their own genome and are an integral part of our cells — lysosomes and centrosomes and Golgi bodies and such. All these different organelles are floating around in the cytoplasm of our eukaryotic cells performing all their various duties in pursuit of cellular homeostasis.

We've got super cells, alright, and a whole lot of them, many different kinds, all connected together, all descendants of the original zygote that emerged from the union of our parent's sperm and egg, who themselves were distant relatives of those first unicellular units of life floating around in the ancient endless primordial ocean.

Sponges may have been the first multi-cellular animal to appear. They're made of unspecialized cells that can transform into any other type of cell and migrate around (like Sponge Bob). They have no nervous system, digestive system or circulatory system, they just do one thing — harvest the nutrients from the water that flows through the holes in their body. This is how they feed and also how they release their waste.

Organisms such as the hydra, a tiny animal less than 1/2 an inch long, can still be found in fresh water habitats and is similar to the sponge in many ways. They're basically a foot with a mouth (which doubles as an anus). Food goes in, gets digested and waste products go back out. Marine microbes took up residence inside the digestive tract of these primitive animals hundreds of millions of years ago, found a happy home (food, water and shelter) and began setting up symbiotic relationships with their host. They were able to produce molecules that the hydra lacked, molecules that they learned how to synthesize from billions of years of floating around in the ocean trying this and trying that, making errors, finding dead ends and then discovering something that really worked — a new messenger molecule! Or a metabolite to help regulate the host's cells.

The molecules that those ancient microbes in the hydra invented are similar to the neurotransmitters, hormones and gut peptides that are manufactured by our own gut microbes. On a cellular/microbial level we are still using the same original messenger molecule language that the earliest cells invented. It's a thing to consider: that even a big brained multi-cellular highly sophisticated organism like us with high speed, high level communications technology is still speaking the original language and using the original network that was invented by the first microbes.

How the human gut works

We eat with our mouths, obviously, and it's not a purely biological function. Our mouths are where we enjoy that wonderful gastronomical event — the meal. We partake of our food with great gusto, celebration and artistry, the art of gastronomy.

Our mouth is also the entrance to the digestive tract and the beginning of the digestive process. All that yummy food starts to get broken down into smaller pieces as we chew and the enzymes in our saliva start to work on it. Thus begins the process of digestion, transforming the carbohydrates into simple sugars and the lipids (fats) into free fatty acids and glycerides that can be absorbed later on in the small intestines. Gulp, with a quick swallow, our food is down the hatch and on its way to the stomach.

The stomach is an acid bath. You could put that hydrochloric acid in a car battery and it would start a diesel motor on a cold morning. The wonder is that the stomach doesn't digest itself, but it avoids that fate by maintaining a protective layer of mucous between the stomach wall and the acid environment.

It's here in the stomach that proteins are broken down into amino acids so they can be absorbed in the small intestines and sent throughout the body. Proteins, of course, are the basic building blocks that are used by all the cells. Liquids pass through the stomach quickly but solids are delayed by large folds that push it up to the top and give the hydrochloric acid more time to work on it.

Once our meal is finished in the stomach, it enters the velvety tunnel of the small intestines where most of the digestion and absorption takes place. As it travels along, twisting and turning inside our abdominal cavity, enzymes manufactured by the pancreas, break down proteins, and bile acids manufactured in the liver emulsify fats so they can be absorbed.

The inner surface of the small intestines is made up of microvilli, tiny fingers made up of even tinier fingers that absorb the digested food as it passes over them and transfers the nutrients to capillaries which connect to blood vessels that carry it to the liver, and beyond to the heart and to the rest of the body. Twenty thousand tiny fingerlike microvilli per square inch is what gives the small intestines its velvety texture. If all that surface area was spread out our small intestines would be the size of a tennis court.

The fats get special treatment. They can't be absorbed into the bloodstream because they're not water soluble and would plug up the works, so they're transported in their own vehicle — the lymph vessels. The lymph vessels transport them to the heart where they also become part of the blood stream.

Finally, after 10 or 12 hours of being propelled along through the small intestines by the peristaltic energy wave, we reach the gate, the doorway, the portal, the ileocecal valve where the small intestine ends and the large intestine, or colon, begins.

The colon, is where the vast majority of microbial residents reside. When you have a gut feeling, that's probably where you feel it, down there in the downtown little people urban metropolis of the colon. Butterflies in the stomach before your recital? Right there. The little people are picking up the message and broadcasting their signal. Our gut is alive with trillions of tiny microbes, they all have something to say. They may be able to listen as well.

When the meal arrives in the colon, there's not much left in terms of usable nutrients. The little people, however, have been waiting for it. They have the nifty ability to break down undigested fiber and turn it into vitamin K, B vitamins and short chain fatty acids, essential nutrients for our body. The colon then absorbs any excess water so it's not wasted and you're ready to poo.

Another part of the digestive system that deserves to be mentioned is the appendix.   It holds a reservoir of friendly bacteria that can be deployed to repopulate the colon in case disaster strikes and the little people get wiped out — diarrhea from food poisoning or that horrible liquid you have to drink in preparation for a colonoscopy. The appendix is attached right at the junction of the small and large intestines so it's in the perfect location to inject friendly new bacteria into our gut. And as a bonus it's made out of mostly immune tissue so it also helps with detoxification.

So that's how it works. The next time you eat something, give it a thought. Everything that's going on down there — the rhythmic pulsations pushing everything along, the digestive enzymes from the liver and pancreas being injected into the mixture at just the right time, in just the right amount. And all the little people doing all their little different things and all the messages they are passing back and forth, trying to be amenable, trying to be good citizens of the city called you.

That gurgling in your stomach when you're hungry or burping when you're full are messages that everything is pretty normal; constipation, diarrhea and cramping are messages that something is wrong. That feeling of satisfaction and completion you get after eating a healthy, well balanced meal, especially when you're hungry — that's a message too. It's our digestive system saying thank you.

The second brain

Embedded in the lining of our gastrointestinal system, all the way from our esophagus to our anus, is a network of neurons called the 'second brain' or the enteric nervous system. As mentioned already, it has a massive number of neurons and is connected to the main brain through the vagus nerve which runs from the base of the brain down to the heart, lungs, kidneys, and ends in the digestive tract.

Why is there such a concentration of neurons around our digestive tract? It seems like 500 million would be more than enough to handle simple chores like peristalsis, turning on and off the digestive juices, opening and closing valves. Five hundred million neurons is ⅔ the number of neurons in a cat's nervous system and cats are pretty smart.

Could this profusion of neurons be related to the trillions of microbes who live in close proximity to them? Of all the microbes that have colonized our body, 99% of them are located inside our gut. And although it's not engaged in any cognitive functions like wondering why life exists or coming up with quips for the barista, the gut brain does provide a broad interface for the little people to talk to us. Its sensory area is distributed over the entire surface of our gut and along that surface trillions of microbes are continuously sending messages. Having a second brain next to the little people is not a coincidence, it's an accommodation.

The second brain was the first brain originally, having evolved in early marine organisms that were essentially a mouth with no nervous system, muscles or skeleton, just a few neurons surrounding it. This at least gave them the ability to react to whatever it found in its mouth — spit it out if toxic, eat it if food. As animals grew more complex, a more elaborate network of nerves developed outside of the digestive system that eventually became our brain.

The first brain was the original organ of sense and response, triggering and being triggered by the cells around it and by the microbes living in it. The first brain stayed in touch with the second brain which gradually evolved and took over sensing and responding to the outer world while the first brain (now the second brain) stayed in the gut and continued talking to the little people in the ambient language of messenger molecules which its ancestors learned in the ancient oceans.

Since microbes devised ways of talking to each other such a long time ago, it's no wonder that they would figure out how to communicate with our cells too. We have been colonized by intestinal microbes for millions of years and they have had plenty of opportunity to develop their own communications channels.

There are three ways known so far that the little people use to communicate with us. One of the channels (as mentioned) is through the vagus nerve by stimulating neuroendocrine cells. These cells are found in the gut and in other organs of our body and produce serotonin, a neurotransmitter. Serotonin has the ability to affect our sense of well being (it's known as the happiness molecule), our social behavior, and our sleep patterns. More than 80% of the serotonin in our body is found in the digestive tract! This is where the little people are working on it. In a study done on mice, scientists found that gut microbes can increase the production of serotonin by 60%.

Another communications channel involves stimulating the immune cells, which are located just under the inner lining of the gut — the dendritic cells. They have tentacles that extend into the gut's interior where they can respond to various signals from the microbes. They have learned how to interpret these chemical messages and determine if everything is ok or if there is some anomaly, in which case they may issue an inflammatory response and prepare to deal with the problem. This inflammatory response includes hormones that are released into the blood stream and travel to other parts of the body including the brain. In this way the little people can affect organs far away from where they are.

The metabolites that the little people use to communicate are produced in profusion. Imagine, for a moment, the diversity, density and number of microbes that are active just in our large intestines — many trillions composed of hundreds of different species packed into a tubular organ not more than 5 feet long. Imagine the nuance in their communication. Their collective genome, for example, has the genetic information to code for hundreds of times more molecules than do our own cells.

In addition to that, the conditions in the gut are continuously being monitored and adjusted by the second brain. Various secretions of the digestive system, the contractions of the gut wall and the availability of nutrients are calibrated.

These constantly changing factors are things that the little people notice and respond to. If the gut microbes are stressed, this is communicated to our brain. If we are stressed this is communicated to the gut microbes.

There is now evidence that degenerative brain diseases like Alzheimer's and dementia have a gut component. The degeneration of brain cells due to these diseases is mirrored by the degeneration of neurons in the gut brain. There is evidence that childhood trauma can not only cause mental illnesses like depression, anxiety and addiction but it can also cause gastrointestinal disorders. The little people have a lot to say and a lot to listen to and maybe that's why we have a second brain.

It's also interesting that the vagus nerve connects with our main brain at the medulla oblongata — the most ancient (evolutionarily speaking), part of our brain. The most primitive life forms are talking to the most primitive part of our brain? I wonder what they are saying? The simpler the organism, the simpler the mode of communication, right?

It's been established that the little people affect our sleep patterns but one of the things I've discovered, to my deep amazement, is that they seem to be able to influence my dreams. I know that sounds nutty but, by the way, we knew hardly anything about the microbes in our gut 20 years ago, not until the NIH (National Institute of Health) started the Human Microbiome Project in 1997 and began to map out the genome — then people started getting interested, doing research and learning all kinds of amazing things.

Anyways, like I was saying, I've had dreams that were so bizarre and frightening that I was compelled to consider what might have caused them. The connection with some food or drink that I had imbibed during the day started to become apparent — if I had eaten too much or the wrong things I would often have the weird dreams and when I avoided that food or drink, my dreams became 'normal' again or atleast not terrifying.

This happened a few times. I tracked it. I know it's purely anecdotal but try it on yourself if you remember your dreams (and if you had dreams like mine I'm pretty sure you will). See if you can figure out   if the little people are responsible and what they're trying to say.

I can't imagine that they are creating the contents of the dream, that's a function of the brain, but they are stimulating the brain in such a way so as to make those movies possible. There's a lot more to learn about the bugs in our gut.

Part of what makes us human

For millions of years and in millions of different species, this relationship between microbial colonizer and their host has played out and proved to be so beneficial that it has survived all the challenges and disasters of the ages. It represents a connection to the original world, back when the earth was young and life was new.

The volcanoes had calmed down and the oceans had formed but there was no life at all on land; in the sea organisms flourished, but only on the microscopic level. The descendants of those first microbes are still swimming around in a ocean, it just happens to be our gut; they are still using chemicals to communicate, it just happens to be our cells that they're communicating with.

We aren't aware of this world because it's invisible and because it speaks in a language that we don't understand (unfortunately), but it's part of what makes us human. Ancient microbes swimming around in our gut are part of what makes us human? Startling news but yes, that's right, at least that's what the current research is telling us about the gut/brain dynamic. "The human microbiota is a fundamental component of what it means to be human." says esteemed microbiologist and Stanford professor David Relman.

One day, no doubt, they will discover other languages and communication modes heretofore unknown that the little people are using to communicate with us and we'll become even more human, or less, depending on your view.

Chapter 4

Han and Hannah

"Let's get stoned and go to Alejandro's."

"Hannah! That's high class."

"Splurge once in a while. You told me you made $200 in one night on tips."

"That was Cinco de Mayo and I was wearing my serape, it has magical powers.

"Really?"

"I think so." Christina has just dumped her armload of books on the table and collapsed on the couch.

Meow is standing next to the empty cat bowl supplicating all who will notice with her eyes. "Yot a soke, ti bata." says Hannah. "You want some dinner Meow? Meow, meow."

"How can you talk to your cat like that?"

"Yeah she understands. You want to use English words all the time? Some people don't speak the English words."

Christina laughs as her roommate fills the bowl with Kibbles.

"There are lots of different languages. You could talk to the trees if you knew how."

"Yeah I guess so." says Christina. "According to Jung all humans are united in their unconscious mind with certain traits and archetypal characters that go all the way back to the beginning of our species and maybe even to the monkeys in the trees and maybe even before that. So yeah maybe we were talking to the trees 10 million years ago.”

"You've got studying to do, right? But you have to get stoned and go to Alejandro's with me."

"You're hilarious. Do you have to get stoned to go to Alejandro's?"

"Nope. But it's my drug of choice. It's better than Xanax or Zoloft, those things mess up your mind."

"And marijuana doesn't?"

"No, it enhances my flow."

"How is your therapy survey going?"

"I'll tell you later, let's get stoned first."

****

The afternoon light was changing into its deeper hues by the time they got in the car and started up. The blueness in the air seemed to cast a calmness over the city and the people of the city or maybe it was just because the streets were half empty, most of the commuters were home by now and out of the traffic, or maybe it was just that Hannah and Christina were stoned.

"How can you explain that?" decried Christina from the passenger seat.

"I can't explain everything. Everything doesn't have to be explained. Maybe there is no explanation."

"Yeah right. No explanation. It's a mystery how a monkey learned to talk and make art and imagine gods."

"Maybe it was a miracle."

"So, ok, here's the deal that I might do my dissertation on. How many of those traits do we still have? I mean a kid, a little kid will naturally climb up into its mother's arms or climb up any stairs in sight, what kind of a kid didn't climb trees when they were a kid?"

"Some of my best times were up in the apple tree reading a book and Toby my dog snoozing in the sandbox."

"Right. That proves my point. Thank you. That was your prehensile stage, Hannah."

"Yeah me and my brothers would jump out of the tree into the sandbox yelling 'Geronimo!'"

"Right. Well that was your lower neolithic phase. Did you shoot each other with guns or arrows?"

"Guns."

"Oh yeah. That's industrial."

****

Alejandro's sits on the new side of town, next to a TGIF and a McDonald's with an Olympic-size playscape on one side. Parking is limited after 7:30 pm on a Friday so they end up across the lot in front of Randall's and make the journey back, past all the parked cars, displaying a fair amount of hilarity and earnest due diligence as if they were on a pilgrimage and had to make the arduous journey through difficult circumstances to arrive at the object of their quest — the cathedral of Alejandro's.

"Ahahahahah." laughed Hannah.

"Finally we are here." intoned Christina.

"We are here." Hannah confirmed.

"Hello. Welcome. Sit anywhere you like."
says the host as they enter the foyer.

"How about on the patio." responds Hannah.

"Good idea." says Christina pointing at a
flowering magnolia tree.

A long undulating trellis covered with
flowering vines unwinds from its source near the
fountain, makes its way across the patio and
curls back into itself by the shady nook where
the two friends have taken refuge. A small
square table made out of bamboo with a woven
mesh top covered with glass and matching chairs
consummate the dining appointments.

"Look at that flower." says Hannah pointing at
the blooming branch leaning down from the tree
as if to get in the picture.

"Ah my love!" Christina touches it delicately
and gives it a kiss as she sits down. "In a flower,
God is revealed."

"Are you doing Rumi again?"

Christina stares at Hannah with a stern face,
"How dare you?" She giggles. "I don't
remember. And it depends on what kind of
flower. It could be Neruda."

"Fricking Neruda."

"What'll it be ladies?" They both look up into
the face of a quite tall waiter standing poised
with his pen in hand. He looks like he's a
university student, possibly a nerd, wearing a
vest, well formed. They look at each other and
then at the menus.

"Uhhh, I don't know what I want."

"You never know what you want."

"Stop it!" says Hanna and mock slaps her
friend by waving her hand back and forth under
her chin and laughing more than she should have

or would have if she wasn't stoned.

"We have a roasted pine nut sauce on angel hair pasta special today."

"Ooh, that sounds good." they both say in unison and then crack up laughing.

"Take a look at the menu and I'll be back." says the waiter as he backs away.

Hannah lays the menu aside and looks at Christina. She leans in close and in a hushed voice says, "I'm not doing therapy anymore. I'm done with my survey."

"Good for you.   Is that good for you?" whispers Chrissie.

"Yes. I have to find it out, my own way out."

"What if you freak out?"

"I still got the pills."

"Umh."

"So that's it."

"Wow."

Hannah looks into her friend's face for a long while.   She has never really noticed how beautiful she is. The elfishness in her crooked teeth that gives the trick to her brown eyes. Her black hair, somehow fashioned into a cut against all odds, framing her face. It seems to Hannah that she is full of kindness.

In that moment she reaches across the table and takes her friend's hand. Christina looks up and responds by clasping hers.

"I know you can do this."

"Thanks."

The waiter returns and drops off the water glasses half filled with ice cubes. "Anything to drink?"

"Hmm. Wow. So what do you have?"

"Here's the drink menu."

"Haha, a drink menu. That's hilarious."

"Stop it, Hannah. She's just kidding around, don't worry. Um, I think we'll have water with lots of ice for now."

"Ok." The waiter leaves.

"So me and Han, we're playing around at his place."

"Oh yeah?"

"Yeah," Hannah retrieves her hand and leans back. "We were having conversation in bed." she smiles, "and we're telling stories like we were Indians camped around the campfire and I'm telling him about my dream. Do you remember? Well I'm at this idyllic place along the river and it has trees and a spring and it's really beautiful, and I'm playing with my friend, we, like, live there. We're children, 8 or 9 years old and we're playing in the stream and all of a sudden a storm comes, thunder and lightening and . . . and the water rises and a flood comes, washes everything away. And we climb up a tree, me and my friend, but he falls off and gets swept away and I cry out to him 'Come back! Come back! Meet me at the springs! Come back!' and he disappears floating down the river on a log and I'm up in this tree crying and crying. Remember? I've told you about this dream. It keeps happening."

"Yeah, you said you couldn't decide if it was a nightmare or a good dream because it was so beautiful when it started out but then it became so terrible."

"And then he tells me his story, ok? He's running through the forest and someone is hunting him, chasing him and he's running for his life and he's wounded so he's hunched over and he's carrying something, like a baby or something wrapped up in a blanket and he's running holding this thing and he's about to get killed when he suddenly comes to this pool of water and dives in. Into a spring."

"Yeah, so is this like his story or his side of your story? In your dream."

"Yeah. Yeah. So that's what I don't know. You know?"

"Yeah. The fuck."

"There's the springs motif . . . and the exile motif. Appearing in both our stories."

"What the . . ."

"Yes. Yeah, the fuck, and you know what's even weirder? His story was a dream too."

"That's eerie."

"I know."

"Are you in love with him?"

"I don't know."

"You never know."

"I never know until I know."

"Even then sometimes you don't know."

"Oh I know."

"Yeah I know."

"Everybody falls in love in a different way. Don't you think so, Christina? How could it be the same way?"

"So every person you fall in love with, it's different."

"Yeah, I don't fall in love with that many people."

"Mark."

"He was hot."

"The guy in the pet store."

"Rebound."

"Chichi."

"I really think he was gay."

"Whatever."

"Any more?"

"Uh, who was that guy when I first met you. You were all into him."

"Daniel. The saxophone player. Hey they all served their purpose."

"Purpose? That's what it is for you? They have a purpose?"

"Yeah, you know fulfill some need or desire. Like Ojo."

"Ojo is just a friend."

"A friend with benefits."

"Ojo has some benefits."

"Right."

"Ok. Let's say that you fell in love with Han, because he met your purposes."

"C'mon."

"Yeah, now you're sharing dreams. Man, that is so Jungian."

"Hey I know you have a B.A. in Psychology from ASU."

"Thank you. Actually it's a BS, ha ha."

"Oh, well at least you can make good conversation and insightful comments while they are filling your water glass."

The waiter has returned and is filling their water glasses.

"There is a direct correlation between good conversation and good tips." says Hannah. The waiter looks at Hannah.

"I bet there is." he says.

"Stop it!" says Christina and whacks Hannah playfully on her hand. The waiter waits.

"So you're in love with Han and you're going to marry him?"

"Whaaaaat?"

"So you're just going to serve your purpose."

Shaking her head, "Hey we all serve our purposes. I'll have the manu with asparagus tips."

"The wagyu?"

"That's it."

"And I'll have the, yeah, the yummy — what was it, pasta with angel sauce?" Christina's giggling as she orders.

"Yes, the, uh, angel hair pasta with roasted pine nut sauce? Good. Excellent choice." The waiter leaves.

"Yeah, so I've got a date" says Hannah. "Tuesday night. We're going to ride. He wants to show me something."

"Hmm."

****

The sun is riding low in the sky with a cool breeze coming out of the north. The two cyclists are making the most of it, top gear, downhill and down wind. Gradually the road levels and they leave the residential area behind.

Han signals with his brakes, "Ha! This is it." pulls off to the side of the road and stops.

"See? Look how it separates itself from the street and the life of the city. It has an entrance, a connecting shaft between it and the city but it is not of the city."

They've stopped at the entrance to a park, astride their bikes. "See how it creates a different light and different sounds than the city does. It has a different spatial relationship, the people of the park than the people of the city,

74

know what I mean?   Here they are crowded quite close together, arms almost touching, spreading and open, roots entangled, not moving from one space to another. In the city there is an assigned distance between people, like quantum physics, minimum and maximum, the subatomic particles must move within those boundaries, but the movement of the particles within those boundaries is constantly in motion, changing the connections and redistributing the information." Han is looking at Hannah earnestly. She peers into the connecting shaft trying to see whatever it is he wants her to see.

"C'mon."

The road curves and disappears into the trees and then another curvy road appears which Han and Hannah turn onto. There are trees on either side, oaks and big pecans and cedar elms. They turn off onto a side trail and follow it to the edge of a shallow creek, stop and dismount. The light is still strong but the shadows are long.   A shallow sound like a log being thumped comes through the air from a distant source.

"It's coming from over there." says Hannah stepping back onto her bike and looking at a faraway clump of trees. "It's drumming."

"Yeah. What is that? Huh. Let's check it out." Han pushes off and follows her lead.

The path moves toward a grove of trees in the distance. The hollow beat grows louder, like the sound of a heart beating, voices gradually become audible, a chanting. They pass through a dense stand of maple and hickory and into a clearing where a group of people in colorful regalia are assembled around a spring. Water is coming out of the rocks in a natural pulsing way, almost like a woman giving birth. It spills over the edge and creates a pool, then flows on and forms a stream. Two kids are splashing in the pool, some others are sitting on the bank. A few adults are standing near the gushing water and singing in a language not known to Han or Hannah.   Their voices are low, almost murmuring and then rise up as if in praise. Their dancing is casual and metronomic, lifting and dropping each foot in succession. The booming is coming from a drum being held by an old man standing in the back, beating out the rhythm with his mallet.

When the drumming stops, everyone is still. No one speaks, even the kids are quiet. Hannah and Han are standing discreetly at the edge of the clearing across from the drummer and the dancers One young man, in blue jeans and a brightly colored shirt, looks up from his reverie and then looks directly at them. Han nods in acknowledgement.

After a few breaths of contemplating what just happened, Han notices that the young man in the blue jeans is moving towards them.

"You probably want to know what we're doing, right?" he says with a smile.

"Yes, I do."

"We're singing to the spirit of the springs, teaching our children the songs. Our ancestors sang these songs before us and their ancestors before them way back thousands of years ago and now we sing to honor them and the water spirit who gave birth to our tribe."

"That's really cool." says Han.

"We're singing to the spirit of the water and teaching the songs to our children in the language of our ancestors. My name's Guy."

He touches his heart and then gestures towards Han and looks into his eyes. He repeats the same gesture with Hannah, looking deep into her eyes. His eye contact seems a bit affected to Hannah but for Han he sees no guile in his gaze.

"Wow. What is the name of your spirit of the water?" says Han.

"Machaganowa is the name of the water." says Guy, "It's the name of the springs. It means beautiful, bountiful, peaceful. This spring is sacred to our people. That's why we're teaching our children the songs so they won't be forgotten. Our people have been coming to this place for centuries to sing these songs like we did today. This is the birthplace of our culture, this is our homeland."

"And your people lived here? How long ago was that?"

Guy rocks his head back and forth and gestures into the air "Who knows."

The singers have begun packing up their gear and calling to their children.

"Nice to meet you." says Guy and moves away.

"You too." Han turns to Hannah, "They lived here. Nobody knows how long ago. Wow."

"Oh yeah."

Walking back to their bikes, Han is commenting, "That was the people. The ancestors of those people were praying to the springs thousands of years ago. Guy said they didn't know long it had been. They've been doing it that way for thousands of years."

"Oh yeah."

"This is the creek that flows through downtown, by the City Hall and the jail and all that."

"Oh yeah?"

"And these guys know, I bet. They know a lot of things about the springs and stuff."

"Yeah, he said sacred springs."

****

Han and Hannah are cooking. "Mmm, kasha . . . slow this down . . . " says Han as he stirs the pot.

"Mmmm yummy yum yum. Hi Choto. Chata nybo, tana," he sings to his cat who strolls into the kitchen when she smells the food.

"You talk to your cat?"

"Oh yeah. We'll start with the base — coconut oil, some mushrooms, hmm kasha, oh yeah that's what i want."

"Here. Add some chili, and cilantro." Hannah dumps what she has been chopping into the wok "I talk to my cat."

They settle in under the big Pecan tree with their meal. Have they entered into the agreement? Are they boyfriend and girlfriend? Han thinks so, Hanna is open.

"I think this was a Garden of Eden event. Paradise. Where everything they needed was provided. Think about it. Everything was abundant, the water, the fish, the animals, the plants, stuff to make stuff with - the river reeds, wood from the trees, the rocks to make tools" says Han. "I want to know about those people, the first people to live here. I want to do a project. Will you help me? We can do a

78

documentary about the old ones and what they knew."

"Yes, I will help you." Hannah smiles. She loves this innocent, spontaneous side of him. It makes her feel submissive and willing which is a nice change from having to be the boss all the time or the bill payer or the accountant or the million little other things she has to do every day to keep her life together.

Han vows deep inside himself to not mess this up. "We can do this." hand slap. Han is smiling his big broad smile now, the one where he just can't contain the energy and feels like his rocket ship is taking off.

'. . . *His teeth stick out . . .*' thought Hanna, '. . . *he's so cute . . .*'

****

Before he has a chance to knock, the door opens and a child squeals, "Han! Han! Han! Han!"

"Hi. What it is little sister?"

She looks at him with a peculiar expression.

"Hey Hailey you want to hear a story about the springs?"

"Yeah! Yeah! Yeah! Yeah!" she's jumping up and down and grabbing at Han. "Come look at my rabbit?"

"You have a rabbit? Where's your rabbit?"

"Come. Come. Come. Come." She grabs his hand and pulls him over towards the back door.

"Hi Omar." He has just arrived at the house of his friend and accomplice Omar. They have a rehearsal time set for 3 o'clock. Han on guitar and Omar on flute.

79

"Well this is a furry rabbit."

"Here hold it." she picks up the rabbit and hands it to him.

"Hailey are you bi-polar?"

Yes I'm polar. Her name is Suzi Q."

"Hi Suzi Q. Doesn't seem like a name for a rabbit."

"What would you name a rabbit?"

"I would name my rabbit . . . whatever occurred to me when i first saw it for the first time. A chana, maybe.

"Achana? That's a good name."

"Well once upon a time, Han starts out, there was a little girl child and her name was Sawana Tati and she grew up at the springs where the water came out of the ground and splashed on the rocks. She was born there. The first thing she heard on the day she was born was the sound of splashing water and she grew up listening to the sound every day and her laughter was like the splashing water and she knew all the animals and plants in that place. One day . . ."

"Do you mean she could talk to the animals." queried Hailey.

"Oh absolutely. She could talk to birds and frogs and bears and trees."

"Bears!"

"Oh yeah. They were big but easy to talk to because they're almost like humans."

"What did she talk to the bear?"

"Hey I don't know. I mean I wasn't there. I'm just telling the story. The way I heard it."

Hailey laughs and points at his face "You have a spot."

"Yes I know that's a birthmark. Everybody has something that makes them unique."

"Oh no, here comes the plot."

"How did you know about plot."

"Mmm I don't know. From daddy."

"Oh I was breaking down the three little pigs for her the other day," says Omar from across the room, "deconstructing the plot. Have you ever stopped to think about it? There really is no plot. The big bad wolf wants to eat the little piglets who employ architecture in their attempt to thwart his stated intentions. That's it. We're feeding our children inferior fairy tales."

"I believe that is true." rejoined Han. "So one day there was this giant thunderstorm. It rained and rained and rained," Han lightly tapped his fingers on Hailey's head and shoulders to simulate the drenching downpour, "The river flooded. Sawana Tati was washed away and her parents couldn't find her anywhere but she floated downstream until she came to another place where other people lived and there she got out of the little boat she was sailing in."

"What boat did she have?"

"You're very astute. I didn't mention that. She made a boat out of, you know, sticks and stuff that was floating in the water and tied it all together with spider web. That stuff is really amazing, strong. She did all this before the flood, well actually her parents helped her."

"Mmm, ok."

"And that tribe was named Oclonoclith."

"Ocolith."

"Yeah and they had a little boy child in that tribe."

"What was his name?"

"His name was . . . Charles. And the little boy child lived in the forest and was born in the forest and knew the trees of the forest."

"So they fell in love."

"Hey who's telling this story? They grew up and fell in love but one day they got separated."

"Why did they get separated?"

"Umh, there was a war and people were fighting. And one of them got lost in the forest. They were wounded. Charles was wounded from the battle with a fierce enemy, fearsome enemy and he ran and he had to escape and Sawana Tati told him to meet her where the laughing waters were. She told him 'Listen to the sound of the water splashing on the rocks and I will be there.'"

"Here's a beer," says Omar, "That's a pretty cool story, did you make it up?"

"This is not made up. This is a real story."

"Did they meet up?" says Hailey.

"Let's practice." says Omar.

"I got a great idea." says Han pointing his finger at Hailey.

"Yeah? Show it to me." says Hailey.

"I'll tell you the rest of the story if you go outside and play for one hour."

"That's not a great idea."

"Hey Hailey." says Han.

"Hey Han." she punches him in the leg and runs out the back door.

"So, do you think Stewart's into it?" asks Omar.

"Stewart is definitely not into it. He's got his job and his girlfriend and he sounded totally not interested."

"Cool. Ampee is down for it. She told me she always wanted to be in a band and that she can sing and dance and be beautiful."

"Ampee can sing?"

"That's what she said." Omar wraps his fingers around the flute and brings it to his mouth, trills, runs up and down some scales to warm up the instrument.

Han strums, searching in his odd way to find some resonance and then hangs out there picking the strings the way he does.

"Wow, I did not know Ampee could sing." says Han and they settle in to the jam, exploring harmony and occasionally dissonance. Themes arrive and disappear like waves on the ocean. Little eddies of melody appear and disappear like bubbles in the surf, rhythms catch on and morph into funkier rhythms.

Hailey appears holding her rabbit and sits on the floor in front of them. They play for her and they play for the rabbit.

Chapter 5

Symbiosis

Visualize Earth's orbital path as a ribbon around the Sun, zoom out far enough to see the entire 186 million mile diameter of it. The Earth follows this path each year in a nearly perfect circle, it varies by less than 2% or about 3 million miles. Holding us here in the habitable zone is a perfect balance of velocity and gravity.

Not only is our earth in a habitable zone around the sun, but our entire solar system is in a habitable zone orbiting the galactic center of the Milky Way. It's far enough away from the deadly radiation of the densely packed core for life to evolve but close enough to be rich in the heavy elements necessary for life.

Our planet congealed out of a giant cloud of space dust 5 billion years ago and turned out to be just the right size and in just the right place in the solar system for it to accumulate an atmosphere and a rocky core, unlike Jupiter which is mostly gas with hardly any solid land and Mercury which has solid land but virtually no atmosphere.

Our sun, our energy giver, our 'Sky God', as the early people saw it, is a star that condensed out of the same space dust but was so large that the intense pressure and temperature generated by the gravity at its center caused the hydrogen to begin fusing into helium — nuclear fusion. Imagine 92 million million one megaton nuclear bombs going off every second — that's our sun. The temperature at the core is estimated to be 27 million degrees Fahrenheit. This energy provides Earth, orbiting a comfortable 93 million miles away, with plenty of sunshine and the perfect temperature to allow life to form and flourish. Our neighboring planet Venus is cooked, Mercury is broiled and Mars is frozen.

Our planet has changing seasons (due to its tilted axis), and movable continents (which create mountains and rivers), it has oceans full of water and the correct atmospheric gases for respiration (so we can have large scale metabolism).

This complex series of fortunate events has resulted in the creation of a planet able to accommodate the primal urge of life. To live, to evolve, to build out, to form mutually beneficial relationships with other forms of life, is what life wants to do. Our biosphere, which supports millions of species of life all at the same time, has developed using the energy of solar radiation, gravity and symbiosis, the energy that comes from being interconnected. Only through this combination of interactions has nature been able to come up with something like us — a creature that is self-aware. A creature who tells stories to its kids and imagines how it was long ago and how it could be in the future, a creature who talks to God and about God — what he looks like and how he made the world, or she. A creature who remembers their ancient ancestors and looks to them for guidance on how to live. We are strangers in a strange land and the strange land is the present, a present that was imagined by those ancestors. Imagined but never seen. How did we come to be like this?

In the beginning . . .

The early earth was not a friendly place. It was super hot, a lot of molten rock, the atmosphere was ammonia and methane and other nasty gases, no oxygen to speak of. It was completely barren of life. Even after it cooled down enough to accumulate oceans, through condensation and icy meteorites falling on the surface, its molten core was still extremely hot and very active. Magma exuded up through cracks in the earth's crust and formed volcanoes, deep in the oceans it formed thermal vents.

It was around these thermal vents, scientists theorize, that the first living organisms may have sprung up. There, the organic molecules necessary for building complex nucleotides essential for synthesizing RNA, were present and the energy needed for chemical reactions was available. The first living organisms to appear may have been non-cellular blobs of protoplasm who, like Sponge Bob Square Pants (if you've never seen the show you really should), took different shapes and forms as needed. They must have contained strands of RNA, the duplication molecule. The RNA molecule, or DNA for later organisms, is able to code for the proteins that are the functioning units of life and is also able to reproduce its own pattern, even improve on it through mutation and adaptation. The RNA molecule was the beginning of life.

The first simple cells to evolve had a cell wall and DNA but lacked a nucleus (or any other kind of organelles for that matter) and existed in an oxygen free atmosphere (anaerobic). There was no oxygen and there wasn't much to eat; the food chain hadn't been invented yet. But the planet was bathed in a beautiful golden light coming from a nearby star and somehow those early organisms learned how to eat light. Photosynthesis! Inventing a way to use radiation from the sun to make cellular energy was a brilliant and innovative breakthrough; one of the most fantastic things to ever happen on planet earth.

In photosynthesis, carbohydrates are synthesized from carbon dioxide and water using energy from the sun with oxygen as a by-product. Green plants inhale carbon dioxide and exhale oxygen. The carbohydrate molecules (sugars) are later converted into ATP and ATP, as you might remember from your high school biology class, is used by the cells to power all the various and amazing activities of life.

When we breathe, we exhale carbon dioxide and inhale oxygen, the opposite of green plants. Deep in our lungs, while doing doing aerobic exercise, you can feel it. This ability of our lungs to provide oxygen to our body is known as the respiratory load and is the measure of how much oxygen is being exchanged for carbon dioxide in the air sacs of our lungs (alveoli). You can feel it. It's amazing. The carbon dioxide is exhaled and the oxygen is absorbed.

It's a circuit, it's an energy pump powered by the sun with photosynthesis and respiration as the positive and negative terminals of the circuit. Photosynthesis makes carbohydrates and releases oxygen, cellular respiration uses carbohydrates and releases carbon dioxide. The energy flows continuously in a circular motion through the animals and the plants. All living things on planet earth are plugged into this circuit and get their energy from it.

Photosynthesis, as it turns out, was such a great idea that lots of species adopted it. They spread throughout the oceans and colonized the land (kind of like the human migration). On land the chlorophyll people found themselves stationary and not able to move around so they spread their branches high above the ground to catch as much sunlight as possible, while underground, on the dark side, their roots formed a relationship with fungi that helped them absorb nutrients.

Today, thanks to that tiny sunlight powered molecule we call chlorophyll and its ability to release oxygen, our atmosphere contains 20% oxygen, more than any other known planet, and oxygen is the fuel that drives this machine we call our body.

The next major evolutionary event in our journey was the development of advanced cells (eukaryotes) with a nucleus and organelles (little micro-cells within the cells that do things). They evolved when larger cells ingested smaller cells and incorporated them into their machinery instead of digesting them. That's called endosymbiosis. If you don't believe me read Lynn Margulis' book 'Symbiotic Planet'. She actually discovered endosymbiosis back in the sixties and nobody believed her then either. When genetic studies finally became available, they found out, whoops, she's right.

Anyways, sexual reproduction also developed around the same time (way more fun than simple division) and allowed for evolutionary changes to happen at an accelerated pace due to the mixing of genetic material. Now we're getting somewhere.

The super cells attached to other super cells and created complex organisms with various features — among them the ability to filter nutrients out of the water (sponges), fly through the air (birds), live underground (worms), construct a solar array in order to harvest sunlight high above the earth, away from the browsers that wanted to eat their leaves (trees) and prowl around in packs using precise hearing, sensitive odor detection and visual acuity to locate large herbivores and eat them (wolves). Oh yeah and also creatures who could communicate using auditory cues with symbolic overtones and tell stories about their ancestors (human beings).

Ever since the Cambrian Era, 500 million years ago, life has been tinkering with multicellular organisms and planet Earth has filled up with an amazing variety of species. This proliferation of life did not come from attacking each other (predation) but by networking (symbiosis). From spiders to sperm whales, from bacteria to bears — all the different species that share this biosphere are connected to each other in some way that promotes life.

Being in relationship allows for communication, cooperation, competition and coupling. We learn from each other and as fellow members of the biosphere, evolve with each other. We, as humans, strive for our highest goals; we have morals and religions. For the little people, who live inside our body and don't have much circuitry, their aspiration is to evolve and make things better too. That's why they mutate so often — trying out different ways of doing things.

Trees and humans

One of the most noticeable members of this planetary biosphere are the trees. We look nothing like them and our lifestyles are completely different, but we have a relationship that is both cultural and biological, and very ancient.

We came out of the trees, they were our home for millennia. Those people living in the trees back then weren't members of the genus Homo, they were apes actually, but they were prelude to the hominids who would come along later once we climbed down out of the trees and started walking around on the ground and growing a big brain and telling stories.

Our fairy tales came from the forest. Those monsters and tricksters and witches and goblins that we saw in the twisted branches as we gathered firewood at dusk to take home to our huts and our hearths, became characters in our stories. We told them around the campfire for everyone's entertainment. Make it good and make it scary, were the only rules, so the kids would get excited and learn something. That's what it was all about.

And later on, after the kids were asleep, the old ones sitting near the fire would speak out and say "Why, that's nothin. This here's the best story I ever heard" and start off on their own tale full of mystery and sex and bravery and humor, to one up whatever the other guy had come up with. In this way we practiced our story telling down through the ages. We saw our heroes and gods and queens and kings in the burning flames and the glowing coals of the fire. Another gift from the trees.

Trees are shape shifters and we imagine them that way in our myths and legends. They appear to be at once a cornucopia of life and then the stark branches of a dead man's hand. In the convoluted halls and labyrinthian walls we find majesty and mystery. We also found bears and wolves and other fearsome predators. We found many creatures there, some were friends, some were food. We were food sometimes too, of course, we hadn't yet climbed to the top of the food chain.

We are related to trees on the cellular level too. Inside our bloodstream the hemoglobin molecule that carries oxygen to our cells is chemically related to the chlorophyll molecule in the green leaves of plants. The only difference is that the center atom of hemoglobin is iron and the center atom of chlorophyll is magnesium. After the hemoglobin drops off its oxygen with the cells, the cells release carbon dioxide into the blood which goes back out through our lungs into the atmosphere where it's absorbed by the chlorophyll in the green plants which then releases oxygen. Oh, I already mentioned that.

We are linked with the trees and all the green plants in this rhythmic dance and we have been dancing this dance for a long time. Our evolution into what we are now from what we were before was assisted by the trees and the green plants. They helped us to be here, unwittingly maybe but not unwillingly. What benefits you, benefits me, was the secret code that was transmitted back and forth between our nascent species and the old ones, the trees, who held up the sky and connected heaven and earth.

The symbiosis of trees and fungi

Trees not only have symbiotic relationships with us, they also form symbiotic relationships underground with fungi. They exchange the sugar they make in photosynthesis for nutrients from the earth that the fungi have gathered. Microscopic threads of their fungal body (the mycelium) spread throughout the soil, casting their nets and connecting the roots of the trees with each other. In this way trees are actually able to communicate and share resources with other trees in their neighborhood.

The mushrooms that we see on the surface are the visible part of the fungi, the fruiting body that sprouts up when it's ready to make spores. Underground, the mycelium is doing the real work. The fungal fibers are so fine and so dense that there could be a hundred miles of them underneath one footstep. In a mature forest the mat operates like an underground internet with nodes and links. The older mature trees being the nodes and the younger trees the links. At its foundation the forest is a communications network with mycelium as its neurons. It monitors and supports the health of its members as if it were an intelligent organism with a brain. See Suzanne Simard, 'Finding the Mother Tree: Discovering the Wisdom of the Forest'. She's done the research.

By some accounts the whole universe is a symbiotic expression

The universe has brought forth life. It took billions of years for this to happen. It could have been a still birth — no atoms, no molecules, no organisms, not much of anything besides a few elemental forces.

Because conscious life exists, the universe is observable and it exists too. They are both concomitant, depending on each other to give birth to each other. The universe is not there if no one is there to observe it, is how physicists describe quantum theory these days. How symbiotic is that? If there were no observers there would be no universe, at least not as we know it.

Maybe when it began it was only one thing, a singularity as they call it, and then maybe the one thing figured out how to divide into two things. Now we've got two things, and they can react to each other and create more things. That was, of course unprecedented, preposterous and impossible. There had never been two things before in the history of . . . nothing and it was audacious. It was revolutionary and so much so that it just kept creating more and more permutations until the universe was full of different things. Mostly hydrogen and helium, of course, being the simplest elements to build, but many others too, iron and magnesium and oxygen and selenium and each element with their own preference and style of attack or how they would interact and the unique consequences of what would happen next. Molecules! Planets! Life!

Maybe the universe began at some point in time with a big bang. Or maybe time was irrelevant, didn't exist yet, or maybe time was part of the big bang. If there was no time then the universe did not 'begin' at 'some point' in time. Maybe the fabric of space and time unfolds out of nothing and then folds back up into nothing. The end of the cycle. Poof. Gone. No time, no space, not even nothing. And then reappears again.

Maybe the universe is like a pulsating bowl of elastic energy jello, echoing and re-echoing from the original big bang of the big bang. That vibration, intersecting and diffusing and diffracting and recombining in the form of resonances that create everything, even anti-matter and black holes and cool stuff that we don't even know about yet.

Maybe the universe came into being with a shriek of joy and has been reverberating with that ever since — from proto-matter to atoms to stars to planets to life to millions of species of life, life in profusion, life in a biosphere, life in a bubble on a small planet orbiting a medium sized star in a large galaxy. If the driving principle has always been to make it better, improve the design, keep the best ideas and let go of the mistakes — then copied into every genetic code is the possibility of possibility and written inside every living cell of every living creature that has ever lived on our planet or ever will is the echo of a joyful shriek.

But then there's entropy. What a buzz kill. Everything is winding down and one day it will just quit. The stars will burn out and the whole universe will go dark and gravity will start pulling everything back together again, until it's no bigger than a pinhole. Then it will blow up again. Maybe.

Maybe the universe *'came into being'* let's say, and not because of a big bang but because of nothing at all. No reason and no reasonableness, it just happened and then quickly calmed down and started making laws — *you can do this but you cannot do that*. Pretty soon strange little 'particles' appeared and strange attractions between the strange little particles. Pretty soon hydrogen was fusing into helium just for the heck of it and pretty soon the universe was lighting up with stars, then the stars burned up all their hydrogen fuel and collapsed, so the helium started fusing into carbon and then it collapsed, just couldn't hold it together anymore and left behind a core of iron which was not fusible so it turned into a black hole and swallowed everything.

The universe had to start up somehow at some point in time if there is to be any logical conception of time at all. Modern physics might have an argument with it but most people would like to have a sense of time that is calibrated and continuous, down to earth, day to day. We want time that runs smoothly and keeps track of things. It doesn't jump around or stop or slow down or speed up.   That's only in our perceptions which is exactly what the physicists would like us to believe — that time itself is a product of our mind. In fact, the whole universe exists only by our knowing it, that it is not separate from our awareness nor can it be.

They are both part of a coherent whole that is continuously unfolding and evolving.   The physical universe and our understanding of it are aspects of the same thing, say the physicists. If you choose to measure a quark, for example, it becomes complimentary and starts to appear as you wish it to be or project it to be in your mind. Subatomic particles and electromagnetic waves are neither particles nor waves but can behave as if they were either.

"When you change the way you look at things, the things you look at change." says Max Plank, the German quantum theorist and Noble Prize winner. "We have to remember that what we observe is not nature herself, but nature exposed to our method of questioning," chimed in Werner Heisenberger, one of the architects of quantum physics.

Well, back to our original point — the singularity longing for its opposite, its compliment, the symbiotic other. That clever trick of multiplying 1 times 0 and getting 2 is unexplained to this day or over-explained. Many theories, there are, for the creation of the universe. Every culture has their own.

Stories of creation

Everything was in chaos and the chaos was in everything. Inside the chaos also was yin-yang.

All the opposites were there, female-male, passive-active, cold-heat, dark-light, all mixed up together in a giant cosmic egg. From the cosmic egg came the giant Phan Ku, the first man, and he separated out all the opposites one by one. He separated earth and sky, light and dark, cold and hot, he separated all the opposites into each separate thing and they became manifest. In that time all things were suffused with the primal chaos, with ying-yang. Phan Ku put the sky in place and carved the mountains. The fleas from his hairy body became the humans.

— Chinese creation story recorded by Xu Zheng, 2nd Century AD.

In the beginning was the Word, and the Word was with God, and the Word was God. The same was in the beginning with God. All things were made by him; and without him was not any thing made that was made.

— Christian creation story, from the Gospel of John.

First, time was born, before the earth or the sky appeared. Time had a name and each day had a name. The days started off walking from the east. The first day produced the sky and the earth from its entrails. The second day made a concourse for the rain to fall down. The third day made the seasons and the weather and the multitude of things. The fourth day forced the sky to tilt and touch the earth so that they were joined. The fifth day decided that everyone had to work. Light was made by the sixth day and now everyone could see what they were doing.

The seventh day created soil and the eighth day stuck its feet in it. The ninth day created the underworld and the tenth day marked all those who were condemned to live there. From inside the sun, the eleventh day made the trees and the rocks. The twelfth day made the wind and called it spirit for there was life in it. The thirteenth day took some mud and made a human body, like ours.

    — Mayan creation story. I love the sense of humor here.

At first there was only darkness wrapped in darkness
All this was just un-illuminated water.
That One which came to be, enclosed in nothing,
arose at last, born of the power of heat.
In the beginning desire descended on it —
that was the primal seed, born of the mind.
The sages who have searched their hearts with wisdom
know that which is, is kin to that which is not

    — Hindu creation story, from the Rig Veda. Translated by A. L. Basham

The creation story is told again and again and don't we teach one to our children as well? 'How everything came to be' is the complement to the four year old's question 'where did everything come from. We teach it by inference, sending our kids to church, temple and mosque. We trundle them off to school before they have even finished their innocent childhood. We teach it by rote, 'God created everything', we say but we don't show them how. We don't bother to mention that creation is happening all the time and so is dissolution, the recycling.

'It's a balance, kids, the universe is here and so are you' is what I would probably say if I had any kids.

Symbiosis as a function of birth and death

Of all the myriad forms of symbiosis in our world perhaps the most lovely is the symbiosis of birth and death. One depends on the other like a lover depends on their partner, they revolve around each other as in a dance. One pre-conditions the other, makes the other possible and intimate. Both are ancient and universal, they complement each other. Death gives meaning to life and life gives death a stage to perform on. How could you die if you were never born?

The unspoken but undeniable fact is this: we all die. What's amazing about it is that it's amazing at all. Everything has been dying for a very long time. And maybe the fact that we consider our death remarkable and noteworthy or at least strange and unusual is because we're not aware of one of the most obvious things in the whole wide world —everything dies. Our bodies turn back into the soil from which they came. Everything goes back to where it came from.

There is an organic burial box, a sort of coffin that you can buy and it has soil and an acorn in it waiting to sprout and you are the fertilizer. Without the death and renewal, life could not go on. It is the ultimate symbiosis.

Death of course connotes illness, decrepitude and senility, all negative things. But this is just a giving back of all that was given.   A slow goodbye to everything you were. Is that not a kindness? Would you rather it were taken away all of a sudden? It's a mercy that we grow old slowly or the shock of it would surely kill us. Besides the next generation is waiting in the wings to come on the stage and do their thing: be kids, be babies and grow up and find a life and have adventures and know truths and find love, just like you did. And then they will die, after bequeathing their genes to the next act. It is a beautiful thing, this ongoing play with different players but on the same stage. Dramatic? Certainly. Funny? No doubt. Rich in theatrical values, without judgment or morality, (it's us who do that), top flight entertainment. Ah the passion, the agony! Ah the bliss, the creativity! Ah the love!

But I stray from my point, as if I was wandering off the path and into the forest, following a rippling stream and discovering a meadow full of wildflowers . . . The coherence of a system that provides seeds at the same time the flower is dying, which then sprout and fruit in their time should give us comfort.

Synchrony is a word not often used, because there are so few occasions that we notice it, but it means something like symphony — like the flower and the seeds, the seasons and the rain, the drum and the strings, the bass coming on, a full orchestral effect, from pianissimo to crescendo to pianissimo again, all the parts moving together to produce feelings of elation and great pleasure.   Life with its accompaniment, death.

Chapter 6

Han and Hannah

Hailey is zooming around in the air like a dragonfly. She's wearing a shiny red dress with green frilly trim and she has wings, she's holding a wand.   This doesn't strike Han as unusual because he's dreaming.

In the dream, Hailey appears as if she were supported by wires that pull her this way and that. He reaches out to touch her but she zooms away to another spot. Her appearance changes, now she looks like a bee or a fairy; she's laughing.

Han can see himself in the dream, he's out of his body now and can see himself lying on his back in the grass.   *. . . well this must not be a dream then . . .* he surmises. He's surrounded by giant oak trees, a small forest of them, sunlight is streaming down through the tree branches. He watches as Hailey zooms around through the air, dancing in the sunbeams as they slant down, laughing in her high-pitched, delightfully,squealy way as she zooms.

She flicks her wand, and a stream of green energy comes bursting out of the tip and hits him in the chest. It feels cool, tingly. He's suddenly back in his body.

As soon as he wakes up, the dream recedes into his subconscious memory. He couldn't find it there if he looked for it. It will reconnect with him at some shining moment when he needs it most.

****

Han is on his bike, working hard. He turns the corner onto Broadway and enters traffic. . . . *damn cars in the road . . . cars everywhere . . . as far as you can see . . . 4,000 pounds of steel and glass exhausting poison gas into the air we breathe . . . just to go to the store . . . a predetermined location . . . point A to point B . . . 4,000 pounds just to take one person to the store . . .*

He races by a grocery store, skimming the light, and comments. . . . *there must be a hundred cars there . . . parked there in the parking lot . . .*

He's on his way over to Hannah's place, they've got a breakfast date at Joe Joe's. . . . she's never been . . . *I can't believe that . . . she's never been to Joe Joe's . . .*

She's waiting for him in the park near her place. Hug, kiss.

"Hey you!"

"Hey you!"

They ride along Broadway, towards city center, Han is telling her all about the ancient people, practically shouting at her so he can be

102

heard over the noise of the traffic. She can hear him fine, she's cycling right next to him.

"And they lived here, all along here, along the river, for hundreds of years, probably thousands. They were adapted to their environment so much, I mean it wasn't like, well it wasn't like this . . . it was full of life, not buildings." They turn off Broadway and enter the Old Town neighborhood, cross the bridge and there's Joe Joe's.

Being a warmish fall day, the door is propped open and they walk right in. A brick wall holds up the cross beams and the cross beams hold up the roof. On the playlist is funky soft jazz.

"Oh, this is how it is." says Hannah.

Behind the counter, three people are attending customers, working the big Italian espresso machine that sits like an altar at the end of the bar. 'La Marzocco' is written in a flowing script on its side. It steams and froths and the baristas adjust its knobs until finally a cappuccino or a latte is produced, the signature drinks of the urban bohemian.

. . . it's a tableau but in motion . . . is how it strikes Han. "It's theatre." he says to Hannah, taking control of the narrative as he usually does when he's around her, "think of it as theatre. Everyone is on stage and acting but also the audience. C'mon let's do a ritual."

"What? Why a ritual?"

"Just anything. something that people feel familiar with that shows your good intentions."

"Like what?"

"Like the paying of the credit card ritual. Then things are good. All good. Everybody is happy."

"Oh I get you. There is a correlation between money and happiness. Even though people say there's not. Actually . . ."

"There's Omar!" Han gestures and they move in his direction.

Omar is sitting at a table with his daughter Hailey, next to the brick wall.

"Hi Han daka." says Hailey as she runs over to Han.

"Hey little small child. What is this?" She hands him a packet of sugar. "Is my name Han daka?"

"Well to her it is, I guess, because when she brings me things and I say 'thank you' she says daka." explains Omar.

"Han daka." she says and squeals in delight.

"Thank you." says Han.

"Is she your girlfriend?' she says looking at Hannah.

Omar, "She's jealous."

"Omar I would like to introduce my friend and accomplice, the beautiful Hannah."

"Ha, ha." says Hailey.

"Hi Hannah." says Omar.

"Hey Omar." hand clasp.

"You are beautiful."

"Oh thank you sir."

"Hailey wants to show you she is four."

"Yeah, I'm four."

"That's pretty good, Hailey. How did you get to be four? I remember you used to be three."

"I don't know. I just did."

"Well you're looking like a mighty fine four."

Hailey shrieks and runs off through the tangle of tables and chairs that populate the cafe. For her they are just above eye level so she sees both the underside and the topside. The underside is composed of legs and feet and shoes while the topside has arms and heads and talking people.

The murmur and clash of the ambient sounds surge and recede like waves on the shore as Han and Hannah and Omar take a seat at their island table moored to the wall and begin their conversation.

"Hannah and I were just talking about the old people, los Antiguos, that used to live around here in our fair city."

"For instance, if they lived here for thousands of years they must have had a rich culture, traditions and learnings and songs and games and stories." Hannah.

"Yeah I was thinking about that. Their storytelling must have been amazing. That was their main form of entertainment right? Sitting around the fire telling stories? Right? No Disney movies, no TV. They were the Disney movie." Han.

Omar, "Well I think their lives were much more balanced and in a rhythm than we are today. De-stressed. Because they moved in the natural world. Nobody had a job or a boss. Think about that, no boss. Nobody had a job. Hey nobody here has a boss, we're kind of doing things . . . "

"I'm the boss." interrupts Hailey who has circled back around after scouting the room.

"Ha, you are little sister." says Han.

"I'm not your sister." she says squealing with laughter.

"Well in a way . . ." Han encircles her with his arm, trying to prevent her from running off, and

says, "Hey Hailey.   Why was six afraid of
seven?
   "It was?"
   "Yeah why was six afraid of seven?"
      Hailey looks at Hannah and touches her
shoulder bag sitting on the table decorated with
beads. Her fingers trace the designs formed by
the beadwork: swirls and lines and circles.
   "Because seven ate nine."
She seems baffled, then bursts out in laughter
and runs away.
   "So what is it you do?" asks Hannah looking
at Omar 'besides barista-ing at Joe Joe's?
      "I'm into Teafullness, it's my own tea
company featuring small family farm grown tea
ingredients from around the world like fennel
and mint and ginger. They're formulated for
medicinal qualities like emotional uplift,
immune enhancement, microbial health." he
rattles off in his presentational voice. "Yeah I'm
having the great Loose Leaf Tea Experience
Thursday in the park, you guys should come."
   "No kidding." says Hannah.
   "And what I think about the ancient people is
that you should talk to Dr. Davidson. He's an
authority, my anthropology professor from the
university."
      "Well we should certainly do that then.
Definitely." says Hannah.
      They talk and quip and sip and enjoy the
ambient sounds at Joe Joes until it's time to go.
Omar makes the first move.
   "Let me excuse myself." he says getting up,
"Someone needs a nap and I've got work to do
at home."

"Nice to meet you Omar and your delightful daughter" says Hannah.

"Hey do you want to ride back to my house?" says Han.

"No I've got to do quarterlies."

"What's that?'

"Oh you know 940's, 1040's, TWC, all that fun stuff."

"Ah, ok, business. See you later then."

"Not if I see you first. Ha ha."

****

Han slips into the street and heads downtown. He's alone, except for the voices in his head . . . *at first there was atoms and they were indivisible . . . then subatomic particles and they divided . . . then quarks and leptons and super strings . . . hey this goes on forever . . . I believe . . . everyone believes . . . it's just about finding something . . . utilitarian . . . tarian tarian multi disciplinarian . . . arian arian endlessly rotating septuagenarian . . . contrarian . . . i find solace in the open sky . . . what about the millennium? . . . ah ! . . .* He gathers speed and cruises down the street, banks onto Main and cuts through the bank plaza and back onto the street. . . . *damn cars in the street . . . watch out! . . . damn cars everywhere . . . my bike works fine and I'm alive . . . it'll keep breaking down endlessly until i ask my subconsciousness to understand more subtle designs of nature . . . I think . . .* He pumps harder until he reaches the edge of the envelope (that's what he calls it when you can't go any faster and sustain it), he attains orbital velocity (that's what he calls it when his thoughts shut down). He stays with it, all the way through downtown breathing and pedaling, no thoughts. To navigate, all you need is stimulus-response and an internal map.

The traffic signal turns red but a quick scan reveals no cops, he rolls through. . . . *why wait for a machine to tell you what to do . . . i'm not a robot . . .* his inner voice comments.

Hardly through the intersection he spots a lone pedestrian walking with a backpack and gives him a hand gesture as he rolls past. In Han's parlance it's a signal to a fellow traveler, to a fellow pilgrim on a journey . . . *each one has their own personal quest . . .* He is comforted by the pilgrim.

The street enters a construction zone with cones and barriers set up to direct the traffic around a giant hole that is being dug in the pavement by a very large machine with caterpillar treads and a long articulating arm. He slows, not to avoid the barriers but to accommodate any unknown events that might transpire in this altered landscape: pedestrians stepping off the curb, motorists getting out of their cars, traffic making abrupt moves. The instinct to avoid danger and be cautious in unfamiliar or unknown circumstances is part of his DNA, bred into him by his forbears, those who came before, those folk hunting and gathering in the wilderness thousands of years ago — the ancestors.

. . . the ancestors . . . it occurs to him now . . . *that's right they were the ancestors of us all and we are their progeny, we carry their DNA . . .*

*even into the city . . . still have their instincts . .
. crazy . . .*

****

Hannah is settled into her office space in the back dining room at the Green Coconut. The restaurant is closed, it's after hours, only Hannah and Suzanne the cake maker are there. They've got the tunes on, Country Western. Dwight Yoakum singing about suspicious minds. There is an open beer on Hannah's desk along with a ledger, an electronic calculator and her computer screen.

Piling chairs upside down on top of the tables Suzi says, "For the longest time I thought heaven and hell were some place you went when you died. Now I think it's right here."

"What's going on?"

"People is going on. My stepfather is a creep and a clueless bastard. I hate him. Jack on the other hand is divine. We went out last night. It was a date without a destination. We just went walking downtown and along the river, stopped at Refugio's. We had a conversation. I never had so much fun in all my life. He's cute. He makes me laugh."

"Hey, ah. Conversation can be better than sex especially when there is conversation *and* sex."

"Yeah. I know like yeah." said Suzi "and he's got his own place. A funky apartment on Grayson but nobody there, just us."

"Hmm. I can imagine that." she takes a deep draw on her beer, "Hell for me is doing paperwork. It makes me want to scream. I just don't know. I know why people live in the street.   No bills, no fucking taxes, no car registration, no license plate renewal, no . . .”

"He's a big guy." Suzi says smiling.

"Oh yeah?"

"Careful and slow. I loved it."

"How slow?"

"Mmmm." murmured Suzi. "Hey, the thing with the thing. Do you do it?"

Hannah laughed, "Oh yeah." She looked at Suzi with admiration for her innocence. "That's the best part. Almost."

"Ok. I didn't know if I was sinning or something."

Laughing again Hannah launches a high arcing shot of wadded up ledger paper at the waste basket 8 feet away, misses badly and reaches for the beer, "You make paperwork fun.".

"Everything can be fun when you're happy." Suzi says and smiles. The chairs are put up and she starts in mopping the dining room floor with slow sweeping motions in time with Lucinda Williams singing 'This Sweet Old World' over the speakers.

"Everyone has a different trigger. It's fun to explore. I can't say I have been shy. They like it. Man oh man."

"What?"

"Oh just thinking about this guy, Omar, a friend of Han's. He's Lebanese or something. I go crazy for exotic ones."

"I thought you and Han . . ."

"Yeah we are. He's interesting. I'm learning a lot."

"Learning?"

"Oh yeah, he's into the ancient people. Something I've often thought about. And we're having synchronous dreams or something. Something weird.”

“What’s weird?”

“Can I tell you something, Suzi? Promise you will not tell anyone?”

“Ok. I love secrets.”

“Han is on medication for bi-polar disorder. Yeah, kinda matches up right.   His father is some rich wheeler dealer and his mother is in a retirement center.”

“Interesting.”

“And there’s something even more than interesting about it. It feels like ghosts in the closet or something. I don’t know what it is.”

“Spooky.”

“Pretty spooky. I’ve never known anyone so spooky.”

“So, is that good spooky or scary spooky?”

“Yeah right. I hate all this numbers and filing and shit.   It's the numbers that freak me out. And the forms and the creepy names like 941 and the TWC quarterly withholding and the FUTA. The fucking FUTA I’ve got to do that next.”

“I’m sorry.”

“Hey put on some reggae.”

UB40 starts up with ‘Red, Red Wine’.

“Han believes that the spirits of the trees are real things, and he talks to them. Yeah. And he has voices in his head. He thinks that they are from some ancient people or something. He’s nice.   Not that closely connected to any consensual reality.”

“Consensual reality.”

“I learned that from Chrissy. We all describe and agree to a reality. Consensual reality.”

"Oh really."

"Yeah, it's psychological."

****

Dr. Davidson was Omar's professor in his favorite class, Anthropology, during his short lived academic career. Ever since then Omar has shared a friendship with him and occasionally a beer and conversation about any subject at all — human evolution for example.

Dr. Davidson's position was that human evolution was inevitable due to the tendency for organisms to become more complex in order to gain a strategic advantage for survival, but also cyclical. Organisms get more and more complex until they become over specialized, overly dependent on too many things and then when some cataclysmic event occurs and they can no longer adapt, they become extinct. Only the simplest organisms survive and start it up again. Omar's belief, on the other hand, is that it's an unwritten book, that every day another page is written on the book of life and humans have the creative potential to write anything they want to, anything they can imagine. It could be destruction or some kind of paradise.

It's the late afternoon crowd at Donner's Micro Pub on the edge of downtown. People are congregated around a large screen with a football game on it, others are clustered in small groups of 4 or 5 carrying on the conversation. Teams of two are playing some kind of throw the bean bag in a hole game on one side of the pub.

Omar, Han and Hannah park their bikes and

112

enter. Dr. Davidson has been expecting them.

"Doctor. The good doctor."

"How are you Omar?   What's new in the hood?"

"Han, Hannah, this is the illustrious and overly educated, infamous from an intellectual point of view — Dr. Davidson. Also author of articles and purveyor of journals."

"Ah, you're too kind. Hello Han." He touches Hannah's hand, "My dear."

Dr. Davidson looks pleased with the prospective audience and ready to get the show on the road. "What'll it be then, the gorse stock or 'call me by any name' porter or the hefeweizen?"

"Lord no, not the hefeweizen." replies Omar. "The tradition here is, if I might explain, the most celebrated and esteemed of the group buys the first round, it then goes to the second most esteemed and so on and so forth. In this way you can identify and maintain the social status of all the individuals in the group while having fun paying for the beer."

"I get it." says Han.

Stainless steel vats are lined up against the back wall with tubes and valves and pipes connecting them to other stainless steel vats and containers in such a way as to be able to brew beer and deliver it to its appropriate destination. A row of wooden casks, stacked and labeled, sits behind the counter ready to dispense the golden sacrament through a collection of taps mounted on the wall with wooden paddles attached. Overhead large fans turn slowly, moving the air, redistributing the scent of humans and beer.

"Tell me about the old people, professor, the

ones who lived here before the Europeans arrived. I want to make a movie." Han picks up his phone and turns on the camera, Hannah jabs him in the side.

"Well they didn't have any guns that's for sure or Christian rituals. They were, umh, how would you say it, bereft of such tools and doctrines so they were, umh, in a way much better off than the Europeans who conquered them."

"Really?"

"Their battles were mano a mano and more about honor than killing someone. Their religion was basically guilt free. There was no hell threatening their poor souls with perdition. Original sin was not their thing, they lived in a complimentary relationship with nature, they were very familiar with the food chain, intimately familiar, not always on the top. Their games and stories, however, were highly evolved. It's likely that they had ample free time for such activities. I'm speaking in generalizations of course."

"Of course. Cheers!" Omar raises his glass and they all clink their newly arrived schooners and drink.

"Did you know that people already inhabited this world 20 or possibly 30,000 years ago? Before humans inhabited England and northern Europe. Did you know there were 100 million people here already in the Americas when Columbus arrived? Did you know that there were 500 nations already here when Columbus 'discovered the new world' and claimed it for King Ferdinand and Queen Isabella? And the pope."

Han looks querulously at him. He continues, "Did you know that there were 100 base language groups and 1000 languages and dialects among all the people who lived here in the new world? In all of Europe there were only 4 basic language groups that all the languages came from."

"Wow. So people have been here for 30,000 years?"

"Maybe, nobody knows for sure, but that many diversifications of language . . . takes a long time. Their cultures are older and wiser in many ways than the people who came and conquered them. They were living in the garden, hunting and gathering. No governments, no taxation, no traffic jams. Everything they needed was provided in the rivers and the forests. Plenty of game out on the prairies too, large herbivores, bison. There were fruit trees and nuts and all kinds of stuff growing out of the ground to eat, and they knew where to find it. Their technology was how to make stone tools and wood tools and bone tools and all kinds of tools to enhance their life. Leisure and having fun were a big part of their lifestyle."

"Well, how do you know that?" queried Hannah who was enjoying her gorse quite a bit. "I mean how can you tell that people had a lot of fun 30,000 years ago?"

"No doubt. Good question young lady. Judging by the known hunter/gatherer societies living today, we can reconstruct what it probably was like for people living that lifestyle long ago. The fascinating thing is that their technology hasn't really changed that much. Maybe exchanged the bow for the spear but they were a pinnacle culture, meaning that their tools and their methods of living were so well adapted to their environment that they didn't need to develop. It's hard for us to imagine. Everything is new. Every day something new. We thrive on the latest and greatest, our economy depends on it."

"So you would say their culture was richer than the Europeans at the time?" said Han from behind his camera.

"While Europe was still under the ice sheets, culture here had been chugging along for millennia. Imagine the tales they told around the campfire. Imagine what their world view was growing up in the forest or by a river or in the mountains somewhere, completely surrounded by nature everyday, from the day they were born until the day they died.

Living with and enjoying the bounty of mother nature was the lifestyle of those people. That was their skill. That's why they recorded their accumulated knowledge into traditions and traits. That's why they made up stories and told them to their children. Their stories were a vehicle for transporting their cultural values to the ensuing generations to keep the tribe alive. They saw time as an ally, a friend, a god, the one who had created the sacred dance and set the first fire alight in the heavens so that people could have light and warmth and could see even in the darkest night."

He grins at Han. "I mean sure they had their wars and stuff." He side glances Omar, "But that's not what it was about. Their stories were about stuff they had learned and was important for the tribe to remember. And the telling of the story with the hero doing things in the world and making things happen, defeating evil — that gave the story its power. Do you get it?"

"I think so." he lowers the camera and does a pan shot.

"The European invaders destroyed all those cultures in order to impose their own. The Tree of Life, holding up the sky and connecting to the earth and providing shelter for the people who lived in between — they chopped it down and replaced it with their own stone tower. Even now on the Indian Reservations there is a terrible problem with addiction and youth suicide. Even now that trauma of genocide and cultural destruction is played out on the generations of today. It affects their psyche as if it happened to them. Do you know about epigenetics?"

"No."

"Look into it. There is a way that the emotional memory of a people is passed down to future generations."

"Jesus."

"Right. Jesus."

****

The morning air was warming up from the overnight low but still cool and it was an easy ride in light traffic to the edge of town. A pigeon came down out of the trees and swooped past them as they gathered speed. The street curved and bent around the hills and then merged into Monmouth Hwy and then out onto FM 48. From there it was an open road.

. . . if you synch up your cadence with your

117

fellow bike riders and fall into the space where you're parallel and equal then it's a sort of perfection . . . thought Han.

They fell into it. They were a unit and FM 48 can be a fast road, both wide and open. Clear and focused, heart and muscles, no thoughts only breathing and listening for cars, they worked together.

"C'mon, hammer down!" says Omar and takes off.

"Oh yeah?" says Han and launches after him.

"You got me!" says Omar.

"Oh yeah." says Hannah.

They sail down the road in single file, no one is able to catch the other. They're all at their limit, and a little beyond. Omar in the lead, Han and Hannah. Miles go by.

Set back away from the road is a small house with a barn behind it, a corral with a couple of horses and a tilled garden.

"Turn off here!" yells Omar.

They slow and turn down a bumpy, unpaved road. Two dogs come running at them, yipping and howling and herd them to the house barking the whole way until Henry calls them.

"Chaka! Hush down. Chono." They immediately quiet and start milling around, inspecting each of the riders with their nose, eventually settling under the Hackberry tree to watch the proceedings.

Henry is standing on the porch with his pipe and emblazoned jacket smiling broadly, "My friend."

"Good buddy." responds Omar.

They lean their bikes up against each other and climb the steps to join Henry on the porch.

Omar embraces his friend.

"It's good to see you. Dog gone it. Just remembering the other day when we went fishing in the lake below the escarpment and the bear came out of the trees and right down to the dock and we got in the boat and went out in the middle of the lake."

"I remember that. We must have been, what, about 10 or 12?"

"Yeah, that big ole bear looked at us like 'what's wrong with you people?" Henry laughs "Good times brother."

"These are my friends: Han Arrizobal and Hannah Ryun. They're doing their project. Hey it's good to see you. It's been a long time."

"Come in, come in." says Henry with a smile. "Hello Han. Hello Hannah."

The living room is furnished with 3 old stuffed chairs and a couple of stiff backs gathered around a low table and some other antique looking furniture, not antique really just handmade and worn. There is a scent in the air of pine and partially burned pine logs are in the fireplace.

"Wow." says Hannah looking around at the interior of their house. "Do you mind if we shoot some video while we talk?"

"No not at all. Make yourselves comfortable."

"Thank you."

Han pulls the camera phone out of his belly pouch and sets up the shot.

"Can I offer you some tea?" says a woman who has just entered the room from the kitchen. "Hi, I'm Gentle Leaf."

"This is my wife."

"This is my husband." All laugh.

"Sure." says Hannah.

"Of course." says Han.

"Hi." says Omar.

"Please." says Henry.

Han is doing a pan shot of the scene. Henry smiles as Gentle Leaf leans down and plants a kiss on his head.

"So, yes, I wanted to ask you some questions and get it on camera to make a documentary about the ancient people who used to live here. We want to get the stories of, that still remain of the ancestors, all those people. What could you tell us about the pre-columbian history and stuff like that of those ancient people, who lived around here, around the springs, what their life was like, how did they live, what was their culture like?"

"Nobody knows."

"Oh great."

"Not really. How far back do you want to go?"

"All the way. To the first people."

"Yeah me too, must have been great."

"Well what do you know that you'd like to share with our viewers?" says Han.

"Who are your viewers?"

"Nobody really, he just does this for kicks." says Hannah.

Han play kicks Hannah with his foot. "Not true, this will be on YouTube and everyone in the world will see it or might see it. Could see it. Possibly."

Gentle Leaf enters with a tray holding six cups and a teapot, puts it down on the low table.

"You have six cups." notices Han.

"This is medicinal tea. Think about that when you drink it. It'll be ready after a while."

"Who is the other cup for?"

"Someone who isn't here or not in this way." Gentle Leaf exits.

"Well there's something," says Henry, "the old people knew the spirit ways. When someone died they weren't gone they were just in a different form, their spirit remained and you could talk to them and entertain them and be entertained. My grandfather used to have conversations with his grandfather right here in this room. I can hear him talking now. Can't you?

"Yup, I can hear him." said Gentle Leaf who had just re-entered.

"You didn't even know my grandfather."

"No matter. I can still hear him."

All laugh.

"They could talk to the spirit of the trees and the spirit of the water, the spirit of the stone, whoever needed talking to or needed to be listened to. They lived in a spirit world where the physical reality was only one level of reality, not more real or less real than the spirit of things. That's how they understood the world. Now we've got science and that explains everything, like spooky action at a distance. Do you know about that?

"Uh uh. What is it?" says Han.

"Quantum mechanics, my friend. They figured out that one particle in one place if it's entangled with another particle will mirror the actions of that particle no matter where it is in space. It could be on the other side of the universe but it will still mimic the qualities of

the other particle exactly and instantly. As if
they were connected. As if they were the same
particle. 'Spooky action at a distance' Einstein
called it."

"Wow. How does that work?"

Henry seemed to be lost in thought. "The
world is not just a bunch of separate entities and
objects existing only in space and time. There is
something more, something that knits together
the fabric of the whole universe and everything.
We have not been able to understand it up until
now. But the old ones did. They knew that, just
put it in different terms. Everything was
connected and everything had a spirit. Today
they might call that super strings, vibrating tiny
little strings that make up basic matter with their
harmonics."

Gentle Leaf rose and walked through the
doorway into the kitchen. Hannah and Han were
listening intently, Omar was on the edge of his
seat.

"I know this from my reading but my
ancestors knew it from their own intuitive
knowledge and from their ancestors. The old
wisdom. Everyone knows it in themselves. We
don't often pay attention to it these days. That's
the big difference I see between now and then.
They had technology and we have technology
but their technology they learned from nature. It
was more like a conversation or a friendship
with different species including the trees and the
birds and their own selves. They could hear and
listen to what we can't hear anymore. Way too
much noise."

Han scratches his head and runs his fingers
through his hair. He checks the video, changes

the shot. "Well what would you consider to be the most important thing to know about the ancient people that lived here long ago." he intones and zooms in closer to Henry's face.

"They knew how to survive, Chato. They knew how to live. That's the most important thing to know." He gazes back into the camera.

Han holds the shot then pulls back and cuts the scene. "Wow. Thank you."

"You are welcome." says Henry. "Now, let me show you the new goat pen."

They all exit through the back of the house and into the yard. Gentle Leaf starts up with Hannah, "That's a pretty scarf."

"Yes, I got it in Guatemala."

"So pretty. Hand made. I can see the weavings."

"Yes, yes made by hand on a loom." Hannah gestures with her hands as if weaving.

"Yes I know what it is. I have one."

"You do? Really?"

"Let me show you."

Gentle Leaf and Hannah veer off towards the barn. Henry, Omar and Han are headed for the goat pen behind the barn.

"Three does and 2 rams. That's my starting. In the Spring I should have 6 or 8 more. Each doe can produce 2 or 3 babies."

"Enterprising." comments Omar.

"Yeah I just want to grow them for wool, make wool, make yarn. Gentle Leaf is a weaver."

****

"Come in. You can see my loom." She clicks on the light.

123

"Wow. You've done these?"

On the wall are woven hangings of different sizes and designs, brightly colored, highly geometrical and highly detailed. They all have a similar spirit but seem to have different possible uses, some are rug size, some are shawl size, some are napkin size.

"Oh yeah." says Hannah, "I love this."

"These designs are traditional Huichol motifs. My people." She turns towards the back of the barn where several windows illuminate the scene. "And these are yarn paintings."

"Oh wow."

Sitting on a work table and hanging on the wall are framed paintings made from yarn and beeswax. "All these designs are related to Huichol stories and myths. Mostly what I read about in books but also from visiting them down around Nayarit and in the mountains."

"Oh so you've been there."

"Yes. The stories are about the peyote pilgrimage and the beginning of the world. The stories are about," she waves her hand as if to indicate all her artwork assembled in the barn, "how to live in the world. They're about the cosmos, the universe."

****

"So that's what it was about, the spring." says Henry back in the house with the gathered throng.

Gentle Leaf is pouring hot tea into each cup and the aroma is wafting into the air in visible wisps of smoke. "This is a mixture of peppermint, valerian, marshmallow, skullcap

124

and . . . lavender. Let it cool for a few minutes.
Add some honey if you like." She places a jar
of honey on the table.

Hannah and Omar are adjusting their tea, Han
is taking his straight. Henry blows on his tea
and takes a sip, Gentle Leaf is holding hers in
both hands.

"Think of an infant nursing on its mother, one
of the very first things we do as a human being,
nursing away on that yummy nutritious warm
milk and our warm mother and being
comfortable and safe. That was pure love,
unrestrained, unbounded. That was the
relationship the early people had with the spring.
Father Sky was above because he was big and
Mother Earth was below because she was soft
and round and gave the water from her breasts."

"Got it. Thanks. Thanks for going over that
again. Even better." Han puts down the camera.
"I have one question about the shaman tradition.
What was that about? Could they really change
into animals? I've read that. They were the
doctors and the visionaries, right? I mean did
they have super powers?"

"You want to know about the shamans?"

"Yes definitely."

"Why don't you go talk to Alma, she knows a
lot about that stuff, all that pre-columbian stuff."

"Who is she?"

"Oh yeah, go see her. She's a bruja. She
might talk to you."

"Yeah, Han, she might talk to you." repeats
Hannah with a smile.

****

It's evening, they are in each others arms, a small campfire is going. The sparks are rising up into the air, the tops of the trees are waving in the wind.

"Han."

"Hannah." he says and hesitates. "Everything is going to be alright, everything is good, I am blessed, I live in abundance . . . of blessings, I am healthy, I am meant to be this way, I am loved, I am complete, I am ok, I am ok, I am powerful.'

"Hey' says Hannah.

"Hi." Han gives her a kiss.

"Are you on your meds?"

"Yeah I'm on that." he disentangles and pulls out his guitar "Listen to this" and plays some chords "Once upon a time, a long long time ago, there lived a boy and a girl . . ." he tells his story over the chords of the guitar, changing with the flow of the story.

"They walked in tune with the sky and the earth and both were reflected in each other, like looking into a still pond and you can see your reflection, they could see each others reflection in their mind."

The changing chords settle into a rhythm with the same chords repeating over and over. The chords become his home base.

"They both went through their cycles and they both formed their map where each one knew where the other was and that they would meet some day no matter what happened and where they were and how they belonged."

He finishes his story, "These days people are disparate and disconnected. Henry talked about his people, I have no people, my family is totally dysfunctional. I live like some kind of a lonely wanderer.   There's the fear of bad brain chemicals and growing old."

"We all have worries, we all have fears."

His phone beeps. He looks at it. "Oh hold up, let me get this." he lifts the phone staring at it, finally puts it to his ear, "Yeah?"

"You know your mother is unwell."

Silence.

 "I'm having her transferred to the Whitewater Nursing Facility."

Silence.

 "Actually she's been there for a few days. I saw her a week ago.   She was incoherent. Yelling. In a most incoherent way."

"Yeah?"

"Oh yeah, terrible things. *You are an asshole. Where did you get that jacket? Are you seeing that woman? Get out of here. Get out of my life.'* Terrible things I won't even say. She's gone off the deep end."

"The deep end of what?"

"Listen Han, there's no use pretending that she will be any kind of a functional mother.   In addition to the schizophrenia, she has been diagnosed with Alzheimer's. She couldn't be left alone overnight. There's no telling what she might do. I think it'd be good if you went to see her."

"Do you?"

"Yes Han, she's your mother."

"And your wife."

Silence.

"Like I said she's been committed. She's not there on her own volition. If she has any."

"No you didn't say that."

"Life is not easy. I've been trying to tell you that."

"Jesus, dad."

"I've got to go. I'm sorry for the bad news. Go see her."

"Right."

Click. Silence.

"That sounded like a happy conversation."

"Real happy. My dad. What an asshole. Jesus, the family I got born into."

"We all have to get born into some family."

They both sit in the silence. Han picks up his guitar and strikes some chords, one after the other, until he finds the one he likes.

Chapter 7

Communicating with the gods

Humans, like so many animals, have the urge, or maybe even the necessity, to come together in social groups and share the feeling of belonging. We have developed extremely sophisticated language skills in order to do this or maybe we do this because we have developed extremely sophisticated language skills. Societies and advanced language skills are co-dependent and developed around the same time. It's estimated that around 70,000 years ago we started talking in earnest, not just to each other but to invisible entities as well, the gods and nature spirits. What exactly is it we have been trying to say and who have we been saying it to?

"Hey, watch out a tiger!" might have been an early phrase spoken or yelled out to our hunting buddies back then. But home around the campfire we spoke of our exploits in poetry and song, we used language to celebrate the hunt and the great adventure and the excellent flank steak.

Stories about brave deeds and mighty heroes have enchanted and enriched our gatherings ever since, not to mention the magical creatures we invented, the dismal swamps we trudged through, the enchanted forests we got lost in and the hidden treasures we discovered. We invented gods and religions. We talked to them and they talked to us. Here's how that happened.

At home in the Garden of Eden

We lived in the Garden of Eden for hundreds of thousands of years, back when we could talk to snakes and walk with God and didn't know we were naked. That was our intuitive knowing phase, that was our living in a state of simplicity now forgotten and almost unimaginable phase, when language was only a whispering possibility and we felt the yearning for something more. From the time our species emerged from among the early hominids of East Africa 300,000 years ago until the arrival of the cognitive revolution 70,000 years ago Homo sapiens minds were as simple as dirt, not dumb but simple, only a little ego, a proto-ego.

Then, as our brain grew larger, we began to get smarter (naturally) and we developed new skills like symbolic logic. Now we could say that this thing represents that thing. Now we could represent. Now we could make marks with paint or by scratching on stones, marks that meant something and whoever would see our mark would know the meaning of it and that the same thing that you were feeling was also felt by them. We learned how to make sounds with our voice to represent things, so that the sound might enter into another person's hearing and cause the same thing that was in our mind to arise in theirs.

It was powerful magic and arguably the most extraordinary development in the entire history of Homo sapiens. Now we could tell stories. Now we could say that this is us and this is not us and this is what happened next because we can talk about it. Because we could represent and imagine and invent things that existed only in our mind, the possibilities of life grew exponentially greater.

Modern humans, us, (who began back there in the cognitive revolution) have invented a whole new world designed by us and for us. But we have also separated ourselves from nature in doing so. We have eaten from the Tree of the Knowledge of Good and Evil. This is how that happened.

The old ones

The early hominids, before Homo sapiens showed up, were fresh out of the trees. The trees had been their home for many hundreds of thousands of years, millions of years actually, but by the time Lucy arrived, around 3 million years ago, we were starting to ambulate.

Lucy was bi-pedal, she stood upright but still showed the skeletal features of a tree dweller. Her fossilized bones were found on the Ethiopian Plateau where the Awash river drains the Ahmar mountains into the Red Sea. Lucy was a member of the bold explorers club, the dreamers, the ones willing to take a chance on the ground because it offered a wider variety of food. But it also offered more predators, those who ate the ones who came down from the trees. On the whole, however, scavenging the occasional carcass and hunting for food on the ground was a more bountiful lifestyle then a diet of fruit and nuts in the trees.

Lucy's brain was only about the size of a modern day chimpanzee but it was about to get much larger. For tree dwelling hominids up to 60% of their blood supply is used for digesting plant material, but meat protein, whether scavenged or hunted offers more bang for the buck and by mastering the art of fire, humans were able to cook which also increased their caloric input. Anthropologists theorize that this change in diet, which may have begun a million years ago among our hominid ancestors, led to larger brain size which in turn would have led to more skillful tool making which in turn would have led to more successful hunting and more calories for our bigger brains.

By 120,000 years ago people were beginning to talk, people who looked like us — Homo sapiens. Maybe they weren't 'talking' talking but they were certainly making sounds and communicating. Since words don't leave any fossil imprints it's impossible to know what they were saying and what it sounded like but not long after that, in a geological sense, they were also 'writing'.

Modern humans

One of the oldest known artifacts that exhibits some kind of symbolic writing is the 100,000 year old Blombos cave stone from South Africa. Scratched into this stone, 3 1/2 inches long and shaped roughly like a stick of butter, are straight lines, triangles and crosshatch designs inscribed by some ancient human. What its purpose is or its meaning might be, is unknown. There are at least 15 other stones or pieces of stones that have been found in the same cave similarly incised and from different time periods, between 100,000 and 75,000 years ago, indicating that this was an established pattern, not a one time doodling.   It would seem that some form of written communication was being practiced way back then in the dim recesses of our pre-history.

The timeline is still being calibrated, but our language development was well underway by the time people started migrating out of Africa 70,000 years ago.   As they moved out and settled in new places, their expressions of symbolic thought began to appear as art. Many examples still remain in the caves that lay along what was then the southern edge of the glacial ice fields that covered much of northern Europe. Caves like the famous Chauvet cave in south-eastern France are filled with realistic paintings of deer, horses, wooly rhinos, bison — the grazing animals that were in the vicinity at that time, and cave lions, bears, hyenas, panthers — their predators. Those caves lay close to the ice melt that created streams and meadows for a rich assortment of grazing animals that gathered there. It was a Paleolithic Serengeti and artistic expression flourished. Much of what we know about our Ice Age ancestors (40,000 - 10,000 years ago) comes from the study of these caves.

The Lion-man, found in a cave in Germany is dated at 35 - 40,000 years old, stands 12 inches high and portrays a half lion, half man figure. Its main features are it's long legs, powerful chest and feline head.   Its eyes are looking straight ahead as if peering into you as you hold it. It's an important clue because at that point in our history we weren't necessarily on top of the food chain. There were lions who could eat us while we were looking for something to eat and I'm sure the names those people had for the local predators were far more descriptive than the names we have for them today.

Encountering a 500 lb. hungry Cave Lion in the wild would be an evocative experience and a heck of a story, if you survived. You might even carve a sculpture out of a mammoth tusk with your flint knife, half lion and half man to remember the event and to invoke the story and the sculpture would hold the spirit of the lion transferred into you by the carving of it and into every other person who held it and told the story.

That could be one reason why the sculpture was made and also why it shows signs of wear as if it were handled extensively and passed down through the generations of story tellers who lived in that cave. You can google this image, as well as the other artifacts mentioned here, it's a strikingly beautiful piece.

The Lady of St. Germaine-la-Rivière and her mysterious necklace were found interred in a cave in the southwest of France along the Vézère River. She lived about 16,000 years ago and when she died her tribal mates buried her with full honors — antler knives, stone blades, sea shells and a necklace made of 71 polished deer teeth, some inscribed with mysterious designs. The markings are arranged in groups and are made up of straight lines, x's and asterisks. What could they mean? Might they have been a proto-alphabet, or maybe mnemonic cues for the telling of an ancient and awesome tale, something that brought comfort and solace to the listener, maybe a primitive version of Gilgamesh, and like rosary beads, helped to keep the sequence flowing?

That would have been of value back in those days as it still is. These days we have voice recorder on our phones and youtube channels on our computer and tele-prompters and televisions and a thousand other ways to record and tell our story. But what if the story went on for five and a half hours and what if all of it was really good and really important and what if you lived 16,000 years ago? The story necklace would have been very handy in that case. And the fact that they placed it around this young woman's neck as a funeral offering may have indicated that the story held particular meaning for her. Maybe it was her favorite story, maybe her totem was a character in the story and she found her direction and inspiration in the telling of the story which she was going to need now that she was navigating the afterlife.

Or maybe it was something completely different; nobody knows. But what is known is that creative expression blossomed during this time, from 35,000 to 10,000 years ago, as evidenced by sites throughout Europe, and not only Europe but also southern Asia, China and back home in Africa.

Through this newfound ability of speech and making art our ancient ancestors were able to invoke the power of the created object, magnify it, bless it and be blessed by it. In its time it was more powerful than the technologies we have today because it enabled early humans to name and harness to their will the natural forces that they found themselves surrounded by. They were able to became a superhero instead of a victim. With the breath of life they could create too: words and meaning. By using interpersonal communication within the tribe they were able to come up with strategies and develop alliances. These two language enabled skills were vital elements in the survival and prospering of the early hunting and gathering people, our ancestors.

A monkey that learned how to talk

We don't really know how Homo sapiens developed their advanced language skills. Crocodiles did not, although they are known to have 20 different vocalized messages. It may have been that some great urge came upon us, or welled up from within us, connecting us in an unbroken chain of DNA all the way back down the line to all those creatures that came before us; all the way back through the spiny lizards, the turtles, the sharks, the jellyfish, the algae to the very first tiny squiggling cells floating around in the water, and when we learned to speak we spoke for all of them. Maybe it was a genetic mutation in our brain or maybe it was a visitation from the star people or a mind expanding collaboration with psychotropic plants that triggered the language explosion.

Somehow we became a monkey who could talk, and in our earliest first beginnings, once we got the hang of it, speech was about praise and glory. It was the beginning of our humanity, it was the beginning of poetry.

Our earliest writings, usually creation myths, are full of praise and glory. Every culture has their own vision of themselves connected to their own pre-history and it is, with few exceptions, glorious and praiseful. These are the stories we told to our grandkids around the campfire so they would know what to believe, so they would know how the world worked and what was their place in it. There was (and is) a deep need for human beings to have a story about the creation of the cosmos and an explanation for the wild and wondrous world we find ourselves in.

"In the beginning God created the heaven and the earth. And the earth was without form, and void; and darkness was upon the face of the deep. And the Spirit of God moved upon the face of the waters. And God said, 'Let there be light', and there was light. And God saw the light, that it was good: and God divided the light from the darkness. . . . And God said, 'Let us make man in our image, after our likeness' . . So God created man in his own image, in the image of God created he him; male and female created he them. And God blessed them, and God said unto them, 'Be fruitful, and multiply.' And God saw every thing that he had made and behold, it was very good."

That's the Judeo-Christian creation story according to the King James version of the Bible. An eminently positive tale full of blessings and good news.

An ancient Chinese text, starts out in a similar fashion to the Judeo-Christian creation story but then shifts into philosophy and social duty. It's called The Huainanzi and was compiled in 139 BC.

"Before Heaven and Earth had taken form all was vague and amorphous. Therefore it was called the Great Beginning. The Great Beginning produced emptiness, and emptiness produced the universe. The universe produced material-force, which had limits. That which was clear and light drifted up to become Heaven, while that which was heavy and turbid solidified to become Earth . . . If we examine the Great Beginning of antiquity we find that man was born out of nothing to assume form as something. Having form, he is governed by things. But he who can return to that from which he was born and become as though formless is called a 'true man.' The true man is one who has never become separated from the Great Oneness."

In the Mayan account of creation as written in the Popul Vuh, it's described this way.

"And the Forefathers, the Creators and Makers, who were called Tepeu and Gucumatz said: 'The time of dawn has come, let the work be finished, and let those who are to nourish and sustain us appear, the noble sons, the civilized vassals: let man appear, humanity, on the face of the earth' . . . . After that they began to talk about the creation and the making of our first mother and father; of yellow corn and of white corn they made their flesh; of corn meal dough they made the arms and the legs of man. Only dough of corn meal went into the flesh of our first fathers,

*the four men, who were created . . . They were
endowed with intelligence; they saw and
instantly they could see far, they succeeded in
seeing, they succeeded in knowing all that there
is in the world . . . Great was their wisdom; their
sight reached to the forests, the rocks, the lakes,
the seas, the mountains, and the valleys."*

Some native tribes of North America believe that the first people came out of the springs on the full moon, emerged from their watery birthplace soaking wet and cold and began an epic journey to the first sunrise. They were the ancestors of everybody. Where did they come up with this creation myth? From looking into the spring and seeing the little minnows swimming around? From contemplating the coming of night and the appearance of stars? Did they intuitively sense that they were part of a great and fathomless world with an ancient beginning, that their ancestors were wise and knew more than they did?

That intuitive wisdom was the kind of wisdom that our ancient ancestors had. Come up with an idea and see if it works. Whatever works is good, whatever doesn't work is discarded. It was through intuitional knowledge that we learned how to talk, it was through intuitional knowledge that we learned how to make a spearhead. It was by being curious and exploring that we discovered how to do these things.

Evolutionarily speaking, that was our only advantage — a big brain. We started developing it a million years ago and it was our big brain that enabled us to negotiate our niche in the biosphere. It enabled us to rise up from being an insignificant little animal to the top of the food chain. We could easily have been wiped out by animals larger, faster and more powerful than us. The tigers, the wolves and the bears would have seen to that, but we mastered fire and created community and we survived.

The functional unit was the tribe, the extended family, maybe 20 or 30 people; everybody helped out, did whatever they could do. They made tools so they could do more things more easily. And our big brain, sitting up there on top of our shoulders, could look around at the sky above and at the earth underfoot, and notice that we were here in between, with the trees. We saw amazing things back then in the primordial world, it's like everywhere was a national park. We saw forests and jungles and mountains and glacial rivers and grassy plains where the animals lived in profusion and the predators that accompanied them.

And we saw possibility too, with our head held high — the possibility to be a predator not a grass eater. And we saw the possibility of choosing between two things, of differentiating, we saw the possibility of entertaining ideas and of representing those ideas in verbal or visual cues. Each one of those stages was a major phase on our road to higher cognition; it took thousands of years for it to happen and to be adopted into the sapiens species as a behavioral trait.

The animal mind sees the world as it really is; whatever their senses tell them, they are informed. But for the human mind we see the world as our brain describes it to us, as ideas represented by words and images. That was the shift that anthropologists call the Cognitive Revolution, Christian apologists call it eating from the Tree of the Knowledge of Good and Evil, I call it communicating with the gods. The wild world around us is not intelligible and relatable until we can name it and make it into words, until we can find patterns and connect elements. Indescribable are the workings of the mind, inscrutable are the ways of the lord. Lutheran hymns came out of the droning of the bees in the garden and the twittering of birds overhead.

And where does this story end, the story of our story-telling? We don't know yet, because we haven't written it yet. We are the storytellers, we can write any story we want. We're the ones with imagination. We're the ones with inspiration. We're the ones that know how to write.

Chapter 8

Han and Hannah

The trees are tangled and dark above his head; it's twilight. Han is walking along a path deep in the forest. In the branches of the trees he sees designs moving, making shapes. He sees the faces of monsters inside the designs and they're looking at him. He doesn't like it. He turns away and tries to run but it's as if he were underwater, he can't quite get any traction. He has a premonition that the trees are giants, real giants, like in Lord of the Rings, and they're conspiring to kill him, but no matter how hard he tries to run, he's still stuck in the mud. The sinister faces in the tree branches become bats and fly towards his head. He's in a maze, and doesn't know which way to go. He's in a labyrinth, no way out.

When he wakes up he's lying on the cot in his bedroom. In the dim light, the shape of the room slowly comes into focus: shelves, clothing, light fixture. He lies motionless, breathing deliberately as if he were trying to purge himself of something, as if he were trying to transition from his dream reality to an awake reality. He puts his hand to his mouth and considers unthinkable things.   Just as he's about to lose himself in the torrent of thoughts, he drops his hand and makes a conscious effort to change the channel . . . *what do I have to do today? . . .*

He throws back the covers and lets the cool air touch his body. Eyes wide open, entertaining reality. . . . *there's something . . .* It's just out of range but he knows it's important.

By the time he gets out of bed and does his yoga, he still hasn't thought of it. By the time the breakfast ritual rolls around he still hasn't remembered, but he's reeling it in, expecting it to pop through at any moment.   While he's carrying the granola and coffee out to the backyard, descending the porch steps, he glances at the pool, the green water . . . *the bruja! . . .*

****

Herbs are hanging from the door posts and sage is smoldering in a clay bowl on the table; it creates a wisp of smoke which swirls around the bruja as she enters the room. She's cooking a caldo on the stove top, stirring it with a large wooden spoon. . . . *there are many ways to cook a caldo . . . si . . .* she speaks to her own mind. Her grey hair and wrinkled face are framed in a head shawl to ward off the chill in the air. She glances around quickly, mischievously looking for more ingredients to stir into the pot.   Her phone rings and she plucks it out of her pocket.

"Hello? Hello there . . . yes."

She moves to the door and opens it partially, peering through the reveal into the face of Han. He's running his fingers through his hair and leaning slightly forward.

143

She opens the door and says, "Come in."

"Hello." he enters, "Thank you. I'm Han. I met your friends, Henry and Gentle Leaf."

She nods her head affirmatively.

"Wow that smells good. They gave me your name and recommended you as someone who could talk about the pre-columbian history."

"Why don't you sit down?" she guides him to a mat on the floor and goes back to her caldo. Her face is gentle but fierce.

. . . what a curious person . . . Han thinks as he watches her.

"Yes, so I wanted to learn more about the people who lived here long ago.   The first people to live here. Along the springs. What could you tell me? About those people. Do you know anything?

She looks at him but doesn't respond.

"I know some stuff already, I know a lot of stuff actually but I'm trying to put it all together into this documentary about, you know, the ancient people." pulls out his camera.

Lying on the table with the smoldering sage are several other objects: a long brown and white feather, a green stone, a wooden stick, some sage bundles, a plastic lighter. She picks up one of the sage bundles and lights it.

"Do you . . . know anything about what it was like? Back then? I mean . . . "

She tilts her head. It has just occurred to her that this young man is crazy, kinda like her.

"Would it be ok to videotape our conversation?" he readies the camera.

"You want to know something that happened long ago?"

"Yeah, yes well . . . what was it like . . . for those people . . . how did they live?"

She blows on the sage and lets the smoke billow up until it fills the room. "They lived day to day like me and you."

"What?" He hadn't heard her properly, couldn't understand her. It seemed to Han as if she had receded into the sage smoke.

"Well. That's it?" he said finally, "I don't want to disturb you or anything. I just thought maybe you heard something."

Han felt himself receding too. Strange thoughts filled his mind: . . . *who is this person . . . what am I doing here . . why all the smoke . . .*

He could think of nothing more to ask her. He sat there for a few minutes, waiting for something to happen, for the bruja to speak or for some brilliant question to arise in his mind but nothing happened, nothing at all and he grew uncomfortable, felt like it was time to go. His leg was cramping from sitting on the floor, he stood up.

"I'm going to, umh, look at the video and see what we got. Maybe we can get together another time if we need more footage."

The bruja was barely visible behind a veil of smoke on the other side of the room tending her caldo as he let himself out.

****

Gray and white, gray and white — the shadows of the trees alternate back and forth across the highway as he rolls down the open road under the dimming sky. He's annoyed,

145

more with himself than with the bruja. In his thoughts he reviews the interview, how it had gone oddly awry, and in fact seemed to have been a total failure.

The negative thoughts slow him down. He tries to push them out of the way and get back into rhythm but they keep coming back in, the miles become longer not shorter.

He feels blocked, like he is at an impasse. He realizes that he doesn't really have a vehicle to tell the story he has created in his mind, it's not transferable from his personal imagination to the world at large, it's out of range, he doesn't know how to do it.

He realizes that he doesn't actually know how to do anything, that he has been a failure throughout his whole life. He feels strangely disassociated from who he thought he was just an hour ago. He can't quite place it at first but a familiar feeling is rising up from somewhere inside him, a feeling that he's afraid of. He's afraid it will take over his mind. The strange odor of it is in his sweat and it makes him sad. The clouds overhead have become oppressive, as if they're allied with this dark power. He notices the clouds and he notices the changing. "Power stroke, power stroke, power stroke." . . . *drive the demon from your mind* . . . "Power stroke, power stroke" . . . *find the edge* . . .

By the time he arrives home, larger and darker clouds have started to roll in, obscuring the rising moon. He notices a text message on his phone from Hannah but can barely summon enough intentionality to answer it.

He strips off his sweaty clothes and dives into the pool, surfaces at the far end and climbs out.

He looks at the sky and watches as the heavy clouds build in the distance. . . . *it's going to rain* . . .   The strange odor has not gone away. . . . *the changing . . . oh god . . .*

****

The tents are set up in an open field next to the Hawthorne Public Library. It's late in the day but people are still selling things and displaying their wares. One tent has hand-rolled herbal cigars and incense, another — paintings made with swashes of thick colorful paint that resemble no recognizable plant, animal or object.   Omar's tent is a bright orange arrangement made out of a military surplus parachute. It's not exactly a tent but it's a place.

Hannah rolls up on her bike and parks it next to the colorful fabric. "Hi Omar."

"Hannah!"

"Your place looks great!"

"Thanks. Where's Han? Did you bring him too?

"Nope. He had to do something. He's working on his project."

"Oh. Ah. Did he go see the bruja?"

"I think so, he didn't want to talk about it."

"So would you like to try some Teafullness?" He looks around at the sky, "Before it rains."

"Oh my god, it's going to rain."

"I know. This is our speciality — Hummer Mint.

"Why Hummer Mint?"

"Because it has power herbs and a smooth mint finish that will give you energy and make you smile.

"Ah." says Hannah smiling, "So you make all these?"

"Yes, these are my formulations."

"Formulations."

There is a crash of thunder in the distance.

"You came just in time to see me get rained out." he hands her a sample of Hummer Mint.

"Hmm, yum. I like this."

"This one is Daily Balance — peppermint to pick you up and ginger to keep you rooted and yerba mate to take it to the next level."

"Wow. I like it."

"Yeah that's what we do, custom formulations from family owned farms, mostly in India and Sri Lanka but also in the States.

"I get it. How's business?"

"We're establishing a customer base."

"Yeah, I know. I know about that."

A gentle rain starts to fall. "Yikes, I gotta get all this stuff in my van."

"I'll help you."

They take down the kiosk and stuff it into Omar's van. The rain is falling harder, beating on their heads.

"Ha! Grab this. Fold it up."

"Ah the Teafullness!" she grabs the display with the samples that has fallen onto the ground.

"Wow. Can I give you a ride?"

"Yeah, ok."

"Throw your bike in here."

They wrestle the bike in through the side door and make a place for it next to the folding tables.

Omar and Hannah sit in the van, dripping wet with rain pelting down on the metal roof. It pours down over the windshield turning it into opaque glass.

"Wow, that was crazy. It came out of nowhere."

"It changed just like that." said Hannah, who's looking out the window at the blurry scene, "Where are you from Omar?" she says turning back to look into his face. "I don't catch that accent."

"Lebanon. My parents came here when i was six."

"Oh wow. Have you ever been there?"

"Yes. I went there with my mom and dad a few years ago. We went camping in the Kadisha Valley where the famous cedars of Lebanon are. Or were. Most of them are chopped down now."

"I know about that. From the Bible."

"Right.

"I don't go to church much."

"Me either."

"Are you a Christian?"

"I'm a nothing."

"Me too." says Hannah, "Can I ask you a personal question?"

"Sure."

Hannah hesitates. "Now I can't think of one." She smiles at Omar.

"You're a funny person." says Omar and leans back against the driver's side window which is now all fogged up as if to get a better look at her or maybe to evade her encroaching proximity. "Hey we'd better get going."

He starts the van, puts it in gear and pulls out of the parking lot. Water is already running in rivulets on either side of the road. They drive in silence, just the sound of the rain beating on the roof and the windshield wipers, *shunk kashunk.*

They reach a low water crossing and stop. Water is coursing over the road.

"This is not letting up, we'll have to take the long route over the bridge."

"A rabbit, look!" Hannah is pointing at the side of the road.

"Sure enough." replies Omar. "When we were in Kadisha I saw a rabbit."

"Oh yeah?"

"It wasn't a normal rabbit though. It was looking at me."

"Maybe this is not a normal rabbit too."

The rabbit was drenched, that was obvious, but what they didn't know was that it had been flushed out of its burrow by the rain water and was wondering what was happening in its world. It was a young rabbit and had never seen such a thing before. It had always found shelter underground but now underground was underwater. It was startled and amazed as only a rabbit can be and was staring at the large object that had appeared in its front yard as if wondering what could happen next. Omar and Hannah were wondering too.

****

Han has been flushed out of the back yard by the rain and is in the living room wiping himself dry with a towel. After dragging all the non-waterproof items from his camp up onto the patio deck under the roof, he is thoroughly wet. He sits down on the beat up couch, the only piece of furniture in the room besides a couple of small tables, and opens his camera function to look at the bruja video. There is only a dark

150

fuzzy picture with darker objects appearing from time to time, the audio is a muffled scratching with some other distant non-discernible sounds.

"Damn." He searches again to see if he overlooked the file. He scans his mind for a clear memory of shooting that scene but can't find one. "What is this? Did I turn the camera on? Damn."

His body sinks into the couch and he listens to the sound of the falling rain. He picks up his guitar and starts looking for chords that will resonate with him and hopefully rearrange his brain connections, but the chords are elusive . . . . *maybe the bruja put a hex on me* . . . he lays down the guitar . . . *my mind is stuck* . . .

All his shortcomings and failures come into focus. . . . *i'll never finish this documentary . . it's just a fantasy . . i've never finished anything in my life . . . i never will . . . i'm a failure . . . jees i'm a failure* . . . Negative brain chemicals triggered by his despondency cause him to spiral downward even further. There is no end in sight. He reclines on the couch, covers his face with his arm and thinks about Hannah.

He wakes up in the middle of the night, still on the couch. A storm is raging outside, the wind is thrashing the trees about, thunder and an occasional flash of lightening. He gets up and goes to the bathroom, then finds his bed and falls into it, burrows under the blankets.

In the morning, the clouds have cleared, revealing a limitless heavenly blue sky. He doesn't notice it as he walks out into the backyard to see what happened. A few small tree limbs are down, scattered around the campsite and everything is dripping wet. The water level in the fish pond is almost to the brim. He scatters some cat food on the surface and watches as the orange and white fish come to the surface and scoop it up. He wonders, . . . *what they do down there at night. . . . do they sleep? . . . do they dream? . . . do they hide in the underwater darkness and wait for morning? . . .*

Slumped down in the wet plastic patio chair, he wonders what happened to his life, how could it be so empty after all those years of searching for something to fill it. He wants to see Hannah but doesn't have enough courage to call her or enough energy or get on his bike.

Finally he begins reassembling the camp, moving the items back into place from under the patio cover. It's a routine chore that he's done many times so it's not hard but it seems like a massive effort.

When he's finished, he puts the coffee pot on and dumps some granola into a bowl. This, at least, is comforting and familiar — filtering the coffee, pouring the milk, watching how the two liquids interact. He carries his breakfast outside and sits down at the plastic patio table. He looks at his bowl of granola, spoon poised, and can't decide what to do next . . . *why was i even born . . . scoops a spoonful . . . just to eat and sleep, watch the sun rise and set . . . why was the universe even created . . . so people could ask stupid questions and feel weird . . .* inserts the spoonful into his mouth, sits motionless, chewing slowly.

He wonders about how the ancient people lived, for the hundredth time, and how they spent their days . . . *did they ever feel like this? . . . no reason to get up . . . no reason for doing anything . . . God . . .*

In his imagination he thinks about going swimming with Hannah, somewhere nice where there's a small river and cypress trees and rocks in the water to hold onto and climb up on and deep pools to swim in and when they get out they lie down in the grass and enjoin their wet bodies and remove their swim suits in order to enjoin them further.

****

Omar's van is still sitting by the side of the road as the sun appears above the horizon.. They spent the night there mainly because it had been raining like crazy and they had been talking about rabbits and life and crazy synchronicities. Now they both are awake and making out. Both have ended up in the drivers seat somehow and their conversation somehow has evolved into wet kisses and the groping of sensitive areas. Actually it has just advanced to oral sex. It slipped out of control when Hannah's button got pushed sometime during the night and she knew she was going in. There is a button somewhere on Hannah's body or maybe in her brain and when fingered it triggers total abandonment and reckless passion. The source of all her problems.

Omar, "Hey this is kind of awkward."

Hannah, "Yes it is." and she goes down on him again.

Omar, "I like you but what about Han?"

Hannah, 'I dunno. What about Han?"

"I dunno."

153

Chapter 9

The Ancient Book of Magic Secrets

Nestled inside a shallow cave carved into the canyon wall of the lower Pecos River near its confluence with the Rio Grande in deep west Texas is an ancient cave painting. The cave is visible as a dark slash against the gray cliff from the Hwy 90 bridge as you cross over the gorge in your car. Inside the cave, the painting still displays its original colors, its strange symbols and stylized people and weird animals and it still looks out from its ancient stone canvas, out across the canyon to the horizon beyond. It portrays, in a language we don't fully understand, the cultural wisdom of the inhabitants of this place long ago.

The cave, or maybe alcove would be a better word, was formed by millions of years of water and wind sweeping around that crook of the Pecos river. At one end, where the rock is smooth — they painted. The composition measures 26 feet long and 13 feet high. It was created 2,000 years ago and is a record not only of the people who lived there but of their ancestors who lived there for atleast 2,000 years before that. This was their monument, their sacred space, their ancient book of magic secrets. We know it today as the White Shaman painting. You can see a portion of that painting on the cover of this book.

When the winter sun falls low in the west, the images painted in red, yellow, black and white, glow and come alive on the cave wall as if the campfire still sparked and surged on that rocky stage and the storyteller still told the story — the power of his voice sounding out over the edge of the canyon and down the river and soaring up to the stars above. And if, as the story goes, the people gathered there to dance with the drums and with the ancestors who were painted on the wall and to listen to the story and the chanting, then no doubt, those people were moved to remember who they were and how they came to be in this place and what they might be able to do next if they all came together and focused on a plan and stayed in harmony with the stars and with the earth and with the flower road.

Who were these people?

They were hunters and gatherers living in small bands of thirty to forty souls in an arid region of about 1300 square miles. Their ancestors had come here from Siberia thousands of years earlier and they too had been hunters and gatherers.

In the hunting tradition, the shaman is a very important person. He's the person who can get inside the head of the animal they're stalking and predict its behavior. Imagine hunting wooly mammoths with a stone tipped spear, on foot, in the snow. You would appreciate every advantage you could get, right? They felt the same way and used their brain, the most powerful tool they had, to be more clever than their prey. They tracked them and followed them on their migrations and peregrinations until one day they found themselves making their way over the Bering land bridge into the 'new world', bringing their shamanic hunting traditions with them.

Of course they didn't know they were in a new world, their world was constantly being renewed, the people who moved, the people who journeyed forth into new lands in search of giant mammoths to kill. That was their obsession, their target and their totem. Mammoths were powerful and not easy to kill but they would try anyway. To kill one was to take its power and those people valued power. That was how they survived in Siberia. Plus there were many other gifts that the totem animal gave — food, clothing, building materials.

And what's even more amazing, the ancestors of those hardy cold-weather campers had come from Africa 60,000 years earlier where they had been hunters and gatherers (and scavengers) for 250,000 years. That's where they learned their chops. It took awhile but once they got it together they moved on up the food chain and then went off to explore other lands.

Central to the development and survival of those ancient tribes was some sort of a shamanic process, a practitioner, someone who had learned how to see the omens and was adept at reading the signs in the clouds and the sky, in the flowing water and the trees and knew what to do next. Someone was needed who could provide practical advice and insight as they moved through the landscape. This was the trick that propelled them from scavenging kills made by other predators to becoming predators themselves and skillful hunters. Once they could kill for themselves, they had their own source of fresh game. Major difference and someone was needed who could talk to the spirits of the animals and ask if it would be ok to take one of them because the people were hungry.

Someone was also needed who could tell the old stories sitting around the campfire with the kids at their feet. The old stories and adaptations of the old stories kept the culture alive as it morphed to fit new environments and 'new worlds'. The White Shaman painting is one of more than 300 that have been discovered in the lower Pecos region and the paintings are almost always populated with what are generally recognized to be shaman-like figures; they are the ones who painted them, pro bably, along with the help of a few apprentices.

When these people first arrived in the Lower Pecos Canyon lands, they encountered an ancient landscape of canyons and plateaus, of occasional rivers and sheltered overhangs. They saw a land with lots of opportunity. Back then it was cooler and wetter than it is today and where the Chihuahuan desert is now, there was grass and trees and game animals roaming about, lots of animals, and that meant good hunting. After they had lived here for a few thousand years they became thoroughly adept at utilizing its

157

resources.   They knew the terrain and the weather patterns and the seasons as if they were a living thing, an ally or a friend and sometimes an enemy.

They knew how to make everything they needed from the resources at hand. Dart points and knives and scrapers were chipped from flint. The spear and spear thrower and the rabbit stick and the digging stick were made from wood or from the stalk of the agave plant and bound together if need be by fiber from the lechuguilla and sotol plants. They made sandals and baskets and nets from the same fibrous plants. Needles, awls and bores were fashioned from animal bones. This high tech lifestyle allowed them plenty of time for games, goofing off and inventing things.   One of the things they invented were the strange enigmatic shapes that they painted on their walls.

They used this imagery to convey their stories, to record them and preserve them in a way that could be read by others. Their stories, or the roots of their stories, go all the way back to the mother country, Africa, where they first learned how to tell stories. The stories and the symbols were passed down from generation to generation, through the ages, with gentle modifications. These were the important stories, the ones that mattered: who are we, where did we come from and how do we live here? The stories and the characters in the stories became emblematized as murals but only long after the stories themselves had brewed and bubbled up in the psyche of the tribe as they sat around the fire and looked into the flames.

A sky full of stars and the sailing moon, a landscape both vast and intimate and traditions both ancient and familiar, comprised their world. Their conception of time must have been profound. If they could count one hundred generations into the past or 2,000 years, which they did, then maybe they could count one hundred generations into the future. That would be us and our progeny. What did they intend to say to us, people they had never met, the people of the future?

The painting has many interpretations but like any good work of art, it's in the viewer's mind that it finds its fullest expression. The artist is only a medium between two points — the creative subconscious of their culture and the creative subconscious of ours. It's in the personal that we find the universal, right? That's what the artist was trying to say, I think, trying to convey something so personal in such an abstract way that some other person, even someone 2,000 years in the future could understand it. The White Shaman wants you to know something and that's why he's standing right there in the middle of the painting looking so enigmatic.

The painting

He's rising up, taking off into his peyote vision, leaving behind his darker side in the process. He has on a tunic decorated with squiggly S shapes and tassels hanging from his arms. He also has, like most of his fellow shamans on other walls, in other paintings, in other caves, no head. But he does have a painted center that extends the full length of his exaggeratedly long torso. This represents, perhaps, his interior spirit or the breath filling his body — the only familiar thing for the shaman to hang on to during his peyote vision, his sense of self, his core reality.

His adherents (or buddies at least) are gathered below him with arms raised in support, cheering him on. His shadow side accompanies him and has aimed a dart in the direction of his rising to support his flight. Even the darker side has a way of helping sometimes if directed rightly and reinforced through ceremony and ritual. This is the story that appears in my mind.

Flowing through the springs and the White Shaman, his darker self and the adherents is a white line that undulates across the entire length of the painting and superimposes itself on everything it touches. And what could that be except for time itself joining together all the aspects of the story and imposing on it the order of the cosmos. And what is the order of the cosmos? I suspect that was their question too and they answered it, to the best of their ability, by painting this mural.

Spread across the canvas and connected by the white ribbon are other figures and symbols: impaled deer, falling figures, five elongated human-like shapes with heads that look like glowing matchsticks holding up torches with their stubby arms, and numerous other objects both larger and smaller than the White Shaman. At first glance it looks jumbled up and purposeless, like items in a child's painting, indecipherable, but that's not true. People have been studying it diligently for at least 25 years (the Rock Art Foundation, the Witte Museum, Shumla Archaeological Research & Education Center), and they have discovered a lot about the art and the people who made it. Let's take a closer look — first how was it made and secondly what I think it means.

How was it made?

It may not be that obvious to us today but back then everything was handmade. There were no hardware stores to buy supplies. The hardest part of the whole process, therefore, would have been the preparation as mentioned in chapter 7 about the Paleolithic art in the Chauvet cave. Gathering the rocks with the pigmented minerals in them, red, yellow, black and white and grinding them down into powder with a mortar and pestle, extracting Yucca juice or something like that to use as an emulsifier so the paint wouldn't dry out too fast, breaking open and digging out the marrow from a deer's femur bone to use as the binding agent — that couldn't have been an easy job; first you've got to track down and kill a deer. And thank goodness they did it that way, otherwise we wouldn't be able to see these paintings two thousand years later. Then they had to construct some sort of a scaffold or ladder in order to paint the upper reaches. The White Shaman mural is 13 feet high and the floor of the cave is uneven and slopes outward. They probably made the brushes from animal hairs or feathers or the nubs of fibrous plants. And once you've got all that together you've got to apply the paint and wait for it to dry so you can paint the next color. This was done, no doubt, with a great deal of ceremony, the making of the painting being a sacred ritual for the maker. It must have taken weeks, plus the coordination of a small team of people, to complete the painting.

There must have been some deep and urgent need at work inside the genius mind of whoever created it. It must have been some primal function of the micro-society to which that person belonged that drove them to do this. There must have been some deep and compelling reason for the white shaman to paint the wall in such a way so that the people who gathered there could visualize their gods and remember their wisdom.

I'm assuming a lot in my interpretation of the painting but when the wind is just right and the night is quiet, you can hear people talking inside the White Shaman cave from the Hwy 90 bridge 1400 feet away. Who knows how far the voices of the singers carried back in the day, down the canyon to other camps and other caves. Who can imagine what that voice meant for those people, living in their tiny nation on the edge of the Chihuahuan Desert depending on the beneficence of nature and their own wits for survival? Courage and confidence maybe? Two things they would certainly need.

Black was the first color he painted (if it was a he), its marks appearing on the rock wall, like the stars in the sky, to guide and inform. It was a dark and stormy night and he was making his way, remembering the story as he painted it and figuring out what to do next. Dots, lines and shapes took form on the empty canvas. Black was the base color, the starting point, the

beginning of the journey. In the ancient Meso-
american traditions, of which these people were
a part, the color black symbolizes femininity and
the primordial world, the time before time, the
underworld.

After the black paint dried, red was applied —
the color of masculinity, fire and blood and the
color of the dawning sky. Then yellow, the color
of the rising sun as its rays broke upon the earth
overcoming the darkness of the night. And
lastly, white symbolizing the midday, the
shadowless world, the zenith before the sun
begins to fall into the underworld again and thus
complete the cosmic cycle of death and rebirth.

In this way the shapes were filled out and
given life. The entire mural was painted with
these layers of colors applied sequentially and of
course in order to paint this way the artist would
have had to know what the composition was
going to look like when it was finished, the
spatial relationships, how the information was
revealed using the symbols and the colors, how
the story would unfold in the viewers mind,
what happened next, the beginning and the end,
and the character development. There are still
many things about the White Shaman painting
that we don't understand, there is still much
more nuance to be deciphered, subtle
interconnections to be noticed, jokes to be
chuckled at.

The artist or the shaman or whoever it was or
whatever group of people it was, were able to
visualize their story on the wall of that cave and
paint it. It was a powerful and amazing thing.
And as they painted, they felt the power and the
amazement. They recognized the feeling that

was overtaking them, it was the spirit of the ancestors, it was the voice from deep within. And as it spoke they listened and as they listened they painted.

What does it mean?

There are many stories layered over each other and intertwined judging by the number of individual symbols in the mural; I counted 101. Tributes and creation stories and heroic deeds of the ancestors and how to walk on the flower road that traverses the painting as a white ribbon, are some of them; cosmic maps of the universe and cues for successful deer hunting and tribal wisdom are in there too. Whatever the wisest thing was that they knew, it was surely in there — *'Hey jack you're going to die, so live now.'* might have been the meaning of the enigmatic black box that appears in some of the paintings in other caves. I can't imagine why else they would paint a black box in their mural; there were no straight lines in their world anywhere much less four of them intersecting at right angles. It's a weird shape and intended to evoke the weirdness of death. Something no one can explain. That's what I think.

That they were experienced storytellers can't be doubted. They knew how to spin a tale and keep it interesting and had practiced that art on a regular basis for thousands of years. They had, no doubt, committed to memory long expansive tales that took hours to tell, or at least until the kids fell asleep, weaving the characters in and out of the action, modulating the drama from high intensity to low, filling in details, making a joke, singing and dancing if necessary and bringing the hero home through the dark forest where the giant bear lived. Only God knows how many hidden layers of subtle cultural references lie still undetected in the painting.

But it's the White Shaman who really commands the piece. It's his voice, his version of the story that's playing. That's obvious. He's center stage in his white tunic with the black center and the elegant 'S' shaped designs. He's the most compelling shape of all the shapes on the canvas and judging by the strength and boldness with which he's painted, it's his story. A story he shares with the 5 torch wielding pilgrims who are journeying across the stage from the place of their birth. The predawn, the sacred spring, the underworld is on one side of the painting and on the other side, dawn mountain and the first dawn and the beginning of time. Must have been an exciting day.

Dawn Mountain looks kind of like a fountain and the Underworld looks kind of like a school bus. Anyway they're on opposite sides and the pilgrims are spaced out evenly between them. The undulating white line, the flower road, goes right through the center of the entire painting, and accompanies all the pilgrims, connecting them to the Underworld and Dawn Mountain and everything in between. It also divides the scene in half. It creates an up and a down, an above and below. There's something. For many ancient people the world was divided into up and down, the underworld and the overworld with human beings living in between like a sandwich.

Just above the White Shaman, a giant caterpillar creature is rising or floating up above everyone. It's twice as large as any other figure in the whole painting. Yes and the deer, the story of the magic deer, some rising, some impaled, some falling; one appears to be accompanying the pilgrims along their journey. These images are the ones with the strongest visual impact and therefore would logically comprise the main theme or themes. Of course who can say with certainty what their intentions were and what it meant to them, unless of course you were a shaman from 2,000 years ago.

As the White Shaman rises up he's just about to touch the giant caterpillar-like creature with his right hand. Others have described the creature as a catfish, but according to most accounts, this is Mother Nature herself, the goddess. She is from the days when the goddesses were more powerful than the gods. She could give birth obviously — what was more powerful than that, the mystery and blessing of life, new energy coming into the tribe. She hovers over the whole theatre-scape with its multitudinous forms. She seems to have antlers or feelers on her head and feet sticking out of her caterpillary body.

One way we have of understanding the painting is by comparing it to known mythologies from existing cultures. According to the creation story of the Huichol and Nahua (Aztec) cultures of Mexico, the first people made their way through the Underworld, cold and wet after emerging from the water. Then they journeyed along the white ribbon to greet the first sunrise at Dawn Mountain to warm up and become fully human just like the 5 torch wielding pilgrims following the magic deer in the painting. The magic deer and the ancient torch bearing pilgrims figure in both stories.

That white ribbon also represents the rope that binds the people to their ancestors, those who came before, and those that will come — the children of the future. It also resembles the ecliptic path of the sun as it makes its way through the heavens between solstice and equinox and hence pays homage to the sun god. But most of all it represents the flower road, the road of the ancestors, the road of truth, harmony and beauty, the ideal life These concepts were shared among other Meso-american cultures including the Nahua and Huichol and by the Lower Pecos people who were related to them culturally and linguistically They were also related to them by the Flower Road where their ancestors had traveled on their pilgrimage from the Underworld to Dawn Mountain.

In Huichol mythology the deer is sacred and brings the gift of peyote to mankind on the tines of its antlers. It's one of the defining traditions of the modern Huichol, who live in western Mexico, and is the basis of the pilgrimage they make every year to the peyote fields, guided by the deer, to find the peyote buttons. In so doing they replay the journey of the 5 Ancestors as they became human so many generations ago.

We may never know all the layers of meaning that are in the painting, some are waiting for future generations to intuit, but it is intact (mostly) and has been recorded and digitally archived. A lot of research has already been done, mainly by the Shumla Foundation and the

Witte Museum, to preserve and interpret the painting, its themes and sub-themes.   Its evocations, however, are the responsibility of the viewer to contemplate and understand, as much as it was for those viewers 2,000 years ago who knew the back story.

In my imagination the play was re-enacted many times on that Pecos River canyon stage with the full moon illuminating the mural and all the stars in heaven looking down while the people danced and the drummer laid down a drum track and the shaman lost track of time and of the mere mortal world and became a god himself and led the people through the portal into the spirit world to revisit the first day of creation and the origin of everything.

Stories of the hunting people

There are at least 18 arrows piercing things in the White Shaman painting. The arrow hit, the moment of impact, was a transcendent experience both for the hunter and for the prey. The stalking, the meditative preamble leading up to the decision and the moment of release and the trajectory. The dull thud and the penetration was something else for those people, something they lived for, aspired to and celebrated. It also meant dinner, high quality protein and a sharing experience around the campfire. If you brought back a deer you were a hero, you and your buddies. The girls would smile at you and tilt their heads. But it wasn't a solo endeavor, it was team work.

The hunt is the primordial template of so many of the team sports we play today — football, baseball, all the throwing sports and track for sure — running, throwing the javelin, the hurdles, the steeple chase, the marathon. Back in the day you and your buddies would 'run down' the deer by chasing it in turns across field and stream. That was some running. Up and down hills, over uneven terrain wearing sandals and carrying your weapon, communicating across great distances with your fellow hunting buddies, rooting them on, hoping for a touchdown while somehow trying to keep that deer in sight and finally when it got tired and slowed down, getting off a shot with your bow and arrow. Thwup! Now it's bleeding and will run slower and be easier to track.

Can you imagine the thrill of the hunt for those young kids, for certainly it was the teenagers who did the running. They could run faster than anyone else and were invincible. Excellent qualities for a hunter and it was certainly more exciting than driving to the store for a pound of hamburger wrapped in paper like we do today. Chasing that wounded deer until it fell and gave itself up to you and the look in its eye as you plunged the knife into its heart and the feeling you felt as you accepted the sacrifice and the deer accepted the sacrifice so that life could go on — that was adventure. That was part of the White Shaman story too.

The story of the shaman

Since the shaman is the most powerful human shaped image in the painting and in many of the other paintings of the Lower Pecos region, let's see what we can learn about his secrets.

According to the lore, he (or she) was able to change into an animal — transmogrification. Stories are told even today about such a thing. Impossible of course. Maybe it was a perceptual thing, where he appeared to be in animal form to those who saw him, but perception is reality right?   In Olmec art, the mother culture of Mexico, there are images of were-jaguars and jaguar-babies, part human, part jaguar.   The Yaqui of northern Mexico call him, the nagual, someone who can take the shape of an animal. I know it's impossible but that's what appears in their paintings: shamans portrayed with the attributes of panthers, deer, birds and snakes. Transmogrification was and is a widely known Meso-American cultural trait.   God knows how they did it. God and the shamans.

But why is it that the shaman is typically portrayed without a head and the interior of his body is painted with strange enigmatic symbols? Could it be that the missing head indicates his mind is blown, his ego lost and the strange enigmatic symbols portray, somehow, the uniqueness of that particular shaman and his powers — who he was and what he could do, what kind of jokes he told and how he spun the old tales, what kind of animal he liked to turn into.   Those design elements must mean something, there is no idle doodling in this painting.

Those people noticed everything around them, not like how we are today. They noticed the subtle changes in wind direction and the subtle smells on the breeze. They noticed the position of the sun during the day and the moon at night, the alignment of the stars and the movement of the animals. They noticed the intricate balance of power between the eat and the eaten, and they noticed the balance of power between individuals in the tribe — early politics. The designs that they drew on their shaman figures may have represented their soul energy or their spirit breath and how they felt when that spirit filled their body. Things are alive when they breathe, that's subtle and profound. When they don't breathe they're dead.   I'm sure they noticed that.

It's hard for us today, with all our technology and all the information at our fingertips, to understand all they noticed.   They were informed by nature and by their fellow tribal mates. There was no media, no government, no 'jobs', no career tracks to pursue and no schools to graduate from.   Everything was taught by mentorship and everyone had an essential role to play in the day to day business of the tribe. The shaman served as a spiritual guide, healer and medium for the people but in another sense it was a truly egalitarian society. Everyone in the tribe was equal because they offered what they could.   It was the children who brought fresh energy into the family and joy.   It was the women who would go out and bring back the edible roots and herbs to make a succulent meal. It was the old and infirm who brought the stories to life for the evening's entertainment and it was the young, the teenagers with their brave hearts and bold steps who, along with the mentorship of the adults, went out and brought back fresh game.

The caves where they took shelter had energy because of their shape and because of the view they offered. The contours of the rocks formed by millions of years of rushing water had a story to tell. The wind, as it coursed through the canyon had a story too. These spaces, human sized and protective, corresponded to their own sense of time and change. The face of the caves opened out to view the sky and the canyon walls and the distant mesas and the river lying at their doorstep.

Well they didn't exactly have a door but the verdant corridor of life that accompanied the river was right there before them. Along that green road the plants and animals thrived — rabbits and snakes and lizards and grasses, and plants, cacti and shrubs and trees. Larger animals came to the river to drink, like deer and antelope and bison. In the river lived fish and frogs and turtles and shellfish. All kinds of resources were available within range of the canyon caves and for the shaman, who was always in search of power, hunted and gathered it in fact, the caves were a place where he could feel the power of the landscape and bring wisdom to his tribe.

Knowledge of the psychotropic plants was a bonus and came about no doubt from serendipitous discoveries while out foraging for food. The effect of chewing on some peyote cactus for example would be like a friendly spirit visiting you and taking you on a journey to another world. Friendly maybe, maybe terrifying — if you ate enough you would have to get past the panther, you would have to die to your old world and be reborn into a new world and there's always resistance to that, the ego.

But this was the source of the power that the Shaman accrued and his major number one secret — he knew that the ego was only a mask and could be discarded with no ill effects and that behind the mask there was an amazing world. The shaman knew that normal 'reality' is essentially an agreement between people, a common reference if you like. When you cross over into the spirit world you also cross over that agreement into a different reality. A person who practiced making that journey through the death/birth barrier (a practitioner) was rewarded with knowledge and could bring blessings to his tribe from the spirit world. That was his job after all.

The shaman's story

So here is the White Shaman's story, or at least my account of it, as it may have been told in that long ago world. The magic secrets in the ancient books of the lower Pecos region are as old as any book made of paper including the Hebrew Bible, the Vedas of India, the Buddhist Sutras and the chronicles of Confucius. They hold the same ancient wisdom, they all are expressions of someone who lived and breathed here on this planet and wanted to say something to the people.

"Once upon a time, there were no people at all. Then the first ancestors came from deep underground and traveled a long ways through the darkness guided by the spirit of the peyote and the magic deer. Finally they came to the first sunrise. They were cold and wet when they arrived at Dawn Mountain and needed the Sun

173

to warm them up and make them fully human. That same path is walked by every person who is born in this world today. First they are in the darkness of the womb and then they emerge, wet and cold, into the light and become alive.

Then the deer sacrificed herself and rose into the sky as the morning star. Do you see? And wasn't that your mom? So when you see that star rising think of your mom and the sacrifice she made to give you life. This is why every year and every day we remember the path they took, the flower road, the road of life, the pilgrimage to Dawn Mountain. We watch the sky and when we see the star rise we remember the journey our ancestors made on the flower road.

Just the same way, kids, we have our ally the Great Spirit who has sacrificed so much so we can have the good life. Every time you pick the peyote or any plant, say 'thank you' for this is all a part of the Great Spirit. Everything is a part of the Great Spirit, you and me and the rocks and the water and the sky. Everyone in the tribe is part of the Great Spirit and they are all walking on their pilgrimage path and so are you, kids. This is the flower road. Walk like the ancestors, head held high but don't trip. Gladness in your heart but ready for anything. Nothing happens in your life that is not given by the Great Spirit. Now go to sleep and in the morning I'll show you how to make a hunting spear. Shhhhhh."

Chapter 10

Han and Hannah

Han doesn't want to get out of bed. There is something wrong with him. Everything feels like a struggle, a sense of futility has taken over his mind. He can't even imagine standing up and moving around. He curls back into his blanket and shuts his eyes. He's aware of his body and the warm blanket he's wrapped in, but that's all.

Slowly the space around him widens, like a curtain opening on a play. . . . *this is the stage, these are the actors . . . earth, sky and trees . . .* he thinks to himself as he peeks out through half closed eyes.

Han is putzing around his camp. Han is playing with his quadcopter, it flies up and looks at him. Han is playing with his feathers, waving them around like he can fly and mumbling like he's consulting an oracle. Han is scrolling through Facebook on his phone without stopping, Han is lying on the ground. It is the safest and most comforting place that he can find. Han is weeping quietly.

He thinks about the old bruja. The way she looked at him and listened to his dumb questions. He felt like he unwittingly revealed to her how fundamentally confused and totally without direction his whole life was. Now he feels compelled to seek her out . . . *ride to the hills . . . find the bruja . . . . . . talk to her . . . . again . . . escape the devouring sadness . . .* He feels a strange, wild freedom arise in his chest.

✱✱✱✱✱✱✱✱✱✱✱✱

By early afternoon he's on his bike heading for the hills and he's flying. He remembers the way and the landmarks confirm his route: the long road out of town, the abandoned building with the rusty tin sign reading, 'Tydale's General Store', the stone wall with the bracken growing on it, the town of Bracken with its handful of houses, the ravine, the river, the bridge. By the time he has climbed up into the hills his rhythm is steady and quick. Standing up occasionally to gain an advantage and keep his momentum he powers through 16 miles of hilly country roads like a madman fleeing danger, seeking shelter.

Finally he sees the turn off. . . *this is the place . . . no car . . . maybe she's not here . . .* He drops his bike in the grassy area and looks at the bruja's house. The path to the front door has tall weeds growing on either side.

He knocks on the door, waits, no response, waits, knocks again, waits, is about to knock a third time when the door opens. She looks at him, he looks at her.

"I am so sad." he says.

"Come in." she says.

She invites him to sit down and makes some tea and serves it to him. She is talking to him in

176

a low sing-songy voice and telling him stories about the old ones. She tells him about the old shamans, how they could fly or appear in the bodies of different animals, about how they had the power to know what was in another person's mind and to interact with them directly without saying any words. She tells him about the medicine used by those long ago people to gain power and communicate with the gods, as she is using it now in his tea. Drink all of it she says and she tells him a story of a long ago warrior.

"A long long time ago there was a warrior and he was lost from his tribe and he got lost on his path and he was running through the woods and as fast as he could but he could not know where he was going. He ran and he ran and sometimes he was chased and sometimes he was running for the bundle he held in his arms. He was hunched over like . . . if he was wounded and he carried the bundle and he ran. And what he carried with him was the wound of a lost love and a child that was not born and a . . . stone that had magical powers and what was chasing him was death and the fear that he would be caught before he could return the stone to its place where he got it so long ago in a faraway place from someone he loved." Han is listening like a spellbound child, sipping his tea.

And when he had finished the tea that the bruja had made for him, she said to him. "Come into the backyard." She led him out the back door and into the space behind her house and there she began to gather sticks and twigs and leaves from the surrounding area and assemble them in the fire pit. It looked like a small house.

And as she worked she continued the story

"He ran until he began to stumble and lose his footing, his legs became weak and his feet could not hold him up and the fear in his heart would not let him go and he ran through the jungle until he came . . . to a spring. There was a pool of water. And he jumped in the water."

Han, of course, knew the story, it was his dream. . . . *how could she know that . . . some kind of bruja trick . . . how could she do that . . .*

"Now look at the fire." she said to him and lit a match and laid it against the leaves and the twigs and the pieces of wood that were assembled there and it glowed and sparked and then she blew on it and it rose up all around her little stick house and devoured it.

Han sat on the ground and watched the flames. The bruja added more wood, larger pieces, trimmings of branches and small logs. Glowing embers appeared at the base of the fire, the flames danced above them and reached into the sky. In the coals he sees a face and in the flames, as they rise up, he sees the shape of a man, and the man turns his head and looks at him. The expression on the face of the man is one of curiosity and openness like a child. His eyes are large and dark, his hair is pulled back and held by a ring. One eye is encircled by a line of red paint and on his shoulder are 4 black slash marks. Han recognizes the man immediately, he is a shaman from 2,000 years ago.

He closes his eyes and the shaman is still there, holding a flute in one hand as if offering it, his costume is draped around him like a serape woven with red and black colors. In that moment he hears a voice in his mind and the voice says "You want to know about how the ancient people lived?"

And in his mind Han says "Yes."

And the 2,000 year old Shaman says "Well I'd like to know what happened to my place."

"What do you mean?" replied Han.

"Where you live now used to be Ana Huappa, the sacred ground, where the creation spirits live, I want to see what happened to it, I want to know how you live here. Show me that first."

****

Han and the shaman are walking on a path. It follows alongside a river.

"When I was a kid I used to play here." The shaman stops and looks at the river. "Yup. And the spring is just up there."

"This is Centennial Park."

"Huh? Ana Huappa is Centennial Park?"

"Yeah, I guess so."

They come to the spring and the shaman kneels down and scoops some water in his hand and drinks. He stands, lifts the flute to his mouth and begins to play a haunting repetitive sequence of notes, ascending and then descending almost the same way but a little different each time, ascending and descending while he dances and sways around his sacred spring.

They follow the river back downstream and it turns into a path that becomes a sidewalk and the trees become buildings and a bridge appears over the river. Cars appear on the bridge, cars appear near and far. A sound like a rushing river fills the air, a road appears.

179

The shaman stops, "What is this?"

"Ah." says Han, "This is my city."

"What is a city?"

"It's a place where people live."

"I don't see any people."

"They're inside their cars."

"What are cars?"

"C'mon I'll show you."

A blue Honda Civic with a bashed in rear fender is sitting by the river. "That's my car."

The shaman looks at it. "Car."

Han walks over and opens the door, gestures to the shaman, "Get in, get inside. I'll show you my city."

The next thing you know Han and the shaman are driving through the city, towards the downtown. The road is made of asphalt and there are buildings constructed of bricks and stone on both sides. There are more buildings, more cars, skeletons of buildings, construction projects, public sculptures reaching up into the air, a university with columned porches, a park with trees and benches, houses, houses, houses.

They stop at a light to turn left and the cars in the right lane swoosh by. Han looks at the shaman sitting in the passenger seat. He still has the red circle around his eye and the slash marks but his costume has transformed into a robe or kimono kind of thing, embroidered with shells, and around his neck a circlet of beads and a headdress with three feathers sticking up in three directions. The kimono is woven with some kind of fiber and dyed bright red, blue and yellow. A bone flute is connected to a cord around his neck and he is playing it, his particular tune that he was playing at the spring, the tune that brings comfort to his mind as he looks through the windshield at the strange world that he does not recognize and listens to the weird sounds that he has never heard before.

The shaman breaks his gaze and turns to look at Han, his mouth begins to form a question, "So where is your tribe?"

"Uh. Oh, we don't really have tribes." The Shaman is staring at Han. He picks up his bone whistle and plays his tune.

They take a ramp and merge up onto an elevated highway and the whole metropolis is spread out before them. Twilight is approaching and the city is starting to glow. They roll out towards the suburbs and exit. Housing developments and shopping centers line both sides of the road; traffic lights, traffic signs, billboards and neon advertising fill the sky. The shaman is watching all the changing shapes and playing his flute quietly.

They pull into a gas station/convenience store with 120 gas pumps. The plaza is laid out in a grid to fuel the beasts that feed there or at least that's how it appears to the shaman. . . . *strange beasts that aren't alive but are alive somehow . . the world contains many wonders, my mentor used to tell me, and the greatest wonder of all . . . is to wonder . . .*

Han parks next to a pump. "Watch this." he says with a smile and gets out of the car. He retrieves his wallet from inside his medicine pouch, pulls out a plastic card that looks like a piece of turtle shell and inserts it into the strange human shaped creature.

. . . like slipping a knife into a deer . . . thinks the shaman. He watches as Han communes with

the creature in some unfamiliar ritual using his hand and then removes its flexible arm. With his other hand he opens a latch and inserts the hose/arm into the rear end of his beast. There is no sound of sucking or mewing that he can hear, just a faint gurgling like a distant creek falling across rocks.

He assumes that the beast is sentient. . . . *if it responds to commands . . . it must have some intelligence . . . awareness . . .* thinks the shaman. *. . . i cannot feel its spirit . . . strange . . . there are no patterns or eye movements . . . no breathing . . .*

The shaman opens the door, gets out of the car and stands next to Han as he fills the tank. He takes in the visuals of being at a convenience store/gas station with the strange human shaped creatures and their long ropy arms feeding the beasts. Bright lights shine down from above while high overhead a noble red and amber circular sign shines out with a furry animal painted in the middle . . . *could be a beaver, might be a rat . . .* thinks the shaman.

"You don't have a tribe," he says, "like that man over there?" and looks at an old guy sitting on the curb near the entrance to the convenience store.

"He's homeless."

"Yeah, that's what I mean."

"What's your name?" says Han.

"Owonomoko. Spelled just like it sounds."

"Ha! You can spell?"

"Yeah what do you think we are fools? We have alphabet, we have language marks on wood and on bone, the stories marked for our children to read to their children."

"Owonomoko, my friend. It is good to know you. As strange as it may be for you, it is also strange for me. I have friends but not really a tribe. Many people are tribe-less in this time. My name is Han."

A large 4 wheel drive pickup with jacked up suspension and four doors drives by and guns its engine. The shaman takes a defensive stance and puts his hand on his knife sheath bound in a leather strap across his chest.

"That's cowboys." explains Han. "Yeah they're loud, but that guy over there he probably lives on the street, finds shelter where he can, makes do day to day."

"Akanomotawah."

"What's that?"

"Exile, without a home. A punishment reserved for only the worst crimes. What crime has this person done?"

"Oh, no crime exactly. Only the crime of being poor."

"In my tribe everyone has a mother or a father or a brother or a sister, or an uncle or a son in law, somebody. The connections are very deep. If you had no tribe you would soon die and your spirit would wander restless through the sky forever."

Han looks at Owonomoko, Owonomoko looks at him. He pulls the nozzle out of the gas intake port and returns it to its home on the mother pump. In the glow of the mercury vapor lamps radiating down from above, the immense concrete parking lot seems like an alien world to Han, just as it does to Owonomoko.

"Let's go." He opens the front door and the shaman, with one jump and a couple of hops, lands next to the passenger side door which he opens with calm deliberation. His movements are performed with such an exaggerated precision that it makes Han laugh. He sits down and the 2,000 year old shaman sits next to him and he starts the car.

They drive through quiet city streets, residential neighborhoods, neither one speaking as the scenes unfold outside the windows of the car. Finally they arrive at Han's place, park the car and go into the backyard campground.

Han speaks to Owonomoko, "Can I make you some tea?".

He nods affirmatively.

When Han returns, the shaman has stirred life into the buried embers in the fire pit and set the twigs aflame, Han sets the tea before him and they sit together.

His costume has become a black and white tunic. A print, decorated with squiggly lines.

The fire grows by degrees.

Han looks at him, "Tell me what it was like in your time."

"Would you really like to know?"

"Yes." says Han and the shaman takes a sip of tea, slowly disintegrates and disappears.

****

Han finds himself back at the campfire in the bruja's backyard, laying on the ground with a blanket over him. He sits up and looks around. She is nowhere to be seen. He is coming down from his trip, the fire has burned down to mostly embers, a few flames. It's dark, the air is cold.

Han rides home consternated, totally amazed

and fairly tripped out. He's still depressed but now his mind is obsessively focused on the peculiar experience he just had. *. . . i just met a shaman . . . in a dream . . . on some kind of a trip . . . from 2.000 years ago . . . and talked to him and just when he was going to tell me the answer he disappears . . .*

The following day is spent in a haze, he's barely functional. He still can't figure out what the shaman was trying to tell him but he can remember exactly what it felt like being with him. It felt like being with a friend, a buddy, somebody you could have adventures with.

He spends the next day working in his backyard, trimming back the weeds, tending the watercress, mixing up the compost, making dirt and spreading it around where the spring garden is supposed to be. It's an experiment.

Later in the day he picks up his guitar and tries some chords, he tries over and over but can't find the chords he needs. His emotional body has been split in two, one half is logical and sad, the other half is open to anything and wild. He doesn't know which one to believe in.

He puts down the guitar and moves inside to the kitchen. A bowl of leaves from the Yaupon Holly tree that grows in the side yard have been drying in the window sill. *. . . they're supposed to pick you up . . .* he thinks and picks up a few with his fingers and smashes them up in his hand. He fills the kettle and heats the water. After the smashed leaves have soaked in the steaming water for awhile he strains them, lifts the infusion to his mouth and smells it, tests the temperature and puts it down.

By the time the tea has cooled enough to drink

he has forgotten about it. Instead he has allowed his mind to take him back into the darkness, the bad chemicals have taken over. He's been transported. He's lost in feelings of meaninglessness and hopelessness. Sadness joins up at last and they're all together. He's crying.

After a while, when he can see again, he pulls out his phone, "hi" send.

Hannah gets the message on the fly, just leaving the restaurant and about to drive. "What's up Hanster?" send.

"wachoo up to ??" send.

"Just running around, on my way home." send.

"can you come by ??" send.

Hannah looks at the message, it suddenly seems like a desperate plea for help.

Fifteen minutes later she parks her car in front of Han's house and turns off the lights. Her mind has considered multiple possible meanings of 'can you come by' on her drive over, none of them were very comforting. She finds Han in the backyard, under the Pecan Tree, in the hammock, with a blanket.

"Han."

He turns his face to her. She can see the tear tracks down his face and the flushed skin and the deep lines.

"Baby are you down?"

He just looks at her.

"Oh no."

The camp is quiet for a long while except for the occasional chirping of a frog.

"I talked to a shaman."

"Oh? What did he say."

"He disappeared."

"Oh."

"It was some kind of herbs that the bruja gave me. I drank the tea."

"You tripped out?"

"Yeah I really did. He came out of the fire and I talked to him. We rode around town"

Hannah spends the better part of an hour talking to Han, trying to understand his strange dark mood, his weird sensibilities, his unbelievable story. It feels oppressive to her, like a toxic odor or the weight of the sky just before a thunderstorm.

"Han I've got to go, my roommate is bringing her friend over and we're going to talk about business."

"Oh, good."

"Take your medication, Han, I know you don't like it. Get some rest. This will all pass, you know that. I'll check with you later. Ok?"

****

Under the protective arms of the big Pecan tree Han is playing some notes, up and down the scale, trying to catch the tune the shaman was playing. He tries over and over, but he's missing a key element. Finally he turns the guitar over and starts drumming on it, a slow deliberate beat, ka thump ka thump thump ka thump ka thump thump thump ka thump. There are birds whistling in the trees nearby, welcoming the night, but he doesn't hear them. Aka, his gray and white cat, walks over and sits under the table but he doesn't see her. Ka thump ka thump.

187

Chapter 11

Money

Human beings love money. Other animals don't seem to care for it. That's distinctive.

Stones are not money and poems are not money. I've tried them both. Pieces of paper are money though. Especially the ones covered with intricate designs and the face of a famous dead person. We have agreed on that, Yes pieces of paper can be money, poetry and stones cannot be. We have certified and assigned value to the pieces of paper, the poetry not so much.

We have created entire bureaucratic departments for the purpose of investigating what happened to our money in case someone takes it or if we lose it, they're called police departments. We have entire business corporations dedicated to tracking our money, where it goes and what it buys, they're called credit card companies. Money is the highest good, valued above all things. We have built temples to it called banks and we spend most of our time pursuing it or thinking about it. It is our religion.

When we speak about the "economy" we invoke our most sacred principles because it has to do with how the money flows.

"It's the economy stupid" was Bill Clinton's rallying cry that won him the presidency in 1992.   Having a job and 'making money' is tantamount to being a good person, a respectable citizen and blessed by God.

Reference to the "Dow", (which sounds exactly like "Tao", the ancient Chinese philosophy of balance and harmony), is a ritual of the nightly news shows. The 'economy' and "the Dow" are terms that have iconic status and stand, like the great pillars of the parthenon, in support of our societies and our world view. So let's take a look at money and see what it's worth.

The history of money

For most of our history there was no money and no accumulation of wealth. Everything you owned you carried with you as you moved through the landscape of your Paleolithic world. Things were simpler. Whatever you needed you made from scratch on the spot from materials you found in situ, wood and stone, plant fiber, shells from the rivers, animals from the forest. Nobody was rich and nobody was poor. Wealth was in the information you had gathered about the environment, the jokes you could tell after dinner around the campfire, the wisdom you could share, some insight into how the world worked.   That made you famous.   It was a currency, coded and archived in the form of story and dispensed whenever needed, deposits and withdrawals, the Federal Reserve Bank of the time. Stories are what we used to exchange value and bring meaning into our lives 50,000

189

years ago.

Of course those early tribal humans did not live in isolation. There were other bands nearby and there was trade between them — barter. I'll give you this buffalo skin for those obsidian stones, I'll give you two strong chickens and a rooster for 6 good Hickory branches strong enough to make bows. Agreeing to a price was part of the process and a form of socialization. It was a chance to get to know the neighbors. But the main problem with bartering is that the value of two chickens and a rooster is very much in the mind of the beholder as are the 6 boughs strong enough to make bows, therefore the exchange rate was never guaranteed and neither was the exchange. Nevertheless, barter was our first means of assigning value to objects in order to trade them.

Commodity money, on the other hand, used common essential items such as salt or tobacco or seeds as a unit of exchange. It replaced barter because of the convenience of having an exchange rate that everyone agreed to. One example of commodity money is in prisons where things are bought and sold with cigarettes, since currency is not allowed. Curiously, back during the days of the American colonies, tobacco was also used as a currency. This idea came from the Indians, of course, who used not only tobacco but wampum (beadwork) as an exchange medium. Chocolate beans (cacao) were used as money by the Aztecs and the Hudson's Bay Company, during their economic colonization of the Canadien north, created an exchange rate for trade with the Indians that looked like this:

- 5 pounds of sugar cost 1 beaver pelt
- 2 scissors cost 1 beaver pelt
- 20 fish hooks cost 1 beaver pelt
- 1 pair of shoes cost 1 beaver pelt
- 1 gun cost 12 beaver pelts

Coins eventually replaced the commodity because it was much easier to carry around and didn't smell. Its value was based on the metal it was made from — silver dollars and gold doubloons. Back in the day, the Romans made coins out of bronze which had a set weight and an intrinsic value — it could be melted down to make into tools or weapons.

Then along came representational money. Money that had no value except what you believed it had; just a piece of paper with writing and symbols in some grand fashion and the famous dead person's face on it. This represented a certain amount of gold or silver which you now owned as attested to by the piece of paper. You were, in fact, entitled to go to Fort Knox and ask for your $20 in gold if you chose to. The US currency was representational money based on the gold standard until the US government nixed it in 1933.

Then came fiat money, which means it has value simply because the government (and God) says it does. 'Fiat' is the Latin word for "let it be done". There's no gold or silver backing it up anywhere, its value rises and falls based on the confidence people have in their government (and God). Even today, on the American one dollar bill, right there in capital letters floating in the sky between the eagle and the all seeing eye; "In God We Trust". Without trust, money as a financial tool doesn't work so it helps if you can enlist God's endorsement as well as that of the Federal Reserve Bank. The Federal Reserve appears on the other side watching over George Washington.

Now we have virtual money, essentially digital data zooming around in the form of numbers inside a computer network connected to other computer networks keeping track of our credits and debits, our stock market purchases and our Amazon orders. You never see anything, only the quiet obsequiousness of the glowing computer screen. That ubiquitous plastic card we carry around in our medicine pouch has become money, and with just a touch, in just a flash it's done, the exchange, the magic has happened.

And the evolution hasn't stopped there, cryptocurrency is the latest and most abstract form of money. It has created an entirely new class of currency, a new way of imagining it. By solving a complicated mathematical problem called an algorithm, value is assigned to the person (actually to their computer address) who finds the solution. It's really hard to do, takes a lot of computing power, and the problems get exponentially harder as new crypto coins are mined, so if you can do it, you should get a reward right? That's called a bitcoin or any one of the other many crypto currencies out there. But the point is you can't just create money willy nilly like the Federal Reserve Bank, it's got to be difficult in order to have value. The network then records each transaction on an open source block chain which is a piece of encrypted code that is distributed to the millions of people with their millions of computers who are part of that block chain all over the world. No one knows who they are or how to reach them so no one (not even AI) can steal it (theoretically).

Does it make sense yet? Bit coins can move seamlessly, effortlessly, from one computer to the other anywhere in the world with no bank fees and no oversight, with complete anonymity and complete confidence. The validity of the transaction is maintained by all the independent, connected computers all holding the same code. Shared computing creates the trust for cryptocurrency.

Yea for money! Or the root of all evil?

So that's the history of money. We are really into money, and always have been ever since we invented it 6,000 years ago back in the Fertile Crescent to keep track of the grain coming and going from the royal granaries. It has fascinated and enchanted us as if it were imbued with magical powers.

In 1519 Cortez landed on the shores of Mexico with 400 men, 6 ships and 88 horses. Within two years he had defeated the mighty Aztec empire, captured its emperor, Cuauhtemoc, and availed himself of all its riches. That story is well told elsewhere and it's a fantastic one, but at some point in the saga one of the conquered nobles, presumably just before he was about to get his head cut off, asked Cortez a question, "What is it that motivates you Spaniards?".

Cortez is said to have replied, "Spaniards have a disease and it is only cured by gold." The disease has not been cured, however, instead it has become a world-wide pandemic.

"Money, it's a gas, grab that cash with both hands and make a stash", advises Pink Floyd in their 1973 classic 'Money'. And even though its value as an exchange medium is unquestioned, money has one serious liability — you can never get enough of it. Its very existence implies imbalance and in that way it has affected and infected our civilizations ever since the time of the Romans and before. Wars were fought for it (and still are). People get divorced, discarded and commit suicide for the lack of it. We build monuments to it: glorious business towers in the middle of our most prestigious cities, and two blocks away the street people live on park benches. Wall Street, the IMF, the Council of Economic Advisers, the World Economic Forum are all top level organizations, they direct the economic currents of out time, they hold together the very fabric of our societies, they see everything in terms of money.

Money has its benefits. It's a useful servant and has allowed us to grow rich and build empires but it also has a corrosive effect. While we exchange our money for goods and services we also codify our darker urges to control and dominate and accumulate as much money as we can. Not that many people even think about that when they're shopping at the mall. It's an enjoyable experience, seeing the shops, deciding on what to buy, making the exchange, thank you, and walking out with a bag on your arm. But if you follow the flow of money all the way back through the wholesalers and the dealers and the transporters and the original producers and everybody else who had a part to play, it ends up somehow that Mother Nature got robbed and everyone else got paid.

Maybe we should re-evaluate our current form of currencies. Are there better ways of doing this? Are there, in fact, other forms of currency that can be used, in reality, not like some wacky urban bohemian poet trying to get a free latte for a poem at the cafe? I mean it seems to me that 'currency' is something we imagine. We imagine it to be real, so it is real. What else could we imagine that's not so prone to engendering greed? Are we afraid to imagine something like that? That might be the first question.

I can imagine it and it's a world very much like the one in which our Paleolithic ancestors lived. I can imagine a world where wisdom and stories are considered treasures and can be traded for goods and services as needed, or other stories. What is a potlatch if not a great helluva party where you give things away to your friends to celebrate how rich you are?

Economy

Without money there would be no economy and no means of becoming wealthy. To better oneself and prosper, isn't that measured by money? "Economy", is derived from two Greek words that translate as "household" and "manage".

We use the word economy to describe the production, distribution and consumption of goods as expressed in a currency, a "dollar value". But the economy also implies the individuals, businesses, organizations and government agencies that maintain and guide the process. It also includes the raw materials we take from the earth (called 'resources' in the economics textbooks) to create the products that we buy and sell (called "goods" in the economics textbooks). Economy is also work, the work that people do (and horses and cows) and the money invested in those people, horses, cows, robots, etc.

These days, machines do most of the work and we just manage them — in the advanced countries anyway. The dividing line between who lives in a first world country and who lives in a third world country is just that. How much labor is being done by human beings laboring away and how much is done by machines. This division of labor is the new caste system. By this standard are ye judged oh nations of the world. If you've got robots building electric cars you are first world, if you're farming rice paddies by hand or maybe with one buffalo in the Mekong delta then you are third world and poor.

If we were "managing our household" in the original Greek meaning of it, no one would be poor and the resources would be sustainable resources. That would be good management. In reality we practice an economic system that is based on continuous growth (capitalism), while living on a planet that has limited and diminishing resources.

The consequences of that situation are only now coming to bear. We're going to have to find another planet to exploit or learn how to live sustainably on this one, otherwise the consequences will be catastrophic. Extinction is what happens when a biosphere can no longer sustain a species. It has happened many times in the history of the earth and it is happening right now to species from frogs to insects to birds. And it's not just the animals – plants are disappearing, no one knows how many because they're not catalogued and monitored. For sure the diversity of our biosphere is being reduced, genomes are being lost. Our safety net, our life line, this garden that supports us with its complex interaction of many different parts, from micro-organisms to megafauna, is being weakened, by us the humans. Our economic system of extracting resources that are not sustainable is reducing the viability of earth's biosphere. Of course on the other hand, it's providing a level of comfort and wealth that people never had before.

Man, we are something else. Up here on top of the food chain, looking out over everything, in charge and in control; but what we don't understand is that we are dependent on all the organisms beneath us on the food chain in order to stay on top of the food chain. What we don't realize is that our economy is destroying the food chain that makes life as we know it possible. We're not managing this well.

So that's the story of money. Han's father has a lot of it. He worked hard for it, as we shall see.

Chapter 12

Han and Hannah

Jack Arrizobal's office is on the 27th floor of the ASB building in downtown San Angelito. There is a view of the city, the expressways and far off towards the horizon, glinting like wheat fields in the afternoon sun, the suburbs gathered around the edge. He's a mover and shaker in the community and he's earned this view. At the moment he's thinking about the Emerald City in the Wizard of Oz and the moment when Dorothy peeks behind the curtain and sees the little magician.

He's sitting in his executive chair with his shirt unbuttoned and his secretary Linda on his lap. His hand is up her skirt. The phone buzzes. He glances at the screen, "It's Han."

She jumps off his lap, pulls her skirt down, straightens her hair, and leaves, Han enters after a short wait. He looks disheveled, his hair awry and his eyes droopy. He's wearing his shirt unbuttoned with a grey t-shirt underneath that says "uck yo". His pants have dirt smeared into them (the result of doing yoga on the ground and not washing his clothes).

"Hello Han, how are you?"

"I'm good dad."

"Are you on your meds?"

"Sure, dad."

"No I mean it. Those things do wonders."

"Yeah sure, dad. What do you take?"

"A little Vicodin occasionally. Son, it's a crazy, violent world out there. Nobody's going to give you a break, you've got to earn it, you've got to be ready for it. And if you don't step up to the plate then there is always somebody else who will.

Han squirming, "Ok, dad." Han is nodding his head. His eyes are focused on the metropolis below. "How's mom?"

Dad nods. "Go see her. She's your mother."

The silence is deafening. It goes on for awhile as if it were a contest to see who can stand it the longest. "So . . . what's up?" says Jack Arrizobal.

"I need some money."

"Son, when are you going to grow up?"

"I am grown up dad."

"But you don't act like it"

"How do you want me to act, like you?"

"I want you to show some initiative."

"I am showing initiative"

"What is your initiative?"

"I'm doing a documentary about the first people."

"Who?"

"The first people."

"Who are they?"

"We're sitting right here, right? In your office, looking out at the city. Before this building was built, before all these people came here there were others living here, there were others who came before right? Track it back, back, all the way to the first people. The first people to arrive here, they arrived at the springs, right, and it was like a fountain surrounded by a pool that was surrounded by trees and it was all full of life. The first people to see that and to live here on the bounty of nature. Mother Nature feeding them all and supporting them, get it? The first people before European culture came and took over, they had their own culture and their own beliefs and their own stories. What was that about?"

"I don't know."

"Well that's what it's about, my documentary. I need some money."

On his way out, Linda hands him a check and says "Here you go son."

****

Hannah is an escapee from fundamentalism but it has done its damage. Her mom visits and tries to counsel her about sex and drugs as if she were a teenager. Her brain was formatted by the time she was six as all our brains are. By the time she was 10, stultifying boredom had been programmed into her circuits through public education and religious services creating a sort of feedback loop that caused spikes in the electricity level. This caused her brain to deform and, at the age of 19 or 20, flip into what some might call a 'personality disorder' or what she knows as confusion, mental stress and a deep anxiety of not belonging.

"Helen, sweetie, all your problems would be so much easier if you would just turn to Jesus. Jesus will make your burdens lighter no matter what's happening in your life."

"I know Mom."

"I'm praying for you."

It's her mom's weekly visit. It's a ritual that Hannah feels obliged to uphold partly because of filial loyalty but also so that she won't pester her the rest of the week. It also expedites cleaning the apartment which is a good idea.

"Hannah nods, "I go by Hannah now, remember. I prefer Hannah."

"But Helen was your grandmother's name. It's a beautiful name. I don't know why you don't want your own name. At least to honor your grandmother."

"Mom, I didn't even know her."

"She was a wonderful woman. I wish you had known her. She taught me a lot of things."

"Well you have taught me a lot of things."

"Well I hope so. I hope I've been able to teach you something Helen."

"Hannah."

****

. . . shostakovich abner doubleday mickey mantle ronald reagan absolute zero dahl hey you . . . Han is bundled up and pushing hard against the wind *. . . lexapro prozac lithium Jesus . . .* the afternoon has not brought clear skies, it has remained overcast and cool, the wind is brisk and out of the north. *. . . hi i'm a tree boy . . . i'm water girl we can both co-exist . . . i support the sky with my leafy branches and connect the earth with my gnarly roots i am so tough that woodpeckers can't peck me . . . hi i'm water girl i am supple and flowing i come down from the*

Han pulls up and parks outside the gray, two tone, stone and adobe, single story building. He secures his bike to a sapling growing next to the ground cover and goes inside the Whitewater Extended Care Facility.

"Here to see my mom, Mrs. Arrizobal."

"And you are?"

"I'm her son. Han Arrizobal."

"She's in 112."

"Thank you."

The corridor is lined with chairs, not easy chairs just chairs and a few of them occupied by residents.

He stops, hesitates, enters the room, looks at his mom. She's appears to be asleep, her eyes are closed.

"Hi mom." He says and starts talking to her. She doesn't blink, she doesn't move. He finds himself talking to her in a stream of consciousness, untethered, going on and on. ". . . and like to shock and confront people, I guess but not to the point where I get a negative reaction from them. You know what I mean? I just want them to react, " he says settling into the one chair provided. Her room is small and includes a bed, a chair, a small writing desk, a small table, a very large TV, a small sink, a very small refrigerator.

"People don't know what to think of me I guess, misunderstood, all my life, but then who has the real script? So people, I dunno, look at me but can't find a convenient pigeon hole to pigeon hole me so just dismiss me. I guess. Who cares. Really who cares?"

He stops talking and looks at his mother. She is lying on the bed in her day dress. Her eyes open when he stops talking. "It's weird mom, I just, I just try to make sense to myself. Sometimes I can't even do that. So, Hannah is, well I don't know, whatever." blink, blink "she's . . . whatever, I can't even say what I'm talking about. Not even to you, mom. I don't know if you even hear me. That's why I'm here. I came to see you. So . . . . I could hear myself talk to you. Dad's fine. Doing his business. He thinks about you. He told me to say that. I don't know if he really does. What do I know? That's my biggest problem right now, mom, what do I know? Forget about trying to say, just know something, right? What do you know mom? Anything? At all?"

Han's eyes start to fill with tears and he turns away. His mom blinks.

****

Hannah and Han are having dinner at Taco Land. It was Hannah's idea. He jumped at the chance to get out of his place and see her. She arranged the dinner because she has something to tell him. Han is talking about his mother.

"And my mother is lying there. They've put her dress on her but she's just lying . . . just lying there on her bed." Han stops talking and puts his hand to his mouth, "It was weird. It's like talking to someone who's not there. And then I thought about — does she lie there all day in her dress on her bed in her room? I don't know."

"Ha, I don't mean to laugh but that's what it's

203

like talking to my mother and she's fully alive.
She can walk around and stuff."

"Yeah."

"No, that's really sad. Isn't there something
you can do for her?"

"Go over and talk to her and tell her the sad
story of my life?"

"Yeah. You could do that." Hannah shifts in
her seat and pulls on her Mountain Gold Pilsner
Light. Their orders have just arrived and Han is
breaking into it.

"So I wanted to tell you, Han, that I'm seeing
someone. I hope . . . you can be ok with that.
Han. Umh. It's Omar. So . . . I'm just asking if
you can be ok with that?"

"Oh."

Chapter 13

Gilgamesh

Once upon a time there lived a king and his name was Gilgamesh. He lived a long time ago but his story is pretty much the same as every human who has ever lived. Just like Han he finds out that he has pretty much screwed everything up and then watches helplessly as he screws things up even worse trying to fix it. Nobody is smart and nobody is dumb, we're just human.

As the story starts out, the narrator (likely Gilgamesh himself) is extolling the virtues of his fair city. "See how its ramparts gleam like copper in the sun. Climb the stone staircase, more ancient than the mind can imagine, approach the Eanna Temple, sacred to Ishtar, a temple that no king has equaled in size or beauty, walk on the wall of Uruk, follow its course around the city, inspect its mighty foundations, examine its brickwork, how masterfully it is built." This is the prologue from Stephen Mitchell's triumphant translation, 'Gilgamesh, A New English Version' and the stage is set.

Soon King Gilgamesh will climb the stairs and enter the stage and act out his role but first the back story, the setup, the underpinnings, the city's beautiful wall.

Back then, in 3,000 BC or so, it was quite a point of pride to have a stout wall. One reason, of course, was so you could slow down any invaders that might want to come across and take the place over, kill everybody. It's the same reason we build walls today except they're usually in our minds. And then there's the other reason we build things — the glory of man. Just like it was back in the day with walls and temples, today we have skyscrapers and soaring expressways and space needles.

That was for sure the state of things in ancient Uruk. Gilgamesh was an impetuous, vain and lustful king, not a great ruler at all but he had the people convinced that he was half divine so he got away with it. He was able to coerce the young men into building monuments all over town to tell everyone how great he was. He slept with every woman in town on her wedding night before the husband just to share his semi-divine seed with the community.

In their oppression, the people called out to the gods for relief. "Help us," they cried, "save us from this tyranny. Our young buck unbridled imperator is ruining our lives". And the gods responded.

Got your attention? Want to know what happens next? This story was written down in 1700 BC and had been on the open mic circuit for hundreds of years before that. They knew how to tell a story. They knew how to cast the enchantment, they could tell when the audience was engaged. There's no need to exaggerate if you're telling the truth. And so they would, they would go on and on about all the trials and travails of old King Gilgamesh. For he was their king after all no matter how arrogant he was or how much he screwed it up. And it was their story, those people who lived back then.

The clay tablets with the Epic of Gilgamesh inscribed on them were found in the ruins of ancient Ninevah where they had lain for 2,000 years, buried under the rubble of the king's library. Those ruins can still be seen where the modern city of Mosul now stands. Or part of it stands, much of the downtown has been destroyed in the Iraq war and counter war, the battle to re-take Mosul after the battle to take Mosul. It's like no one there ever read the story of Gilgamesh.

Start the story

"Oh Gilgamesh, humans are born, live and die" says Shiduri, the divine bar maid on the beach at the edge of the world. "a lifetime is the gift given by the gods to humans, not immortality. Enjoy your life, have fun with your children, love your wife, eat good food and dress up once in a while; fill your house with music and dancing because one day you will be dead." There it is, the epic wisdom from 3000 BC, the great treasure that Gilgamesh found on his arduous journey. And the story was discovered right there in Mosul where they have been killing each other back and forth, wrecking the place.

Anyways, it took Gilgamesh a long time to figure it out too. That's why his tale was so popular, mythic. He's a bonehead, oblivious to what is obvious to everybody else. Even in his regal setting, his royal finery, his brave bold persona, he's a bumbling idiot, making careless mistakes with profound consequences. So human. Anyways, here's what happens next.

Let the women fix it

The gods respond to the people's outcry in a way that only the gods can — they create something and set it in motion, like a spinning top, to see which way it will go. Anu the main man of all the gods, the father figure, sends a memo to Aruru, the mother goddess, the one who created human beings.

"Here's the situation Aruru, can you do something with this? Oppressive king, arrogant youth, mother a goddess."

"Sure." she says and gets right to work. She fashions a human out of clay who is the perfect opposite of Gilgamesh and sets him down in the wilderness where the wild animals are. Job done, send a few dreams, let it play out.

'Perfect compliment' would be a better description of the human she created. This primal human, Enkidu, has the power and strength of a wild animal just like Gilgamesh but the innocence and sophistication of a donkey. Gilgamesh on the other hand is strong but super civilized, supreme among mankind, surpassing all kings, the son of a goddess, blah blah blah. His resume was familiar to everyone in Uruk.

Enkidu bows down and drinks water from the watering hole like the animals do, he eats grass like they do, he runs with those people, it's his posse. His body is covered with hair and when the trapper sees him he is shocked to the point of fright. The trapper runs home and tells his father about the wild man and how he is totally freaked out right now and is never going back out there.

His father, an older gentleman no doubt, says, "Calm down, get your wits about you son. Here's what you have to do. Go to the big city, Uruk, and tell the great King Gilgamesh what you saw. He will know what to do."

"Ok, dad, I'm on it. Always wanted to go to the big city." and off he goes.

Meanwhile back at the royal palace, Gilgamesh is having a restless night. He awakens after a particularly vivid dream and goes to see his mother, she's good at interpreting dreams.

"Mom, I dreamed that I was walking down the street and a comet fell out of the sky and landed at my feet. It lay there like a giant boulder, too heavy to lift. Everybody in the neighborhood showed up to look at it. They were kissing it like it was a baby. I wrapped my arms around it and began caressing it like a lover. It was the weirdest thing."

His mother replies, "My dearest son you are about to encounter a companion, someone who will share your adventures, someone you can love. Someone your equal but your opposite, someone who thinks like you but in a different way."

"I love you mom. Thanks. Thanks for always being there for me." Gilgamesh was a spoiled child if you don't know that yet. His mother is a goddess, Ninsun and his father is the mighty warrior (now deceased) Lugalbanda. So it's hard.

Meanwhile at the back gate the trapper shows up, "Can I speak with Gilgamesh?"

"What's the nature of your business?"

"Well . . . wild man."

"Wild man?"

"Wild man in the wilderness."

"Wait here." the gate keeper leaves.

Gilgamesh is sitting in his rooftop gazebo looking out over his fair city. Ishtar's place, greater even than his own palace, the orchards and the gardens — well watered and fruitful, the lovely buildings, people strolling the wide avenues, the plazas, the markets, the river — all can be seen from his vantage point. He's pleased but at the same time it's all so familiar.

He gives a signal with his hand, "Bring in the man who wishes to speak."

The man enters and kneels before Gilgamesh, "Lord there is a great hairy man in the wilderness. He wrecks my traps and turns the animals free. He runs with the antelopes and drinks with them too. I cannot believe my eyes. I don't know who he is but he frightens me. My business is ruined."

Gilgamesh shifts his broad shoulders, straightens his broad back and looks at the man. The news excites him. He rises and approaches him.

"Go to Ishtar's temple, it's right over there, and get Shamat the love priestess. Take her out there where the wild man is and show it to her. Tell her to lie down and open her legs, tell her to take off all her clothes and use her love arts on him. He will come to her and she will have control over him as she teaches him all the ways of a woman and then he will be tamed and the wild animals will leave him and know him no more. Then she will bring him to me."

Well after that speech, as you might well imagine, that is exactly what he did. He hiked back out to the wilderness area with the beautiful Shamat, the temple priestess, and began searching for the wild man. On the third day they found him drinking water at the watering hole and Shamat laid down where he could see her. She removed her robe and she spread her legs and she showed the wild man what the secrets of a woman are and he approached her. He got hard as a rock being young, virile and a virgin and they proceeded to copulate right there on the ground. She kept him hard for 6 days and 7 nights, she knew more than a few tricks. When it was over he went to rejoin his friends the animals but they fled from him.

"Don't be concerned with them." she told him, "Do you want to roam the plains with wild animals all your life? Now that you know what a woman is let me teach you a few more things, let me take you to the great city of Uruk where people dress in brightly colored clothes and dance in the streets every day. Let me show you something amazing."

And she did. She taught him how to eat bread and drink beer and wear clothes and speak properly. And she told him about Gilgamesh.

"Listen Enkidu, in the great city there lives a great king. He is splendid, handsome and stronger than any man. No man is his equal. He rules the city for his own pleasure and no one can stop him. I will lead you there and you can see for yourself."

Enkidu is fascinated by this account and with his new found knowledge of women, eating from a plate, drinking from a cup, speech, logic, and now jealousy, he's curious to discover what more wonders exist that he doesn't know about yet.

"I will go with you to see this king and this splendid city where the people dress in brightly colored clothes and dance in the streets every day. I will meet this king and I will yell in his face *'I am more powerful than you are! Nobody is more powerful than me!'*"

The big city

Well, alrighty then. The trick worked. Was Shamat instructed in her role, how to bring the wild man to the big city, or was she using her intuition, or was she just proud of her home town? She was a devotee of Ishtar, the goddess of love and war (two not dissimilar enterprises) and Uruk was an Ishtar city. Amongst all the gods she was the best loved, her shrine was at the very center of the city and shone like a jewel in the sun. If Shamat was part of the conspiracy then the gods were working through her. She braves the journey to the outback, gets humped by a wild man and then focuses on civilizing him and bringing him to the king, not an easy task. Certainly she felt a higher calling. At any rate she did a splendid job and the next thing you know, Enkidu and the temple priestess are entering the city to the amazement of all who see them. Everyone in the whole neighborhood comes out and crowds around him, they kiss his feet as if he were a baby.

They happen to come across a wedding party, people eating and drinking. Lively music is being played.

Enkidu inquires of one of the celebrants, "What's happening here?"

"This is a wedding, man." says the celebrant.

"And where is the bride?"

"She waits in the bridal chamber for Gilgamesh to come and take her before the husband can enter."

Enkidu is outraged (he has also managed to develop a social conscience). He storms to the bridal chamber and stations himself in the doorway like a giant boulder. Gilgamesh arrives to do his thing and sees this hulk of a man standing there. "My man, you are in the way. Move aside."

"I'm not your man and I won't move aside." replies Enkidu. Whereupon they commence wrestling like two young bulls.

This would be very interesting as an animated movie, maybe a Celebrity Death Match, because according to the story they tear the place up, knock down doorways, crash into walls, bust up the market stalls, and shake the houses to their foundations. Neither one can break free from the others grip and neither one can dominate the other. Enkidu wrestles Gilgamesh to a standstill except for that trick move he puts in at the end, no wild animal could have known that. Only the cunning of human beings adept at politics and stage craft and mendacity could have come up with that trick. So anyways Gilgamesh trips him up, throws him down and pins him with his knee.

Enkidu lies there looking up and says, "Dude, you are awesome and worthy to be king as established by the gods."

Gilgamesh says, "Dude, no way. You are way more awesome, you've got hair down to your knees and you are the strongest man I've ever wrestled."

They become fast friends, which was the whole point of the conspiracy the gods had cooked up — Aruru the mother goddess and Anu the father of all the gods and their beautiful daughter Ishtar, the flirt. All the gods wanted Ishtar but she knew what she was worth (more about that later). For now the balance had been restored in Uruk and the people got their relief. Gilgamesh had a companion, his beautiful Enkidu, and they were inseparable.

If you can imagine the wonders of being in the big city for the recent immigrant, Enkidu — everything was new and amazing. For Gilgamesh, who grew up there and knew every street and alley, it was familiar and well known. Always the same wall, in the same place, always the needy supplicants, always the same musicians. A new adventure was what he needed and now that he had a worthy companion . . .

Let's go kill a monster

"Hey Enkidu let's go kill a monster. Old Humbaba dwells in the sacred forest scaring off anybody who goes there. I say we go kill him and rid the world of that menace."

"Oh my friend, listen to me." says Enkidu, "That's my old stomping grounds, I know that place. Humbaba is terrible, his breath is like fire, his voice is like thunder, his jaws are death; when he walks, the trees tremble. Let's not do this my friend for I am afraid and unsure."

"What you're lacking in confidence I will make up" says Gilgamesh, "I must make a name for myself so I will be remembered forever. I must prove to the world that I have no fear of death. My story will be broadcast throughout the whole world and no one will challenge me. C'mon let's do this thing, lets go for it. What if I am killed in the forest and you're not there, you're here resting at home, what would people say? No, you've got to come with me, we can do this together. I know we can."

The plot deepens

Gilgamesh calls everyone in the city together.

"Listen, people, I've known you all since I was a kid. All you old guys, I've listened to your counsel. My buddies, we've fought together on the parapets of our great wall. My kinsmen, my townspeople, hear me. Now I'm going to do something on my own. Me and Enkidu, we're going to kill the monster. We're going to the sacred forest and we're going to take him down. Humbaba, he's terrible, a menace to society. Give me your blessings and I'll re-join you at the next New Year's Eve celebration in our great city."

Then Enkidu stood up and looked at the assembled people and with tears in his eyes spoke, "Please, please people, persuade the king not to do this, not to go into the sacred forest and kill Humbaba."

Then the elders spoke, all with one accord, "Gilgamesh, re-consider your rash plan of action. You are young and your heart is restless but why do you wish to embark on this folly? Humbaba is dangerous and has been put there by the god Enlil to protect the sacred forest. His breath spews fire, his voice is like thunder, his jaws are death. He's horrible to look at, just one glance can kill a person."

But it was all to no avail. Gilgamesh basically laughs off the old men and then says to Enkidu, "Are you still afraid my friend, or are you ready to die a hero's death? C'mon." They march off to the armory to forge some new weapons — something guys do.

Axes, knives, swords — all kinds of high quality stuff is made for the expedition and buckled on. "Let's go see my mom and get her special blessings before we leave." says Gilgamesh, "She's a goddess."

So they do that. Ninsun is at the rooftop altar burning some incense to Shamash her favorite god and offering intercessory prayers. She already knows what's coming. She hugs her son and says, "You are so special. I have already asked Shamash, the sun god, to protect you on your way. Enkidu, come here son. I love you like my own child, you are like a brother to Gilgamesh. Go with him and protect him on his dangerous journey."

The two young punk warriors, hand in hand, set off for the sacred forest and monster adventures. At two hundred miles they stop and take a break, grab something to eat, at four hundred miles they make camp and dig a well, at six hundred miles they stop and take a break, at eight hundred miles they make camp and dig a well. They're in a rhythm. They cover a thousand miles in one day. They've got energy to burn and they're on a mission to kill a monster.

They reach the sacred forest on the fourth day. It's thick with cedar trees towering above their heads. From its interior they can hear rumblings and thumpings.

"Let's, umh, make an offering to Shamesh," says Gilgamesh, "before we go in there."

A giant voice comes out of the sky and says, "Go now! Attack! Don't delay. This is your chance before Humbaba sets his defenses."

"Who is this?"

"This is Shamash, the sun god."

"Is there anybody else up there I can talk to?"

"No! Go now. Attack Humbaba before he puts on his 7 cloaks of illusion."

They stand at the edge of the forest peering into the depths, listening. It has become eerily quiet all of a sudden. They enter the forest and stealthily creep along a trail formed probably by Humbaba himself, deeper and deeper they penetrate into the gloomy woods. They unsheathe their knives and grip their axes tightly. They can smell the presence of the monster like smoke in the air, they can hear the beating drum of his heart reverberating through the ground. The passion of the hunt stirs both of them and urges them on. Reckless abandon supplants their courage. They look at each other, clutching their weapons. Humbaba is nearby.

They climb up a hill in the heart of the forest and suddenly — there, in a clearing, stands

Humbaba, 50 feet tall.   His face looks like sheep's intestines and his eyes blaze with fire.

"Hello young men", he says cordially, "prepare to die."

Gilgamesh freezes, his feet can't move, he's unable to raise his arms so filled with terror is he.   Enkidu sprints around behind him and climbs up his back and begins hacking with his axe on the monster's neck.   The monster gives out a terrible shriek and throws Enkidu to the ground.   Gilgamesh finds himself and attacks by climbing a tree and leaping into his chest.

"Unk!" retorts the monster.

Slash, slash, plunge, plunge responds Gilgamesh with his knife.   He swats at Gilgamesh with his huge hand but misses as he jumps up to his shoulder.   Enkidu picks himself up and starts hacking at his Achilles heel.   He kicks him away. Gilgamesh climbs into his hair and the giant roars with such ferocity that sparks fly and trees fall.   He grabs for Gilgamesh who is burrowing through his rich locks trying to evade his hand and catches him by the leg.   He holds him suspended in front of his terrible face, his mouth open, his gaping craw, his terrible teeth.

Suddenly the wind begins to blow from the east and from the west like a hurricane. Shamash has arrived as promised to help Gilgamesh in his quest.   The giant is blinded by the ferocious wind and turns this way and that. He falls to his knees as Enkidu manages to hew through his tendon. Gilgamesh evades his grasp and jumps up on his neck holding a knife to his jugular vein.

"Don't kill me Gilgamesh." begs the monster,

"Have mercy. Let me live here in the sacred forest. The great god Enlil put me here to safeguard this place. Don't kill me and I will give you riches beyond measure."

"Kill him Gilgamesh! Do away with him!" yells Enkidu.

"If you do this I will curse you, I swear by the gods. They will call down their wrath upon you and you will be sorrowful beyond measure."

"Cut his head off!" cries Enkidu.

Gilgamesh was written in a time before computers. Before pencils, before paper. They used a system of writing that had a stylus and you made impressions in wet clay with it — cuneiform. That means the writer must have had a fully formed idea of what he was trying to say in his head and was able to get it down before the clay dried. There were no backups and no corrections. Writing itself had only recently been invented in ancient Sumer where the city of Uruk was located. Imagine how many times the author had heard this story and read about it in different versions that were floating around the valley. They have found copies of this tale in several different archaeological sites of ancient Mesopotamia. Imagine how he approached the writing of the death scene. He knew what had to happen, Humbaba had to die to set the curse, and how to kill him off? What was the final blow? How do you paint that picture?

Gilgamesh swung his axe and sliced into Humbaba's neck, blood spurted out 10 feet into the air. He swung again and the monster's eyes rolled back into his head. He swung again and the head came loose flying through the air and landing by a fallen cedar tree, still charred and smoking from Humbaba's monstrous roar.

The two heroes embrace and with a shriek of victory hold their weapons high. The clouds descend from the sky. A soft wind comes from the south. A gentle rain begins to fall on the trees and the mountains of the sacred forest.

When a goddess hits on you

Ishtar, the flirt, was waiting for him when he got back. She liked heroes.

"Gilgamesh, c'mon and be my boyfriend," she boldly uttered when she saw him bathing all the grime and grit of the monster killing expedition off his body in the public baths. "I'll give you a chariot of gold and horses as swift as the wind to pull it. I'll give you luxury gifts that you can't even imagine: Gucci luggage, Armani tunics,"

But Gilgamesh, feeling full of himself, as usual, responded, "Ishtar, everyone you take as a lover you turn into a frog. I don't need that in my life."

"Louis Vuitton wallet, Aviator sunglasses.

"That's cheap crap."

"Live in my temple."

"I already have a place."

"All the kings and princes will bow down and kiss your feet."

"People already bow down and kiss my feet, girl. Take a hike, you're over rated."

Ishtar flew into a rage, "Over rated! I'll show you who's over rated. How dare you!" and off she goes to the celestial realm to Anu father of the gods.

"Daddy, Gilgamesh insulted me, he must be punished."

"You probably deserved it, sweet cakes, c'mon
. . ."

"No!   Give me the Bull of Heaven or I will
release the undead from the gates of hell and
they will eat every living person on the face of
the earth!"

"Gees, calm down. Ok, ok you can have the
Bull of Heaven. But you have to return it."
"Thanks daddy."

Into the city of Uruk crashes the Bull of
Heaven, smashing down the gate and goring
everyone in its way. It bellows a great bellow
and the earth opens up and swallows a hundred
warriors. It stamps its feet and the foundations
of the houses collapse. Gilgamesh and Enkidu
hear the commotion and come running.

"Damn, the Bull of Heaven!" cries Gilgamesh.
"Let's kill it!" cries Enkidu.

Round and round they go circling the bull, not
giving it a chance to charge. Enkidu grabs its
tail and plants his foot on its hindquarters. "Kill
it Gilgamesh!"

Gilgamesh grabs its horns, does a double back
flip over its head and lands on its back, draws
his sword and drives it deep into the soft spot
behind its ears. Blood gushes out and the bull
falls. It breathes its last mortal breath and with a
violent spasm, expires. They cut its heart out
and offer it as a sacrifice to Shamash.

Ishtar is watching this from the top of the wall.
"You have killed the Bull of Heaven!" she
screams at the top of her lungs.

Enkidu tears off a hind leg and throws it at her.
"Yeah and we would do the same to you if we
could catch you."

They both laugh. What a great joke. Ha, ha.

Ishtar takes off to the celestial realm and calls a council of the gods. They all come together from wherever they were: tripping out with the satyrs in the meadow, playing with the nymphs in the stream, flying through the sky with the clouds, talking with the dryads in the forest . . .

"Oh gods," she begins, "something must be done. First Gilgamesh and Enkidu killed Humbaba the guardian of the sacred forest put there by Enlil to scare away people and protect the sacred trees, and now they have killed the Bull of Heaven. Someone must be punished. Someone has to pay. I suggest we kill Gilgamesh. He's such an ass."

"No, not Gilgamesh. Enkidu must die." responds Anu "for Gilgamesh is 1/2 divine besides the story is not finished yet."

"Ok fine. Kill Enkidu, that will be even better." smirked Ishtar.

The dream

"Oh my friend I have had a dream." says Enkidu waking up in the middle of the night.

"Huh? What was your dream about, dear friend?"

"I dreamed that there was this bird or a person dressed like a bird with feathers and a beak and he was pecking at me, tearing the flesh from my body and he ate my flesh right down to the bones. Then he dragged me down to the underworld where people were eating dust and drinking mud. There were skeletons everywhere and the bird people were walking around going 'caw caw caw caw. It was horrible."

"Ah Enkidu," said Gilgamesh with tears in his

eyes, "that is not a bad dream. The gods never send dreams to the sick or dying only to the healthy. Your dream means exactly the opposite of what it seems. It means that you will live a long time and while others may die you will stay strong and healthy."

"Oh Gilgamesh, in my dream I called out to you for help but you did not come. I cried out for your assistance but you were not there."

Gilgamesh is feeling something that he has not known before. He who was the mighty king of everybody is touched by something that he doesn't understand — a deep and abiding love for another human being and at the same time he feels the sting, he feels the arrow penetrate his heart, and wound him as he feels that thing being taken from him. No one has ever wounded Gilgamesh before. He is a little bewildered, like the beast when it takes the first arrow from the hunter.

"Why are you crying Gilgamesh, why are you weeping?"

"Listen Enkidu, that's not a bad thing. That's a sign that your friend is always with you. We can never be separated. I will always be there for you. Because . . . this day. Because we are . . . together, soulmates, Keedu, we have fought the monsters together, we have battled Humbaba, we killed the Bull of Heaven."

Enkidu looks at Gilgamesh and Gilgamesh looks at Enlidu and silence overtakes both of them.

The next morning the sun rises but Enkidu does not. Gilgamesh sits in a chair next to his friend. Nearby, the altar to Shamash has a fresh offering on it — incense from the sacred forest is burning. The smoke wafts through the room like a swirling spirit.

What happens next is that Enkidu dies. There's no nice way to say it. He stops breathing and everything. Gilgamesh is unable to accept this unalterable fact. *He looks like he's still here, the friend I know,* he thinks to himself. He touches the body, it's cold, he shudders. *His eyes are staring up at the ceiling but they don't see, his beautiful mouth is open but nothing comes out of it.* He is fascinated and horrified at the same time. Hours go by. Enkidu doesn't move.

He leans closer and looks at his face for any sign of motion, any twitch or pulse. A fly crawls out of his nose and a deep groan emerges from Gilgamesh. He is stricken with the gravest emotion — doom, fear of death and demise, of turning into lifeless corpse with maggots crawling out of his nose.

He cries out, he wails, "Enkidu! Enkidu! You came out of the wild chaparral. Your mother was a gazelle and your father was a lion. You knew not of the ways of the world but I taught you. You knew not of the ways of adventuring but we ventured together. Enkidu! We shared everything even the secret thoughts. Enkidu I mourn you. The great walled city of Uruk mourns you. The harlots of the temple mourn you, the stars in the sky mourn you. Enkidu! I loved you!"

This went on for quite a while, the moaning and wailing and weeping. After 12 days had passed and the body had been interred and the funeral rites had been performed and the people of the great walled city had gone back to work, the great king Gilgamesh sat on the edge of his bed and stared vacantly out the window. His body had run out of tears and he could no longer weep. He felt as dry and empty as a dead leaf blowing in the wind.

Road trip

A dark foreboding in his chest was all he had left. The fear of death oppressed his mind. He looked around at his palace and his possessions and saw only impermanence and dissolution.

"Must I die too, like Enkidu? Must I become lifeless and still, unable to move?" He rose and shed his royal garments, tossed his crown to the floor, he picked up Enkidu's discarded clothes, the skins of wild animals and a belt of snakeskin and covered his own body with them.

"I will find the ancient wise man who lives beyond the edge of the world and ask him for the secret of immortality. He's supposed to know." He walks out of his palace and out of his city, through the splendid gate in the splendid wall and sets off on foot into the wild outback carrying only a small back pack and an extra pair of sandals.

And so he wandered and roamed, always to the east, in search of the old man who knew the secret of immortality. The story had come to him in his childhood of old Utnapishtim who had survived the great flood and was given eternal life by the gods because he saved all the creatures, two by two, in his wooden boat. It was a myth, a children's story but maybe it was true, maybe there was someone like Utnapishtim. Gilgamesh trudged on, his heart

225

heavy, full of sorrow and the terror of death, not knowing if he would ever find him or if he even really existed, knowing only that he must try.

He crossed deserts and mountains, he fought lions and snakes. He endured more hardships than any man ever did before or since and he felt more sorrow than any man ever could or ever would.

Finally after many months of hardships, traveling around, he arrived at two huge mountains known as the Twin Peaks. Their peaks touched the heavens and their roots spanned the underworld. There at the entrance stood two scorpion people, a husband and a wife, guarding access to the tunnel underneath the mountains, which is where the sun disappears at dusk and reappears on the other side at dawn. The appearance of the scorpion people was so horrible that just the sight of their faces could kill an ordinary person, but Gilgamesh steeled his nerves and approached them.

"Why do you come here and who are you?" demanded the scorpion husband.

"Gilgamesh is my name and I am the king of great walled Uruk."

The husband and wife consult with each other, "Well you look like shit." says the scorpion wife, "Why have you made this arduous journey over deserts and mountains and endured more hardships than any man ever has or ever will?"

"I have come to find my benefactor and my teacher, Utnapishtim, who knows the secret of immortality for I am terrified of death. Ever since my friend Enkidu fell sick and was taken into the underworld where people eat dust and

226

drink mud, I have had no relief and no rest."

"Well you're out of luck my bedraggled friend.' said the scorpion wife, "No one has ever crossed these peaks or passed through the tunnel underneath."

"No human being can survive such a journey." said the scorpion husband, "Your quest is at an end. Go back."

"I can't go back. There is nothing there but the memory of my friend who has died. Show me the way to cross these mountains or I will surely die trying."

The scorpion couple talked between themselves in whispered tones. Then they turned to Gilgamesh and said, "If you can run through the mountain before the sun enters you might make it. There is a tunnel but it is dark and long. There is no light to guide your way. Through this tunnel the sun travels at night to reach the other side of the world. If you enter before the sun sets and make it to the other side before it rises you will survive, if not you will be burnt to a crisp."

Gilgamesh ran into the tunnel, he didn't hold back, he ran for his life. Ever downward he went, There was darkness all around him. Fear arose in his heart. He stumbled and fell against the rocks. He cried out in anguish. He picked himself up and ran on even faster, he ran at the limits of his endurance, at the limits of his endurance he ran. For one hour he ran, for two hours he ran, for four hours he ran until all his hope was extinguished, for 10 hours he ran on blinded by despair. For 12 hours he ran and just as his strength was about to fail him he beheld in the distance a faint glimmer of light. He ran towards it stumbling and exhausted. He felt a faint breeze of fresh air and suddenly there was a flash of light and he found himself falling face first into the Garden of the Gods.

There was soft grass and there was the smell of the earth. He raised his head. There were trees full of ripe fruit sparkling like jewels. There were clusters of grapes growing on the vines, dates dangling from the palms. And there, on the beach at the edge of the world, sat Shiduri the bar maid at her bar.

If you can imagine a Corona beer commercial with a little thatched hut, a tub of ice cold beers and white sandy beaches with sparkling water — that would be Shiduri's place. She might have been a goddess — or atleast the archetypical bar maid that appears throughout history serving up brews. Let's see there's the serving wenches of the old medieval English pubs, no doubt the mead halls of old Beauwolf as well, they were there tapping the casks and serving the carafes in Viking Scandinavia, the geishas of imperial Japan, the satorial women of Gengis Khan, and back all the way back to the first woman serving up drinks — our mother. Maybe that's the symbolic purpose of having Shiduri's bar in the story next to the garden of the gods on the beach in the middle of nowhere. Maybe Gilgamesh needs to have an encounter with the 'mother' and learn some wisdom from her now that he has passed through his dark night of the soul. Maybe he's humble enough to receive it now. But when she sees Gilgamesh with his torn up clothes and weary worn face and his battered body she runs into her hut and bolts the door.

She climbs up to the roof and looks down at

Gilgamesh. "Go away you bum! Get out of here! Leave good people in peace." and starts throwing rocks at him.

Any trace of humility that he might have had up to that point completely disappears and he becomes outraged, "Hey! Do you know who the fuck I am? I am Gilgamesh, the king of great walled Uruk!" he yells back.

"Oh a great king are you? Well, great king, what do you want here, I have nothing but beer."

"I can see that. Look, come down here so I can talk to you?"

"And what is it you wish to speak to me of, oh king?"

"I wish to find the way to the ancient wise man, Utnapishtim. Only he knows the secret of immortality and from him I must learn it before death overtakes me like it did my friend Enkidu."

"Gilgamesh, humans are born, live and die" she says, "a lifetime is the gift given by the gods to humans, not immortality. Enjoy your life, have fun with your children, love your wife, eat good food and dress up once in a while; fill your house with music and dancing because one day you won't be able to enjoy it anymore."

"What are you saying? Your words have no meaning. My heart is sick with the fear of dying and all you have to say is enjoy yourself? I must find the wise man even if I have to cross the ocean, even if I spend all my days wandering and searching the wilderness with an empty heart."

"Well now that you mention it, that is a distinct possibility." says Shiduri, "But look, on the other side of the ocean is where the old man

229

lives. Unfortunately for you no one has ever crossed that ocean on their own. There is neither road nor map nor compass and it is boundless."

"Well how did he get there?"

"Good question. With the assistance of the boatman of course, and his boat, crewed by a strong brave crew and that is the only way to cross the ocean."

"Where is this boatman? Take me to him."

"Take yourself to him. He's off in the forest chopping wood with his crew."

Gilgamesh sneaks stealthily along the forest path, his axe in one hand, his knife in the other. He swoops down on the party when he finds them and begins hewing them apart. He attacks every single crew member and cuts them up into small pieces. Finally only the boatman is left, hiding behind a tree.

"Come out boatman, reveal yourself."

The boatman steps forward.

"Take me across the ocean to see my kinsman the ancient wise man, Utnapishtim who knows about immortality."

"You just killed my crew."

"I know. I'm sorry."

"How are we going to cross the ocean now?"

"I don't know." Gilgamesh sits down on a stump, his face in his hands. "I always wreck everything. I don't know how to behave. No one loves me. My only friend is dead."

"Stop complaining. Everyone has problems. Look, here's what we can do — go chop down a hundred trees from the forest each a hundred feet in length, trim the branches and bring them to the boat. I've got an idea."

So Gilgamesh chops down a hundred trees a hundred feet long, trims all the branches, brings them to the boat moored on the edge of the boundless ocean.

"Ok, put them in the boat and let's go. Grab one of the poles and push off and when that pole is spent let it go and grab another, push off with that one until it is spent then let it go and grab another."

Across the sea their track was marked by a trail of poles where Gilgamesh had given a mighty shove and let go. When all the poles were used up he grabbed the boatman's cloak and made a sail out of it and in this way they sailed across the ocean.

They arrived at the other shore and there on the beach stood a man — old, with white hairs and a beard. Gilgamesh jumped out of the boat and went up to him. "I am looking for Utnapishtim, my kinsman and mentor. I am looking for the one who knows the secrets of immortality and is not afraid of death."

"Why are your clothes so ragged and torn?" says the man, "Why is your face so ravaged by the desert sun and by the bitter cold of the mountains? Why are you roaming around like a crazy person? What are you looking for?"

"I will tell you why I'm roaming around like a crazy person. I'll tell you why my face is ravaged by the desert sun and by the bitter cold of the mountains. I'll tell you why my clothes are ragged and torn. It's because of my friend who died and is no more. Now my heart is afraid of death, that it will touch me too and I will become no longer living. Oh death has taught me fear but not wisdom. I'm looking for the wise man. The one who can tell me how to overcome death and put my heart at ease."

At this point in the story he is no longer a king or a ruler. He is a supplicant, a beggar. Maybe the boat trip took it out of him. There would be no logical reason to put the wise man at the end of the earth except to facilitate the image of Gilgamesh at the end of his rope. The distinct possibility of dying before ever finding the wise man must have occurred to him by now. To cross the ocean implies some mythic element that those people understood, living near the Persian Gulf 5,000 years ago. They traded with the Indus River Civilization in southeastern Pakistan which was either a mountainous journey or a long sea voyage. They understood the vastness of the sea and the epic nature of a journey across it.

The wise man spells it out for Gilgamesh

"Why do you trouble yourself with grief and pain?" says the old man, "Have you ever paused to think about how much you've been given. This human life of yours, your magnificent body, the hopes and aspirations of the gods are all in you. Even sweet death you are given and not even the gods know that, for knowing that they wouldn't be gods. Love and the pleasure of friendship and the meaning of conversation are given to you. Even time and the turning of the stars are given for your measuring. Revel in your life, celebrate and sing. This is my advice to you. Only the feeling of profound gratitude can outweigh the oppression of death when it comes. Practice it every day and you will become good at it. You will find yourself shielded from sorrow but not from pain, protected from evil but not from disasters."

"Utnapishtim!" Gilgamesh falls to his knees in the sand and looks up at the old man, "I came all the way here just to hear you say that? That's all you've got?"

"Let me tell you a story. Come inside my tent, Gilgamesh. Have some cool water."

Utnapishtim's wife brings him a pitcher of water "Here you go Gilgamesh, son. You must be worn out."

"Once upon a time, long long ago in a land far far away" begins old Utnapishtim, as he embarks on his epic tale of saving all humanity from the great flood, kind of a Mesopotamian Noah. He hasn't recited it in a while since there's no one around except him and his wife, so he pulls out all the stops and tells the grand tale with all the flourishes and finally comes around to the conclusion.

"And finally the rain stopped and the wind died down and the boat came to rest on solid land. We opened the door and saw the sun in the sky. We made an offering to Aruru and Shamash right then and there and we got blessed with immortality for our great deed."

Utnapishtim stops, pleased with himself, and looks at Gilgamesh. "That's what happened to me. That's how I got immortality, me and the Missus. Now you tell me Gilgamesh, what god is going to grant you such a boon? And could you receive it if they did?"

"Absolutely. Yes I could." replied Gilgamesh, "You can test me in any way you like to determine my worth."

"Ok. Sit here and stay awake for 7 days and 7 nights and afterwards we will determine what is your worth."

"That's easy." said Gilgamesh, "I can remain alert and ready for a lot longer than that."

Mrs. Utnapishtim brought him a pillow to rest on and Gilgamesh closed his eyes and fell fast asleep so exhausted was he from his long journey.

Seven days later when he woke up he jumped to his feet, "I just closed my eyes for a second. I wasn't sleeping."

"Look", said Utnapishtim, "each day that you were asleep my wife baked a cake. You can see the first one is already moldy and the last one she baked is still fresh. Would you like some cake?"

When Gilgamesh saw this he knew it was over, that he would never get the gift of immortality. Downcast and with an empty heart he went to the boatman. "Let's go. Let's go back. I have failed. I have no more business here." They boarded the boat and set sail.

"Oh sweetie," said Mrs. Utnapishtim to her husband, "he came so far and endured so much. Give him something."

"Ok." he agreed. "Gilgamesh, come back!" he yelled, "I have a gift for you."

When Gilgamesh heard this he turned the boat around and returned to the shore.

"Look, kid." says Utnapishtim to Gilgamesh, "You're not a bad kid, maybe a little . . . OCD. I'll tell you what — if you dive down to the bottom of the ocean and grab the magic plant, it's the one with spines. Bring it up and you've got it. Whoever partakes of the magic plant will live forever."

Gilgamesh immediately dove down to the bottom of the ocean, grabbed the magic plant, the one with spines and brought it back to the surface.

"Hey look at this," he says to the boatman, "the magic plant! It can imbue life so I can live forever. I'll take it back to my city and test it on an old man and see if it works. Then I'll use it on myself and become young again."

They sail across the ocean, they walk across the land. At two hundred miles they stop and take a break, grab something to eat, at four hundred miles they make camp and dig a well, at six hundred miles they stop and take a break, at 800 miles they make camp and find a spring.

He leaves the plant on the ground and bathes in the water, washing himself in preparation to enter the great city of Uruk. A snake, smelling the captivating aroma of the magic plant, stealthily slithers up to it and carries it away. As it goes it sheds its skin and disappears.

When Gilgamesh comes out of the water, he sees that the magic plant is missing and then he sees what the snake has done. He sits down and weeps. "All my hardships have been for nothing. Now the snake has stolen the magic plant and I will never find it again. Why was I so careless? I'm almost home and now I have lost everything."

Homecoming

The next day Gilgamesh and the boatman see the city in the distance. It comes closer and closer as they approach the main gate of the great walled Uruk.

"By the way, what is your name?" says Gilgamesh to the boatman, "So I can introduce you to my people."

"Urshanabi, the servant." replied the boatman

"Urshanabi, we are here. The great walled city of Uruk. See how its ramparts gleam like copper in the sun. Climb the stone staircase, more ancient than the mind can imagine, approach the Eanna Temple, sacred to Ishtar, a temple that no king has equaled in size or beauty, walk on the wall of Uruk, follow its course around the city, inspect its mighty foundations," he says as they pass into the city.

"Behold the great city" he continues, "where people dress in brightly colored clothes and dance in the street. Where a man finds pleasure with his wife and joy with his children, where there is music in the streets and people dress up for dinner. Where a man can find peace and prosperity for all the days of his life."

At seeing their king, the people of the city crowd around him, yelling loud cheers and exultations, touching him and laying down soft carpets for him to walk on.

They have a big party in the city center and Gilgamesh tells them all about his adventures. He introduces his friend, Urshanabi, the servant, who ferried him across the endless ocean and forgave him for killing all his crew.

"He's a great guy." Gilgamesh assures them and they drink wine and make music and dance. Gilgamesh is implored to tell his story yet again and he does — this time even better.

Chapter 14

Han and Hannah

Han is lying in his hammock. Han is reading his book. Han is diddling with his guitar, lost in his fantasy of what the ancient people were like. . . . *they had their own technology too . . . things they could do with wood and bark and river reeds and talking to the trees . . they could fly . . . they could turn into animals . . .*

He pulls his quadcopter out of the basket, retrieves the controller and turns it on. It rises into the air and looks at him. It zooms out over the pool, it ascends to the top of the big pecan tree. From his screen on the controller he can see the whole neighborhood. He does a high level scan, circling and then drops fast, brakes and settles in over the pond like a dragonfly. Han practices being a dragonfly darting here and there, he lifts up into the sky does a flip and brings it down with the intention of landing with a quick scoop but it comes down too fast, hits the ground and skids into the pool. "Damn!"

He rushes over to rescue his toy and trips on the glass kerosene lantern, which shatters and spills kerosene across the concrete patio. "Fuck!"

At the edge of the pool he reaches down as far as he can into the water and grabs the quadcopter but it slips out of his fingers and disappears into the dark green water.

"Shit!" He runs over to the shed and grabs the pool net. He casts and casts and finally snags it, pulls it out of the water and holds it up as the water drains out of the plastic chassis.

"Damn." He carries the copter over to the round plastic patio table, places it in the center of the table and looks at it. He opens the battery compartment and detaches the battery, lays it on the table. He retrieves the controller from where it was dropped and places it next to the quadcopter. "Fuck." he says in conclusion.

Two hours later, after changing the battery and drying it out as much as possible including 10 minutes in the oven on warm, he flicks the on button. There is no response. He pushes the throttle lever forward but it doesn't whir, it doesn't rise, it doesn't fly. He sets the quadcopter down on the ground and smashes it with his sandaled foot. Parts of it fly off and land in the dark stain of the spilled kerosene and shattered glass which he still hasn't cleaned up.

The emotions crash down on him, again. He feels crushed by an immense weight that comes from nowhere. He feels disoriented. The sense of loneliness and abandonment, his familiar ghosts, have found him. He fights back, he gets on his bike.

Once up to speed, he assesses the situation. . . . *it's a clear day four o'clock . . . thursday . . . crisp wind out of the northeast pushing me , , , damn cars in the road . . . always damn cars in the road . . . the faster they go the farther they*

*have to go . . . it's a never ending spiral of
insanity . . .*

He turns onto Broadway, towards downtown,
passes buses when they slow, takes on cars . . .
*there are different modes of riding . . . loping
like a wolf across the prairie, going at a speed
you can sustain all day, not fast not slow . . .
then there's pushing the envelope going hard at
a speed you can't sustain very long . . . there's
hammer down full outa my way going as hard as
you can . . .*

Han accelerates, gets into double breathing as
the oxygen debt builds up and the pain
comes. . . . *it's good pain . . . you can trust it . . .
when that ends you're over . . . switch on a
different mode . . .*

"Clear lane! Clear lane! Give me a clear
lane!." he yells from the curbside as a large
sedan passes him taking up most of his lane. . . .
a *full size bison back in those days was 7 1/2 feet
tall and weighed thirty five hundred pounds . . .
imagine hunting one of those with your stone
tipped spear, you and your young punk
buddies . . . if you missed . . .*

The buildings of the downtown city center
grow larger incrementally. The city's skyline
changes from a horizon of buildings to a forest
of buildings. He turns left onto Commerce to
inspect them, their glass facades, reflecting and
revealing both at the same time . . . *like an
ancient shaman . . . the three windows . . . the
three worlds . . . underground on ground and
above ground . . . the three reasons . . . birth . . .
life , , , and death . . .*

The buildings merge and morph in his
peripheral vision as he passes them.   The

canyon-like walls of the street rise up on either
side. He downshifts and takes the corner at St.
Mary's against the light. . . . *bike cops are
numerous downtown . . . watch out . . .* The
rumble strip in the center of the street slows him
down and he pulls off into Main Plaza, an open
space decorated with fountains and statues. The
Cathedral of St. Almond Butter occupies the far
end . . . *here we are . . . homo sapiens with all
our high level language skills and all . . . we
don't even know who we are . . .*

Street people have installed themselves on the
benches and under the trees with their bags and
blankets, regular people are strolling around in
couples or small groups with kids, some are solo
with a dog. A couple of bike cops are moored
nearby. He stops and dismounts, fastens his bike
to the light post with a steel lock and walks
towards the cathedral.

Its real name is the Cathedral of Saint
Alexander but the light brown colors on the
flowing robes of the statue at the foot of the
nave evoked the association in his mind years
ago and it stuck. Han is not a believer in any
specific religion so precise names are
unnecessary. His form of worship consists
mostly of sitting quietly in a pew somewhere
between St. Almond Butter and Christ and
weeping softly under his breath. After having
done this for awhile and having gone over most
of the sins and mistakes he's committed recently
he finishes with a prayer and leaves. He still
feels unworthy and wretched but like he's had
company at least.

Outside the church, the sky is growing dark;
twilight . . . *crepusculo* . . . The world seems

curiously strange and wholly indifferent to Han, the trees stand in a row and hold witness and are indifferent. Nowhere in the plaza can be seen ghosts or apparitions, nowhere in all of the downtown area are there tigers stalking him, or angry mobs chasing him, or helicopter gun ships targeting him with hellfire missiles from above but still he feels hunted and vulnerable.

He climbs up on his bike and pushes off, the rhythm settling into his mind, distracting his thoughts. Around the corner and down a dark street he goes, across a creek, through Bank Plaza, does a turn around the flags, banks onto Commerce Street, heads for the parking ramp and climbs 9 levels to the top.

The sun is about to disappear below the horizon. The city is laid out before him. He feels the space as pure emptiness, he feels it inside himself, he feels it as a vast unchartered space with no direction, no way to orientate. He leaves, disturbed by the feeling and descends each level almost too fast trying to squelch the feeling, trying to drown it out or distract it or defrock it or disempower it or something.

. . . the Esquire is open . . . he muses upon exiting the parking ramp onto Losoya. *. . . stores are shut and restaurants are open all along the boulevard . . . that would be market street . . .* He turns on Market, cruises a few blocks and pulls over.

Inside the Esquire a long wooden bar stretches out all the way to the back. Bar stools are attached to it and on the opposite side of the room, booths are available if privacy is desired.

Han sits at the bar. "Hey. The bartender needs a menu." he says looking at the bartender. There is no response. Han slumps on his stool. He puts his elbows on the bar and bows his head as if in benediction but instead of praying runs his fingers through his hair and holds his head. The bartender drops a menu on his next pass.

"Let me know if you have any questions."

"Yeah umh . . . what is the purpose of life?" responds Han looking up.

"Well about the menu anyway. I don't really know that."

"You don't know the purpose of life?"

"No not really."

"Damn it."

"Uh, I'll come back and get your order."

The menu is divided into two columns and when you fold it out, six columns. . . . *too much i just want a beer . . . i don't want to read about it and every beer and its title . . .*

On the menu each beer is listed with its name, price and alcohol content. The IPA rating is also noted. Below the Belgian Stout is a short description of the beer — its heritage, its friends and acquaintances, its standing in society, its brave adventures and its noble accomplishments. Same with the Clear Water Blonde and so on.

. . . everything is a story yeah right . . . i wrecked that one sure did am i free to go now fuck . . . what the fuck jesus she's banging omar fuck what the hell . . . damn i messed it up should have stayed on damn it should have stayed on for awhile . . . Jesus what the fuck . . . fuck omar she fucks anybody jesus . . . focus don't think about that don't drive the nails in deeper . . . go with the flow be alive remember what she said i hope you will be ok that's what she said i hope you will be ok . . . i'll call her . . .

*no that wouldn't be a good idea just be ok . . . ok
be . . . separate yourself from all you are
perceiving to be . . . the observer . . . feel let it
flow accept . . . right . . . just feel it don't call her
let it be . . . tomorrow maybe . . . i'm having a
hard time . . . i'm not sure . . . fuck . . . fuck . . .
fuck . . .*

"So what'll it be?"

"I'll uuumh, have an IPA."

"Ok." says the bartender sizing him up to see
what might fit.

He returns after a few minutes and pours the
beer into a glass, up about half way, and leaves
the bottle. Han looks at the label, it's the picture
of a ram with a big rack of horns and its head
lowered, an angry look in its eye. Han pulls out
his phone. He takes a picture of the label, he
takes a picture of the backlit bottles lined up on
the shelves behind the bar. He looks at the
pictures. He wonders why he took them.

He sits on his bar stool with the glowing wall
of bottles floating in front of him, a 16 ounce
IPA beside him . . . *a member of the human race,
in the modern world, safely ensconced in a
modern city . . . high and dry but in reality
drowning in a whirlpool of grief . . . a maelstrom
of regret . . . i'm underwater . . .*

He picks up the phone and calls Hannah. It
rings and rings but there's no connection. He
orders another beer when he gets the barman's
attention.

He taps out a text message. "wow what
happened to the love" drinks his beer half way
down and sends it.

Ten minutes go by and she responds, "I can't
love everybody."

Han is looking around at the bar, his eyes come to rest on the backlit bottles. The feeling of abandonment overwhelms him, the feeling of loss, the feeling of desperation mixed with humiliation takes over. Shame comes in late but mixes well with the others. Bad memories from the past that he can't control are inflicted on him by his own brain chemicals that have been eviscerated and traumatized by various negative experiences and conditions throughout his life, mostly in his childhood. Experiences and conditions that he could not fathom at the time but now that's he's grown up and learned how fucked up he is all those experiences are much more fathomable.

Fifteen minutes later he taps into his phone "ok so maybe we can get together sometime" and sends.

"Not right now."

Han is staring into his empty IPA glass as if it were an augury, as if he might receive information from the bubbles at the bottom. It's not a conscious thing, more of a furtive thing, a rabbit taking shelter in the foliage and sitting very still, kind of thing. Han feels like that rabbit, and the feeling that's stalking him is out there, like a hunter, trying to find him. It's a crazy feeling, and scary.

He taps out a message. "oh thanks / that's great / i'll see you around / i guess geezus that's fucked up". He hesitates, reads the message over again, calibrates, he sends it and turns off the phone.

There's a football game on the TV: the team with grey piping and green uniforms vs. the team with black trim and red uniforms. Both teams line up facing each other, digging and pawing at the earth and then, in a moment of truth, collide with great exuberance. A runner struggles forward through the trench where they fight, staggers and falls. One of the enemy soldiers is holding onto his leg, another crashes down on him just as he hits the ground.

Below the TV set, the illuminated bottles swim on, row after row like good little soldiers, and he remembers something from a long time ago, a moment in his childhood when he was lost in a shopping mall. His mother and his brother were somewhere but he couldn't find them and he was so ashamed at being lost that he hid behind a booth selling jewelry next to the Penny's entrance and pretended to be invisible. He remembers looking at the different colored stones in the bracelets and necklaces hanging from wires and slowly turning. He remembers crying in his little hiding place because the feeling of shame was so sharp, like something cutting him and the burden of being invisible was so heavy.

"You want another one?"

"Yeah I guess so. Hey who's playing?"

"The Barracudas against the Sea Lions."

"Oh." *. . . barracudas against the sea lions who would win that battle . . . barracudas against sea lions who would win that . . .* Han thinks about it for a long time while he drinks down his beer. The red and green bottles glow. He pays the bill and goes.

Up on the bike, he navigates through downtown, around the traffic circle and back to the river. The trail forms a long uninterrupted pathway out away from the city and down river and he gets into it. Not so easy after three beers but he still has the rhythm thing so he checks in and winds out. Six or seven miles later he throttles back and turns it off, exits the trail and rides back towards town on the surface streets.

The funky south side gets less authentic and the city gets denser and denser as the city center approaches, finally he is among the tall buildings again. He makes a hard left onto Presa and slows, splits the parked cars and the traffic and turns into an alleyway. Sub-streets between the main thoroughfares provide a place for the dumpsters to sit and collect trash from the downtown restaurants and retail establishments.

In between the dumpsters sit two men, backs to the brick wall. They are each braiding long fibrous leaves. One is making something that looks like a cross, the other appears to be making a sombrero. They are singing.

"Ya me canso de llorar. Y no amanecer. Ya no se si maldecirte." they sing in unison. "O por ti rezar. Paloma negra. Paloma negra. Adonde, adonde andaras."   As the song ends the sombrero maker exaggerates the last line with a dramatic flourish. They both think that's pretty funny.

"Yo veo el espíritu del cuerpo" says the sombrero maker, "Todos ellos están marchitos. Sus cordones están sucios, no están conectados."

His buddy lifts up his construction and shows it to his friend,"Oye, mira esto. El Arbol de la Vida."

"Si, es dificil de hacer. Es duro vivir en las calles." advises his friend, looking around at the tall buildings and the alley.

"No hay lugar donde establecernos", says his buddy. "No hay donde descansar. Para reponer la energía. Todo es seguir".

"Es un ambiente hostil."

"Sin agua, sin un santo patrón. Solo cemento. Híjole, hasta la popó de los pájaros huele raro." Laughter, "Hasta las aves se sienten raras aquí!"[1]

"I'm tired of crying. And there is no dawn. I don't know whether to curse you anymore." they sing in unison. "Or to pray for you. Black pigeon. Black pigeon. Where, where will you go." As the song ends the sombrero maker exaggerates the last line with a dramatic flourish. They both think that's pretty funny.

"I see their spirit body." says the sombrero maker. "They're all shriveled up. Their strings are messy. Not connected."

His buddy lifts up his construction and shows it to his friend, "Hey look at this. The Tree of Life."

"Yes, It's hard to do. The streets are hard." advises his friend, looking around at the tall buildings and the alley.

No place to settle." says his buddy. "No resting place. To collect the energy. Everything is taking."

"Harsh environment."

"Without water, without a patron saint. Only cement. Wheeeie. Even the bird poop smells funny." Laughter, "Even the birds feel weird around here."

Han slows to a stop when he hears the singing. When there's a pause in their conversation he makes himself known and speaks to them "Como estas."

The two men stop working and look at him. "Hola amigo." says the man holding the half finished sombrero. He's wearing a blue shirt with long pants. He has an odd looking fedora on his head and a long braided pony tail of black hair coming out from underneath it. On his feet are a pair of sandals also made from some kind of fibrous material plaited together.

"Nice, man." offers Han, having no better idea of what to say to them but eager to initiate some kind of contact.

"Nice man." says the man in the fedora.

His friend laughs at this as if it were the funniest joke he had ever heard, then turns to look at Han. He's is in a similar costume and wearing a Panama hat made out of light colored woven straw. His feet are bare. "Ponch, pachuco low rider." he says nodding towards Han and they both laugh.

"Allow me to introduce myself, señor. I am Ponch and this is Theo making his cross." At this remark, Theo erupts in laughter and pounds the ground with his hand. "We are from Sonora state and have come to see your city."

"Welcome." says Han.

"Thank you my friend. We have heard much about this place from our comrades and so here we are. We have come to see el Norte." he says with a flourish.

"El Norte." repeats Theo.

"Yeah?"

"Oh yeah. Where I come from only two houses is called a city." Theo laughs. "Here in this place there are houses as tall as trees. It's like a jungle here. Don't you agree?"

Han looks at both of them, suddenly suspicious, unsure of their intentions and what his agreement might entail. "Yeah, I guess so. Well what do you think of our city?"

"Fantastic." says Ponch. "So many people living together in the same basket. In Mexico we have a saying, 'Mas burros, menos helotes.' Do you know what that means?"

"No."

"The more people the less for everybody, but here everybody has more. It's fantastic."

"Yeah more for most people, not everyone." says Han.

"Everyone has more except the people who lost their energy, their spirit animal."

"What's that?"

He removes his fedora and runs his hand through his long black hair while gazing up at Han. "Look! See that?" he points at the sky between the buildings.

Han shifts his stance and looks up at the sky, catching a glimpse of a hawk in flight.

"Imagine being a hawk. The hawk stalks his prey, watches it carefully maybe for hours or days and calculates the best chance to get it with the . . . smallest amount of risk. Then he makes his move, no hesitation, completely focused. That's how you do it my friend. If you don't have a friendly animal to teach you the way, you're lost."

Han "Ah. Yeah. Good point. I can see that. Yeah. I'm lost."

"You're welcome." says Ponch, who replaces his hat and continues working on his palm leaves. Theo keeps his head down and focused on the folding and bending and the points of tension in his cross.

Han gets in his toe clips, "See you later amigos.".   They nod and their conversation resumes.

"No compa, nosotros podemos crear un paraíso aquí. Nadie tendría que trabajar, nadie estaría incómodo, ni sin algo que comer. Con toda esta tecnología?"

"Si, a lo mejor podríamos vivir junto al río."

"A orillas del río, exactamente!   Pero si hubieras visto a Jorge anoche . . . ¡chale ! Estaba en tan mal estado que se que se hubiera caído al río y ahogado ahí."

"No dude, we could create a paradise here. No one would have to work, no one would be uncomfortable or unfed. With all this technology?"

"Yeah maybe we could live by the river."

"Down by the river, exactly but if you saw Jorge last night, oh man was he messed up. He would fall in the river and drown."

. . . that was interesting . . . Han rides out of the alley and turns away from downtown. He heads for home. . . . *from Sonora . . . . . . seemed like they were . . . visiting or something . . . making straw hats . . . in the alley . . .*

Everything is puzzling to Han. *. . . why can't things be obvious? . . .* He's tired, he's worn out, the wind is in his face. *. . . of course it's in my face . . . it's always in my face . . .*

He feels like everything is against him . . . *what was that bruja about? . . . that was crazy I*

*have no idea what happened . . . gees I messed
up . . .*

He pumps harder, trying to make the voice go
away and leave him in peace. The hill at the
entrance to his neighborhood has a strange
outward curve. He takes it too fast, brakes hard
to avoid the cars parked there, feels his bike skid
out from under him and goes down in the street.

"Aarrgh!" Bang. It's all over, his bike
somehow landing on top of him with one leg
through the frame.

A car stops, the passenger side window lowers,
"Are you ok?" says a voice from inside. Han
finds it annoying to be asked by a motorist if
he's ok while he's lying in the street trying to
figure out if he's ok.

"I'm ok." he says after a moment.

He slowly picks himself up and counts the
number of places where blood is seeping from
the abrasions and contusions caused by
slamming into the pavement and sliding to a
stop. The total is four: knee, shoulder, hand,
elbow plus a sprained thumb. He picks up his
bike, which seems to be functional. He taps his
bike helmet which is still intact and slowly
walks up the hill.

Once home, he showers off the blood and
cleans the wounds. He cuts fresh aloe vera from
his front porch and uses it to make bandages for
his raw skin.

Lying down on the futon where he once made
love with Hannah, he feels all the aches and
pains, explores them. talks to them . . . *it's gonna
be alright . . . it's gonna be ok . . .* He thinks
about Hannah. He thinks about the whole world
and why things happen. *. . . why people do what*

they do . . . why do I do what I do . . . He finds no answers to his questions and he finds no solace in his musings. His wounded knee throbs and his shoulder has an insistent sharp pain. His thumb aches. He thinks about his life. He questions his sanity. He wonders how deep sadness can go. Finally he falls asleep and dreams about a ram with giant horns that's chasing him.

****

Hannah is returning from a hike when she sees the call from Han. She's on a camping trip with Omar and they have just climbed all the way to the top of Mount Archibald and back. She veers off the trail and looks at her phone, puts it on mute.

"That was amazing. Those shapes high up on the rock. What were they — airplanes?" she says as she lays down an armful of sticks and branches that she gathered for the fire.

"The circle shapes on the other side with the wavy line and the V-shaped people." says Omar.

"What was that?"

"Haven't figured it out yet." Omar's contribution is a pile of stones that he has just arranged in a circular pattern. Earlier in the day they had built the little lean-to shelter leaning against Omar's van, just enough to shield the fire and magnify the sounds coming out of the surrounding hills

That was the idea - go to Mount Archibald, see the cave art and make a fire. Everything was quite in order as far as she could see. Then messenger beeped.

252

She looks at it "God!"

"What?"

"It's nothing." she says, "It's nothing any human being hasn't gone through."

They get the fire going just as night descends and the dancing, writhing light fills their little camp.

"I know you're going to say it was a natural formation" says Omar "they look like natural formations but there were shapes in there."

"No there weren't." says Hannah laughing, "They weren't even in the guide book."

"Hey, they don't know everything."

"Yeah but they know quite a bit." Hannah had moved over in front of Omar and laid down there and leaned her head on his knee, "Lets look at the stars."

"There aren't any stars yet."

"There's one." says Hannah pointing.

"Ha, ha. There is no star there."

"It's a figment one. Of your imagination."

"Oh . . . a figment one. Ha ha." he leans over and kisses her, "there's a figment."

"I got that figment." says Hannah and rolls over on her stomach.

"Hold that thought." says Omar, gets up and heads for the bathroom which is behind any tree close enough but far enough away.

"I've got to get some blankets and turn off the solar array." he says when he returns and hurries off behind the van.

Hannah pulls out her phone and for some perverse reason or maybe just recklessness, reads the message.

She doesn't want to deal with it, she very much doesn't want to deal with it. . . . *it's the most frustrating thing about boys . . .* she thinks. "I can't love everyone." she sends.

"Sorry I took so long." Omar reappears.

"It's ok. I've been talking to Han."

"Oh."

"How's the solar array?"

"I shut it down."

Messenger bings again. "It's Han." she looks at the message and types in "Not right now."

"Hi Omar."

"Hi Hannah."

The fire ritual, exploring the other person which is what she likes to do, begins.

Han likes to wonder why people act the way they do and tries to figure out different stories for how they got that way.

Hannah smells Omar and gets horny. Omar gets horny.

Han can't figure out if trauma is passed down from generation to generation or starts new each time.

Hannah has disconnected her rational mind, which is what she likes to do. She has become some kind of an animal, a wolf perhaps, or a deer. It comes in phases.

Han questions whether his brain is working right.

Omar slips off his fold up camping chair and onto the ground.

Han is casting pebbles into the pool of his mind, watching the ripples grow.

The first real star comes out over the distant hills but Hannah doesn't see it.

Chapter 15

The Nature Pool

We need to find contentment if we are to be fully human. We need to find our rhythm. We need discourse: talking to each other and to ourselves in a meaningful manner. We need to feel our existence and be grateful. We need to notice things. We need to see the sky and we need to find our quest, something that compels us. We need to see the trees, something that grounds us and we need to see the world we live in, here below, as the song goes.

I do a lot of my seeing and introspection and peace finding while sitting on the backyard porch looking out over my little biosphere or walking around inspecting the various features of my quarter acre residential lot here in San Antonio.

The nature pool is the main feature of my back yard and consists of an old in-ground swimming pool that has been converted into a fish pond next to a fan shaped enclosure filled with gravel and held in place by a low wall of concrete blocks — the bog filter. A pump at the far end of the pond sends the water through a pipe and into the bog filter where microbes embedded in the gravel digest the waste products of the fish and turn them into food for the water plants growing there. The filtered water then tumbles back into the pond, aerating the water for the fish. Inside the pond reside goldfish and little black minnows plus two turtles.

The nature pool, in reality, consists of the entire backyard: the pecan tree, the willow, the hackberries residing in the groovy nook back in the corner, the ligustrum, the possum haw, the holly trees growing alongside the house and the dirt they all grow in populated by microbes, fungi, ants, beetles, worms, mites and fleas, among others. The birds, the bugs, the frogs, the possum and her joey and every other living thing large and small that has decided to make this place their home; even the gentle breeze that comes and goes and the sky above are part of the nature pool.

From my station at the plastic patio table on the back porch I can sit and observe all the comings and goings of this miniature world. Thoreau trekked two miles out into the woods and built a cabin alongside Walden Pond. I already had a cabin so I built the pond next to it and here I sat on many a pleasant evening observing the wildlife and the twilight and the doves brave dive and the occasional swishes of the fish.

Kybo the cat has accompanied me on some of these reveries. She is the one who taught me the art of sitting and witnessing the world. She has the brain for it and can do it for hours. Mine is wired differently, doesn't have nearly so much focus but I do the best I can.

Winter

It's a drizzly, chilly, cloudy, winter day in the nature pool. The sky is a hundred shades of grey and random drops of water are splashing all around, exploding on contact and disappearing into the ground. Some are landing in the pool creating bright rings that expand and diffuse, some are landing in the driveway where they find their way to the street and into the gutter and on their way down to the river and to the sea, the heaving, thunderous sea. Water above, water below and in between, water alive: us, the critters, the plants and the humans, we're all made of water, mostly.

The frogs are dropping their winter song — 3 longs and a short, a sort of semaphore to the lengthening nights and the chilling weather. Soon they will find their underwater bower and bed down for the long night, dream and drowse the way frogs do, hibernate until spring comes with her warm currents and wakes them up. Then they will emerge into the world and sing again.

I don't think anyone knows what it is that frogs sing about when they gather around the pool, chirping and trilling away with all their strength, but my guess would be the dreamtime — what they felt when they slowed way down and slept underwater for 3 months. But what kind of dreams could their little amphibian brains possibly have created for them? Or was it maybe some kind of a blank screen where nothing at all was seen? That would be a compelling image — a blank screen. Ideas and thoughts would reflect on a blank screen.

Maybe frogs don't have thoughts. Hmm, but then how do they think?

Well anyways, all those dreamtime frogs have manifested around the pool and are doing their rhythmic chanting, their primordial ritual, their all night long call and response group orgy. Yes, by the end of the night they will have climbed up on top of each other and had sex, setting up the next generation of dreamers and singers in the nature pool.

The rain has stopped but the wind is still moving through the sky. The clouds are turbulent. The day dims as twilight arrives. Imperceptibly at first, a darkening of the mood more than of the sky, but then things start to disappear, the darkness comes out of nowhere and overwhelms the light. The sparrow couple make their way back to their home under the eaves.

It's vespers, the time of transformation, when things that are seen become unseen and unseen things become seen, like a religious ritual or a magic trick. Although it happens every night, we usually don't notice it, only the after effects of 'day' and 'night'. We live by that: the day and night cycle, the rising and falling of the curtain across the stage, one day done, one more act complete, intermission, a pause while the stage crew re-arranges the set. Then the sun returns, the curtain rises, same play, new act.

The frogs have settled into their groove — choruses and chants; their refrains and descants are interspersed with silence, quietude, a moment of reflection perhaps.

What the microbes are up to

It's morning. Light has come, filled the air and chased sway the shadows.   In the bog filter watercress is thriving.   It's like a miniature jungle in there, looming over the gravel and over the hiding places of the frogs.   It has grown higher than the wall itself and is falling over the other side like the Hanging Gardens of Babylon.

Under the gravel, the communities of bugs and bacteria live according to their laws. I know of the microbial life by studying about bog filters. *Nitrosomonas* and *Nitrosoccoccus* are two genera of bacteria that are common inhabitants due to their ability to oxidize ammonia. That's not an easy task, it takes several steps and a bunch of enzymes that they make themselves to do the job, but there's plenty of free ammonia floating around from the waste products of the fish so it's a good deal. Metabolizing ammonia into nitrites is how they get their energy.

The resultant nitrites are digested by *Nitrobacter*, another genus of bacteria, who have been waiting in the wings to take over. They get their energy from oxidizing the nitrites and turning them into nitrates. Nitrates, you might recall from reading the ingredients on the back of that bag of plant fertilizer you brought home from the nursery, is plant food. Therefore the waste products of the fish are taken up as nutrients by the roots of the plants.

All this I have learned and even more I have visualized about the microbes and their busy little communities interacting within the gravel bed, each microbe clinging to a niche or swimming around among the debris with its flagellum, grabbing nutrients from the water, communicating and calibrating with other microorganisms using their signaling molecules. I visualize an industrious and vast population of little people working day and night, in concert, seamlessly, their little chemical factories humming away, turning ammonia into nitrates. They don't mind working hard, they're the little people.

In the fish pond, which forms the lower level of this aquaponics experiment, different microbes of varying designs are pursuing their various lifestyles. Cyanobacteria, amoebas and paramecium, diatoms and dinoflagellates are present in all likelihood, spirogyra with its twisting spiraling green fibers and oscillatoria with its oscillating tendrils. Larger species, too, like dragonfly nymphs (they sting) and the voracious rotifers (tiny strange little animals that can completely dry out and then reconstitute themselves), co-habitate fresh water ponds like this and take their turns in the food chain.

Turtles

There are turtles. Except right now they're hibernating. They're at the bottom of the pool, buried in mud. I can't see them but they are, presumably, comfortable. Turtles, as it turns out, can hibernate underwater for months at a time by breathing through their anus until the warm water returns and they resume their active lifestyle of basically hanging out all day.

The ancients believed that turtles had something to do with creation. The Chinese used them for divination. They would put a turtle shell in the fire (presumably after making turtle soup) and then read their augury by the cracks that appeared. In the Iroquois culture the world rests on the back of a turtle. According to the story, Sky Woman fell through a hole in the clouds and landed on Big Turtle floating in the endless ocean whereupon all the animals came together to help her. One of them, Toad, managed to swim all the way down to the bottom of the ocean and bring back a mouthful of mud which Sky Woman used to make the Earth as a home for all people.

There is something enigmatic about a creature who is equally at home on land breathing air and underwater breathing in the water. Turtles must have some kind of special knowledge, unbeknownst to us humans, about the underwater realm, the primordial world, the world where life began 3 1/2 billion years ago. Certainly they must notice the two worlds and a portal of some sort as they pass between them, a doorway between one and the other, a moment when everything changes.

The fish, who live only in the water, may not even be aware of water. Like us humans, who live on land and on water and everywhere else on this intricately connected biosphere, yet barely notice that we live on a planet. We are oblivious to what is most obvious. Although if someone was asked the question on a TV game show: 'Do you live on a planet?' They would say, 'Yes, I definitely live on a planet'. I think the turtles can teach us something here. I'm not sure what it is.

How the chili pequins do it

Winter turns red the chili pequins that grow on the small bushes underneath the hackberry trees next to the fence. They are planted there by the mockingbirds, for they too love the small red fruit. Apparently they have no sensitivity to the intense heat they generate otherwise it would be hard to imagine how they could gobble them down — by weight one of the hottest chilis. But like the squirrels who planted the Spanish oaks in front of my house (to provide shade and protection assumably), the mocking birds deposited the seeds (after passing them through their gut) in places that get enough sun but not too much, where they are accessible and create nice borders. It's amazing, kind of like exterior decorating.

Maybe it's the slant of the light that calls forth the red, the low sun. They look, in fact, like small decorated Christmas trees with their bright red orbs nestled among the green leaves; the berries are ovular, actually, and orangish red. I pluck them for tossing in the breakfast tacos.

At this season the sun rises to about 37° above the horizon before it goes down again. I can see it through the trees and it's about noon right now, the high point. That's just a guess, it's less than 45° about that much. Back in the day they used to measure the angle of the sun and track the movement of the stars across the sky and navigate from those two celestial events using an astrolabe. That plus a compass and you could find your way across the vast uncharted oceans of the world, as Magellan did in 1522 in his wooden sailing ship or at least some of his crew mates did; he got killed by natives in the Philippines.

The ancient South Pacific Islanders could navigate across thousands of miles of open ocean using the sea currents and the smells and the sea birds and the stars to guide them, along with some simple devices they invented. Navigation for them was an art, a meditation, a process of constantly monitoring the signs and signals and remembering their meaning. The information that they needed to remember was embedded in their songs and stories which in the telling, each to each other onboard the ship, became the navigation and the way finding. This is how they did it, traveling to distant islands in their double hulled canoes with sail and oar thousands of years ago. From the Hawaiian Islands to Fiji and Tonga, to Vanuatu and Tuvalu they navigated, singing their way along, and to all the other islands that humans inhabited back then.

I navigate with google maps strapped to my bicycle handle bars. I can find my way home when I'm totally lost on the south side after dark with my phone. Or GPS in my car, same deal. Keying off blipping satellites 22,000 miles overhead in geosynchronous orbit.

The chili pequins can do none of these things as they navigate the seasons, only the slant of light and the night time temperatures and whatever other clues a chili pequin notices. But when it's right they send a message to the bud: *Be fruitful and multiply, turn red and proclaim: come and eat me."* And they do come, the mockingbirds come and eat them and carry off

the seeds so they might sprout forth anew in the
Spring.

Trees, hawks and cats

Sitting on the back porch I can see the stark
silhouettes, of the bare trees against the pale
grey sky. Their shapes evoke something in my
mind, a feeling . . . something about our earliest
fairy tales perhaps. Those old stories came from
the forest, and the elves and the dwarves have
inhabited our human mind ever since. And the
witches, oh yes, the witches; it's the witch's hut
in the woods.

Trees and humans go way back. We have a
common ancestor, a billion years ago, that was
not a tree or a human but passed along the
possibilities for both. If you are 'rooted', in the
parlance, it means you have established your
connections within the society around you and
don't want to move or be swayed. So it was
with our ancient friends the trees, who found a
way of living together in great communities with
their roots embedded in the ground, absorbing
water and nutrients and exchanging information
with each other while holding themselves firmly
in place.

There is a sharp cry from the Blue Jay and a
kerfluffle in the tree tops. The doves dive for
cover and right behind them a hawk zooms
through the branches of the pecan tree with a
wild look on his face. He seems to have lost the
ambush attempt but is enjoying the chase.
Staying in practice with those low level flying
skills and having fun with it. Poor doves get it
from below and above. There are other

predators.

Kybo the cat is an ardent and stealthy hunter of the order Carnivora and can grab doves out of the air with her lightening fast reflexes and needle sharp claws. She's descended from many generations of predators, and is perfectly suited to her niche.

She also maintains order in the household, makes sure everyone gets fed and that their are no issues in the tribe. Here is the current roster of cats at the nature pool (not counting strays or raccoons). Tee Tah, the black and white, Kybo's play buddy. They lick each other if she's in the mood, otherwise Tee Tah just hangs out under the tree, or in the leaves, or on top of my car, or on the foot stool inside. She knows how to find her spot and sleeps there for hours, meditates, whatever. I have never seen a more relaxed cat.

Miatti, the black cat, also lives here. She spent her kitten-hood on the street having been abandoned by her previous owners when they left town. She likes to be aloof and not let anybody smell her butt. She also bites. She likes to act snooty and above everybody else or atleast she used to until Kybo gave her an attitude adjustment one day — swatting her in the face with lightening fast paw punches. It only took a couple of sessions.

Now everybody is in harmony. Except me. I still struggle but I try to learn from the cats. How to sit still and witness the world. Maybe, if I'm quiet something will occur to me, maybe I'll notice something I never noticed before, maybe a hawk will come blasting through the over-story with a mad look on its face.

Spring

When the Spring rains arrive, the ground cover piles up like snow drifts against the fence and against the trees in the back yard. Cleavers and vetch and assorted flowering plants spread out and reach for the sky. A former embankment transforms itself into a maze of morning glories. The feathery green buds of the possum haw in the groovy nook alongside the fence bubble up out of their stems. Other trees take longer to wake up; the big pecan, the Spanish oaks, the willow, the hackberries wait patiently for their cue, wait for the grey wet skies to touch their roots and the warm weather to unfurl their flags.

Mosquitos appear, having somehow survived the winter weather. The turtles float to the surface and lounge on their pickerel weed porch. The fish announce their presence with tail splashes, the doves coo, the mocking bird sings, the waterfall falls into the water and Spring is in full bloom.

Over against the gray cedar fence, the false day flower blooms, her purple wings open wide, her anthers wave in the breeze, stigma ready to receive. And behind the bloom, that resembles the face of an elven princess or a woodland nymph or a meadow fairy — a single green leaf unfolds, circular at the base, and fits around the lady's face like a cowl.

By late afternoon she has lost her courage — the purple wings curl up and scrunch down around her shoulders. Her stamen and pistil still show but she looks startled or maybe spent. Maybe she got visited by the bees and got the seed and doesn't need to look pretty anymore.

Maybe they sprinkled fairy dust on her ovaries so now she drags her purple cape close around her and drops her purple curtain and lowers her purple flag of availability. *I don't need any more fairy dust and I have no more nectar to give.*

Food chain

Kybo, the ardent and stealthy hunter, exits the cat door. She has been inside on the bookshelf above the computer napping but now she seems to have a purpose in mind and probably not to smell flowers. She strides across the porch and off into the wild backyard.

The backyard holds a rich assortment of habitats for her to explore, from the falling down old fence over by the water tap where the anole lives, to the scrum pile where the loose brush and leaves are piled up and things burrow down and bury themselves, to over by the groovy nook (my shady grove) in the far corner next to the alley where shadows mix and mingle at twilight.

The main habitat and source of things to kill is the pool, either the frogs who come up out of it to feed or the doves who come down to it to drink. She has eaten a few frogs and I worry about the sustainability of the frog colony living in such close proximity to Kybo. One frog I discovered behind the TV — it was fine, just covered with dust. I helped it back into the pool and it swam away.

The fish live somewhere near the center of the food chain, protected by the water, but by no means immune to predation. The lesser green heron is fond of the minnows that swim at the surface and visits occasionally, the egret too but less often, Kybo rarely. The raccoons, though, they can get a fish anytime they want, a big one.

Adjoining and common to the pool, the jewel, the oasis, is the concrete skirting and the laid bricks that surround it and make up a proper border with the yard. It is around this circumference that Kybo sets up her patrol. It leads to the shallow bog filter where the doves come down to drink. They splash and preen and sip water and toss it over their backs with quick head ducks and this is where Kybo, the ardent and stealthy hunter, sneaks up from behind, under cover of the wall or the heavy grass and jumps on them with her terrible claws. It must be a moment for the cat, grabbing that soft fluttery bird with your claws fully extended, getting your jaws on it, tasting its blood. And for the dove certainly a moment, when struggle becomes futile and you just become still and let the cat eat you.

Fortunately, today, no doves are thirsty and no ambushes are set. I have deep sympathy for the murder victims, Kybo has none, doesn't have the circuitry. One time Kybo brought home a freshly slain anole, a small green lizard that lives around here, she laid it on the dining room floor and snarled like a wild tiger trying to get it to move but it couldn't. It had no more life.

Yes, the food chain is happening for sure. In the pool microscopic predators are eating microscopic prey. In the nicely trimmed front yards of the neighborhood, hawks are ambushing squirrels, dispatching them with a quick blow to the back of the neck with their sharp beak and carrying them off. Down by the river, raccoons are eating the baby ducks if they

can find the nest. Kybo eats anoles. So it goes.
From my perspective as a mid-sized animal who
buys his food at the grocery store and carries it
home in plastic bags, it seems really dangerous.

The deep end

From my back porch I can witness the willow
bending and behind it the hackberries moving
and above it the big pecan tree waving its leaves,
each branch and each leaf moving with its own
motion and yet moving all together, as if they
were part of a great conversation, inspired by the
wind.

The deep end of my backyard is surrounded by
hackberries, it's like a cove, and sometimes the
wind gusts and the branches dance wildly, as if a
great joke had been passed between them, and
then they settle back down again into a gentle
conversation with the blue sky as their witness.

There are infinite shades of blue in the sky, if
you really look, and the moving and shaking of
the green leaves is infinitely varied and the
breeze is infinitely nuanced, bursting and
swirling and dying down again. Intimations of
infinity is what nature is.

The way I was raised, nature was something to
look at, not necessarily something to appreciate,
certainly not something to interact with. It was
there but it really had no bearing on our lives
unless there was a storm or a tornado, then it
was something to be feared.

About the closest we ever came to interacting
with nature was our annual excursion out into
the countryside to see how the corn was doing.
Since both of my parents grew up on the farm,

they were well aware of the dictum 'knee high by the 4th of July'. That was considered a good omen and an acceptable level for field corn in southern Michigan. I also remember my mother's lone fashion advice — never wear green with blue.

I accepted it as some kind of an absolute as I did all else at that age — the plan of salvation, the one, two, threes and A B C's of public education, the heroic stories of Christopher Columbus discovering the New World, the taming of the American West. It was not until many years later that I questioned my mother's fashion advice. I noticed, in fact, that blue and green were everywhere, the trees against the sky as they are in my backyard right now, and how pleasant it is. I strayed from the path of my Baptist past. I discovered movies and marijuana and ecstatic disco dancing. I lost faith in the patriotic myths and blue and green became my favorite color combination.

The algae grows green and thick as fur around the edge of the pool. There are teeth marks where the fish have gnawed it off the tile. The water is a light dusky green from the free floating algae suspended in it. Algae, my friend, ubiquitous and persistent, resilient and helpful, cooperative. It aerates the water and feeds the fish, it transforms sunlight into carbohydrates, it's a first responder and the beginning of the food chain.

The backyard as theatre

Moto and Rocket, the yellow bellied slider and the red eared slider that I picked up from the turtle rescue lady out in Bulverde, are sitting on turtle island, a stack of concrete blocks I erected in the middle of the pool for their convenience. Both turtles are aligned with their heads held high, and in the direction of the back porch, the direction from which I appear, to bless and inspect the world. I am the great god, I suppose, who lives in the great house and causes Meow Mix to rain down from above.

The lesser green heron is hiding behind the pickerel weed, fishing for minnows. Her bill is sharp and stout as a rapier and just long enough. It's attached to her head, even with her eyes so she can strike whatever she's looking at and never lose sight. And she got one! A squiggly little guy from the shallows.

Kybo emerges from the kitty door to join me and the dove and the grackle, who had both been stealing cat food, fly away. She canters across the back porch and the heron flies up into the willow tree to digest its minnow.

It strikes me with some force — the theatrics of it. How, on this small stage so many different life forms come, act out their roles and exit. This little biosphere in my backyard containing two curious turtles, 10,000 fish, 10 million microbes, a lesser green heron, a small but terrible cat (a couple of more cats), raccoons under the house, doves and grackles (who come and go), blue jays, mocking birds, an occasional owl, maybe a hawk, possums, frogs, toads and squirrels — this nature pool, this gathering of life forms, this co-habitation zone, this biological matrix, this garden — contains so many expressions of life, so many competing and cooperating species.

Frogs in the pond

The bounteous watercress has died out and gone to seed. Let us now praise famous things. It's already re-sprouting. Its tiny green leaflets are lifting up out of the water towards the sunlight, its slender newborn blades are poking through the gravel.

Jewel blue dragonflies buzz over the pool, hovering above the hydrilla and landing on the tips of the purple flowered pickerel weed that populate the edge of the pond. They want to know if there is any nectar left. The hydrilla, floating on the surface, forms mats made of interlocking tendrils that spread out across the water. Two lily pads are attempting to push their way through the mat with their probing tendrils, trying to break through to the other side and sunlight.

Springtime also brings back the toads from their winter slumber buried beneath the earth in the groovy nook. They appear after the first heavy rain and when night comes begin their rhythmic chanting — as sincere as the medieval acolytes in the Chartres Cathedral singing to God and the angels 800 years ago.

They (the toads) devise a kind of harmonic convergence with their droning that creates resonant frequencies. It is in this convergence, I believe, that they acquired their power, or atleast their motivation to help Star Woman create the world and concurrently to perform the procreation ritual. That biological act will ensure that life continues in the nature pool. All the energy of their warty little amphibian bodies is focused on making that connection. Now they're feeling the attraction. Now they're mating, hooking up, jumping on top of each other. Not to assume what goes on inside a toad's head, but I can imagine it's pretty urgent.

I have spent some pleasant nights under the mosquito net in the backyard falling asleep to the pond music. If the frogs and toads happen to both be singing then the symphony usually starts off with a soliloquy from the frogs over in the bog filter and then the bass beat starts up from the toads over in the pickerel weed, providing a consistent rhythm section. As the frogs explore their riffs from their carefully chosen hiding spots close to the water, the toads call out as if in response.

It's not quite enough cover for the frogs, though, as it turns out. Kybo caught one the other day with her stealthy and ardent hunting skills and ate it. Must have been a taste sensation.

At the time I thought, 'Well the frogs will adapt to this somehow.' But the pattern continued. The frogs were seemingly unable to avoid the trepidations of Kybo. And Kybo, having noticed the spring time arrivals, was unable to resist her predatory instincts. They were fair prey being smaller than her and palatable. She was into frogs.

After about the third frog, I began to realize that they were in dire danger. They had to come out of the water to feed and Kybo was going to jump every last one of them. There were going to be no more frogs left in the pond at this rate.

So I had a talk with Kybo. It was heart to heart and I thought it went pretty well, but several days later there was another dead frog on the patio and I realized that she hadn't understood a thing I'd said.

Imagine being the last of your species on the planet and about to go extinct. You can't mate because there are no others to mate with. You can't have a conversation because you are the last one. You can't say good morning or good evening because you are the only one to hear it. I thought a lot about extinction and what that must feel like, being the last one of your kind and there you are.

And this is what happened to the frogs in the pond, they all did disappear and it was quiet. No more frog calls. The toads left too, I don't know why.

Summer

Several consecutive days of hot, dry weather have driven gentle fragrant Spring away and installed King Summer in her place — a more forceful and aggressive god.

In the summer the flowers die off and the green grass turns brown; it shrivels away hoping to retain some moisture in its roots and make it to a better day. The ground cracks and cakes, especially in the front yard where it gets full southern exposure. There it turns into a desert.

But sometimes, if we're fortunate, the precipitable moisture coming up from the gulf hits the cooler air moving in from the north and the summer sky billows up with rain clouds and there are thunderstorms, like the one brewing up in the sky this evening.

I imagine the birds and the willow both

waiting on this storm in their own way, sensing it in their own way and me, sitting here on the back porch with the weather radar on my phone, sensing it in my own way. The sun has fallen beneath the horizon and the sky turns a dark-grayish blue. It feels as if I were in the middle of a great forest. Nothing moves, nothing rustles, it's quiet. As the pressure drops, everything is attracted to the center. The thunder begins far off in the north and a gentle rain falls. Just for a few minutes. That's all.

The bugs come

The next day I notice that the small blue dragonflies have also returned to the nature pool. They crawled out of their aquatic nymph phase in the water and are now fully formed. They're darting around, hovering over the pickerel weed plumes, cavorting with the big red ones.

Let me tell you something about dragonflies. First of all their wings are made of extremely thin but rigid layers of translucent chitin (the same stuff that makes up the exoskeletons of insects) and has veins running through them which gives them strength and flexibility. They are attached to the flight muscles in such a way that they can change the shape of their wing and the angle of attack as desired. This bestows dragonflies with both speed and dexterity — they can hover, fly up or down, side to side, forward and backward. They can operate their two pairs of wings independently, the front pair counter-rotating with the back (hovering), or in tandem (super fast flight). They have extendible mandibles and grasping claws. They can catch other insects in flight, take them to their perch, tear their wings off and eat them head first. If dragonflies were the size of a human they would be the most fearsome predator on earth. They could eat small dogs and cats, grackles and pigeons, squirrels for sure. I appreciate their beauty and their flying skills and their ability to eat mosquitos. And the fact that they're small.

The mosquitos are definitely back. Mosquitos have a sensory organ that can detect trace amounts of CO2 from a person breathing 50 yards away. That probably explains why there is a steady supply of them. I have killed 5 but others man the breach even as their sisters lie fallen nearby. They have been bred by evolution's wisdom, to fly low and stay around the ankles, rarely coming up high enough for a clean shot. They are also sensitive to light changes as when an angry hand moves into position above them. I'm not angry anymore, just curious.

Will mosquitos go away if you tell them to? Someone proposed this idea in a recent conversation at the cafe. It's mid-afternoon in the groovy nook, just after two. I decide to do an experiment.

2:16 pm Zero mosquitos but I'm sure they're on their way — equipped with their highly sensitive carbon dioxide detectors.   Trees breathe out oxygen, humans breathe out carbon dioxide.

2:17:36 First arrival, I panicked and tried to kill her, missed.

2:18.05 Mosquito #2, I calmly instructed her with a fore finger gesture 'Hey You' and she flew off.

2:18.13 She came back. I killed her.

2:19 Mosquito #3, I have her blood on my hands, didn't know her name, where she was from, if she had any kids.

This may be a process for both of us. I understand that mosquitos want to suck my blood to make eggs for their babies and what i want is to not get my blood sucked. The classic dilemma, usually sorted out by the strongest and smartest. I guess that would be me.

But in our way of thinking (the humans), it's not the survival of the species, it's about the survival of one — me. For the mosquitos it's about the survival of the species. Whatever it takes to keep the gene pool alive, whatever it takes to keep making babies and so they risk their lives. They know they might die, apparently, judging by the speed with which they get airborne and out of the way before the descending hand obliterates them, yet they do it anyway.

The citronella candle seems to have worked better, it certainly wasn't my mosquito language skills.

Groovy nook

The willow tree overlooks the waterfall and leans out towards the hackberries. The hackberries come in from the other side with the possum haw along the fence line. It is a great green cathedral in here, what I call the groovy nook. Three small plastic pools have running water and tiny fish, a wrought iron bench; a floor made of randomly placed bricks and stones comprise the nave. The trees are fully leafed out: dense green, lighter green, grayish-green, sun speckled green, iridescent green, they all rise up into the sky, in a congregation of green leaves. They form a copse.

The branches of the trees are connected to the trunks and the trunks are firmly established in the earth. It's a symbol and a sign; it's a system. The ancient people believed that the tree of life stood at the center of the world and connected heaven above and earth below and that in between, in the shade of that tree and in the bounty of nature, the humans lived.

In the small ponds, the branches of the trees are reflected and the sunlight glowing through the translucent leaves dapples the ground. It's a grotto, with the healing fountain flowing, like Lourdes. It's an altar to the nature goddess, whatever her name might be: Ishtar or Venus or Gaia or Ninsar, Pachamama or Aphrodite or Asase Ya, the earth goddess of the Ashanti people who live in the big tree rain forest of central Africa.

The temple-like features of the groovy nook are not lost on me and I worship here, when I'm not killing mosquitos. When the citronella candle burns bright and there are no mosquitos, I look out upon the fish pond and its quiet light.

The raccoon comes to dinner

Evening returns and the raccoon appears, looking for dinner. He lives under the house and comes out for cat food. Tonight he seems nervous and quickly disappears back behind the couch that sits on the back porch. He prefers to dine alone, I so totally understand that. These days human interaction seems to be the exception, friends fall away and my reclusive persuasion takes over. It's powerful, but who is ever really alone? We have our thoughts, our intimations of God, our aspirations and all these critters that share the bio-habitat with us. We've got our microbiome, the little people inside us. You can talk to them.

I think everything is good. I think life and death and entropy are all ok and part of the alphabet, part of the environment, part of the universe. I think night has arrived. It's dark out here. In the shelter of the light cast by my porch lamp, I sit and listen. The wind is moving the trees around, against the background of the dark sky. The raccoon comes back, hungrier and bolder, and begins stealing nuggets from the cat bowl.

Summer monsoon

They say the tropical monsoons are moving further north; I can vouch for that. We've received 2/3 of our annual rainfall in the first 3 weeks of September. The groovy nook is flooded and can't dry out. The ground is so saturated and spongy that I hesitate to step on it in case I might sink in and destroy whatever is growing there.

In the front yard, delicate new life is coming up from the ground everywhere, a profusion of different plants. Some old friends like lantana and morning glories, some new ones that I haven't seen before — bastard cabbage and standing cypress. The bastard cabbage has bush-like branches that spread out and are tipped with yellow flowers. The standing cypress grows tree-like, straight up and strong; it has flowers flaring out all the way to the top. It's like springtime in fall.

Mushrooms are popping up out of old logs and assorted detritus, it's good to know they're here, that their tiny mycelium threads are alive and well underground.

Fungi, as you may know, is neither a plant nor an animal, it's fungi and it's responsible for breaking down dead stuff and creating new soil. Fungi can make new soil out of rocks which is what it did a billion years ago when it was one of the first living organisms to venture out of the water and onto the land. The truth is, fungi will make dirt out of us too, one day, if they get a chance. Fungi will make dirt out of everything it can, we're not special and dirt is the basis of the food chain on planet Earth, atleast for terrestrial animals. How awesome is that?

I'm not unhappy about having a monsoon season in San Antonio. From my view sitting outside on the back porch in the twilight watching the drizzle fall out of the sky, splish splash into the pool — everything looks good. I'm listening to it tip tapping on the roof. The world is wet and everybody is happy except for maybe the commuters driving home through the rain, sitting at the light inside their steel and glass cocoons, next to each other but cut off from each other and from the pleasures of nature. The raininess, the smells in the air and the capricious wind are all lost on them. Instead they're listening to the 6 o' clock news on the radio.

Rain and more rain has fallen, flooding the streets and nourishing the lawns and tonight, a miracle has taken place — the frogs have started to sing again. I thought they were extinct, gone forever, victims of Kybo's predation.   I had mourned their passing, but here they are, resurrected.

Three bass notes and a chirrup calls one, *chirrup chirrup* comes the response and the evening concert begins. The frogs, light of heart and nimble of voice, call back and forth to each other, *creeeek, clockaclacka, creeeek, chockalaka laka kalaka.*

Autumn

It's Fall, and the canopy of the pecan tree goes from green to yellow in two days, like it flipped a switch and the juices stop flowing and the leaves start dying and falling off.   I enjoy watching them fall. It's tragic but lovely. Just now I'm wondering about the leaf and how did it feel when it dropped?   Does it hold on with every bit of its energy to the branch or does it let go easily and accept the falling? And how does it feel now?   Does it feel accepted by Mother Earth who has gathered it to her breast, or does it feel rejected by the tree who let it go?

I'm anthropomorphizing, of course, but that's what we do, we're the humans. We want to know about everything in our terms. We have convinced ourselves of our own myths — that we are the crown of creation, that we are the king of the world, that God looks like us and thinks like us.

What a happy coincidence given all the

creatures that "He" created. But maybe "He" appears to each creature in their own image so they can recognize "Him". God anthropomorphizing humans. "Yes and I write books too and I get mad but it's righteous anger."

Two doves come down to drink, flutter down from the trees above and settle in the bog. Their grey and white costuming makes them appear somewhat angelic — their beautiful heads and their wings. They dip and sip from the shallow water and take off again on their angelic wings. They don't dare stay too long, Kybo shares the same grey and white coloration and leaps out from under the bushes to snatch them up. I don't suppose the Inca Doves enjoy that at all but maybe their sense of things is different, being not the crown of creation, being just one of the creatures and firmly ensconced in the food chain, neither on the top nor on the bottom.

Animals seem to possess an amazing amount of acceptance. No one is really trying to climb up the food chain, they just eat where they are. The squirrels eat acorns that the oak tree provides from above but also from above comes the hawk and eats them. So, is 'the above' good or bad for the squirrel? Not having eaten from the Tree of the Knowledge of Good and Evil, of course, they cannot answer this question but simply accept and eat and are eaten.

We have courts and lawyers and judges to determine what is good and what is bad and after 8,000 years of trying we still have not reached a verdict. Maybe our species with its high powered intellect is doomed to ask questions it can't answer. The questions it can answer we tend to ignore like 'why am I alive' and 'where did I come from' and of course 'where am I going next'. We're here because we are here and we came from nowhere and we are going to nowhere. I can say that with confidence because in human language the word 'where' indicates a place or a space or a condition that can be described. We didn't come nor are we going to any place that can be described. That's not just my opinion, it has been verified by all the people who have tried — thousands and millions of them, everyone, really, throughout the millennia. That we are here can be verified by looking in a mirror. Recognize that person? They have your face and your shape and your voice.

Curiously enough, gorillas do not recognize themselves in the mirror, chimpanzees sometimes, dolphins and elephants, I'm not sure, ravens — they'll try to steal the mirror and bring it to their mate as a gift. I wish someone would bring me a mirror as a gift, or maybe they have. Maybe every person I ever met was giving me a mirror to see myself in some new way that I had never seen before.

The season changes. Leaves carpet the ground. Acorns crunch underfoot. It's been a mast season with all the rain that fell earlier in the year. The universe spins on, stars explode and galaxies collide while elsewhere tiny organic organisms look "up", although there really is no up in the universe, and wonder why.

Chapter 16

Han and Hannah

It's night and the stars are out. Han is sitting next to a small fire he has built in his backyard. He's looking up at the night sky and thinking . . . *sparks are coming out of the fire and sparks in the sky . . .*

His feathers are scattered before him in the grass. He's binding them together with wires and threads into a talisman of some sort, a shield, or an art object.

Urban adventures are playing in his mind . . . *the city at night . . . flowing through the streets and the alleys and the parks and the parking lots of the downtown urban center . . .* He's narrating the memories as they pass by . . . *finding safety in the swiftness . . . of my steed . . . arriving at the destination . . . the plaza by the park . . . the church and the steeple . . . taking notice of the people . . . the weather . . . the vibe . . .*

He mulls this over . . . *looking for gratefulness . . . affinity . . . symmetry . . . .* The feathers, white and brown, gray and blue, sort themselves out as he works. He chooses them one by one and ties them around an arc of bamboo he cut from the alley and split into four pieces. Two pieces form the top arc and the bottom arc, the other two hold them apart or pull them in to form a circle. The feathers are arranged in such a way that they point inward towards a center or maybe a place of gathering.

Colder air has arrived and the small campfire is a comfort. He works with the feathers and seeks comfort. He goes to his bed under the pecan tree and seeks comfort.

Morning comes and the sun climbs high into the sky but but he's still lying on the futon beneath the pecan tree. Finally he throws off the blanket and emerges from his cocoon. It's almost noon.

. . . what am I supposed to do now . . . Each day seems like a huge block of unformed wood that he's supposed to carve into something . . . *ok, now what do I do . . .* Then the hammer drops and he's underwater again, lost, untethered, trying to get back to shore, back through the day so he can fall asleep again. Sweet oblivion.

His days have been like that. The brutal onslaught of the maverick brain chemicals triggered by the disastrous romance with Hannah has rendered him incomplete and inert.

Putzing around the camp is about all he can manage and that only in spurts. The rest of the time is deep thoughts and catatonia and despair and weeping. He hasn't ridden his bicycle. His project is abandoned. He hasn't picked up his guitar except for once when he tried to play something, tried to remember the shaman's tune.

. . . he played his flute whenever he felt distress . . . anxious . . . in need . . . he played the same

song . . . the same rhythm . . . . the same sequence . . .

He picks up the flute that Hannah gave him and tries to recreate the tune but the notes are all wrong.   He sits in his plastic patio chair and thinks. He looks around: his feathers, his stone collection and farther away his bike, his hammock, the pool, the trees, the sky. Nothing triggers a response in his mind, nothing means anything to him. Everything is nothing.

****

One day, in mid fall, after a cold front had just moved through and he could see his breath hanging in the air, after he had grown weary of crying, didn't have any more tears to cry; he got up from his cot, numb with the cold and with the despair of his darkened mind, and got up on his bike and rode out. No destination in mind.

When his legs got in rhythm, he could feel his cardiovascular system kick in and his speed increase without even trying. The blood flowing into his brain was 20% more oxygenated than it was a few minutes ago.   He balanced his breathing against the oxygen debt he felt growing in his chest. *. . . stay on the edge . . . pass that bus . . . damn cars in the road exhausting poison gas into the air we breathe . . . focus . . .*

He took the corner using the bike's centrifugal force to maintain his speed, careful not to spin out of control and crash, past the art museum with the sculpture made out of twisted I beams welded together *. . . looks like a collision . . .* Endorphins, released from their tether, sail off

287

across the synaptic gap to the nearest shore and the feeling that he is seeking slowly creep into his brain. Obliteration, pure awareness of breathing, only seeing and noticing, only listening, no thoughts. His body feels warm.

Click, click, down shift, he turns off into the park and brakes, follows the path and finds himself back at the spring. He drops his bike in the grass and sits down on the wooden bench. The splashing water is flowing like it always does. There is no one around. Leaves rustle in the trees above his head. One breaks loose and falls spinning to the ground. Han watches it and contemplates life. His contemplations have become a morass, a labyrinth, a dark place, but his mind is so habituated to think deep thoughts that he can't help going there. It's the bane of his existence, or atleast that was the last thought to enter his mind before he stood up and methodically took off all his clothes.

One deep breath and then another and he plunges into the pool. The water is cold but also peaceful, quiet. The only thing he can hear is the buzzing in his ears. He grabs hold of a rock and stays underwater as long as he can. A minnow swims by in front of his face and he watches it.

Finally he releases his hold and floats to the surface, his breath coming fast and deep. He's treading water and turning in a circle as if the world around him had just been created and he's seeing it for the first time.

"Aaaeeeyaaaaaah!" he screams with all his might and climbs out of the pool.

He's talking rapidly, as if there were an audience — an audience of trees and plants and water. "And this is where the ancient people lived. Oh yeah. They lived here, right here at this place." he informs them. "They made their stone tools and their arrowheads and they hunted deer and buffalo. They gathered pecans and caught fish."

He raises his hands as if imploring the congregation. "They found life in abundance. They knew how to live, they knew how to survive, man. They lived together in a tribe and they were all connected. Each one with one another." His voice is rising, filled with urgency. "They knew how to make things, whatever they needed. They felt the spirit of the trees and the animals and the water and everything around them. They knew how to heal each other."

A crazy smile emerges on his face. "They could fly." he says flinging his hands about. They could dance with the sunbeams."

An image of Hailey passes through his mind in that instant, floating up in the air among the sunbeams as it was in his dream and he's speaking as if to the whole world, to the sky and the trees, his voice choked with emotion and tears streaming down his wet face, "And they found their circle of life here and they saw their spirits of water here and they lived their life here."

He shakes off the water, dries his face with his shirt and looks at his phone camera as if he just understood something, grabs it and starts recording. "They lived in peace." he says into his phone, "those people lived here, right here next to the spring and they found their comfort in nature. They played music. They told stories. They could talk to the trees, they could talk to the birds, they could turn into a mountain lion or a raven. They knew . . . how to be alive."

He aims the camera at the water. "They knew how to make everything. They could heal each other! They were all connected! They were all connected!" he yells out to no one in particular. "Whoop whoop whoop whoop!"

He clambers into his clothes, still wet, gets on his bike and rides as fast as he can to Hannah's place, running through traffic lights, skimming through intersections, zooming down sidewalks, flowing like a ghost rider, using all his anarchist bike skills in celebration of his epiphany.

He rings her bell. She's home. Out of breath and disheveled, he's still damp but excited, when she cracks open her door. "I have to talk to you." he says.

"Are you stalking me?"

"No."

"I don't want to . . . talk to you . . . right now."

"Why not?"

"Because. I don't feel . . . that . . . "

"Feel what?"

"C'mon. Don't play games."

"I'm . . . not . . . playing . . . games. I want you to help me."

"How can I help you?" says Hannah.

"You can help me edit the movie. I want to finish it and show it in my backyard, have a party. I need your help."

She looks at him, "Edit the movie?"

"Yeah." He pauses, drops his arms, stops gesticulating, realizes he can't force her to agree, that he's powerless. The only power he has is desperation, he needs her to agree.

"It just needs some final editing." the words tumble out of his mouth before he can stop them. "We have to finish this. You can help me. We can work together."

****

The sun is riding low, the light is changing, the wind is rushing through the leaves in the small oak trees outside the front entrance of Hannah's apartment; she opens the door.

"Ok. C'mon in, let's look at this thing."

"Yes!" says Han with a big smile and goes inside.

"You're wet."

"I know."

"Here's a towel."

The editing process is composed of viewing the clips he has collected on his phone and laughing. Some of them are remarkably bad, out of focus or too shaky, easy to sort out. Some of them are marginally useful and noted. A few of them are both recognizable and informative.

"Oh yeah, that's when I was being crazy. Nuke that." Han.

"No let's save it." Hannah.

"Oh geez." says Han, "Here's the landscape shot from approaching the spring."

"Good one. I like how you shot through your spokes."

"Yeah, special effects." Han.

"Where is that street person at?"

"That's downtown."

"I'm not sure that's part of it."

"Oh yeah it is. That's part of the ambiance."

"Alright."

291

"What about this interview with Henry, remember that?"

"Oh that was good.   And Gentle Leaf." Hannah is smiling, "What's this?"

"Umh. I forgot. Oh yeah me riding my bike."

"Ha!   It looks like you're in a washing machine."   Hannah is laughing, "Ok we gotta keep that."

She looks at Han, for the first time really since he arrived, "Ok save all these clips, download them to your laptop and synch it up."

"With what?"

"With some music or something."

"Right, right."

"What's the smokey part about?"

"It's something you can't see."

"Oh that's good."

"Yeah I thought so too."

"Where's the one where you're talking to Hailey in the cafe, where's that?"

"Oh that's back on . . . let me find it."

Han scans through the videos on his phone, finds Hailey and Omar, selects it and watches. Hailey is cute as a button and talking like an adult not a 4 year old. Omar is fathering without interrupting.

"Umh, could we leave this one out?"

"Why?" says Hannah although she knows perfectly well why.

"Oh."   says Han looking in her face, "I'm sorry for everything."

"Keep it." says Hannah, "we need it."

Han selects all the apparently useful ones and prepares to put them in a cloud file. He works quickly with one finger and pushes send.

"I got it."

"Super cool."

"I will let you know. When the party will be." he looks at Hannah, he tries to relax and feel whatever it is he is feeling. "I will let you know."

"Ok."

His head is bowed, he holds the phone to his chest. He takes a deep breath. He leaves.

****

It's the Backyard Film Festival on a full moon night in October. Han is introducing the film to his gathered friends in the backyard.

"And people lived there for 15,000 years, right there where the spring is now, and all along the river" he says getting up to speed, "It was beautiful there, people, it was a Garden of Eden. Everything they needed was provided. And what did they know? All those generations growing up there, each child gathering some wisdom from the forest, from the animals, from the water and from the stories of the elders, and passing them on to their children and their children passing them on to their children. They had some awesome stories to tell, no doubt. There were animals all around. The habitat was the same for everyone. Humans weren't separate from nature. They knew all the animals. They could talk to the animals . . . So anyway that was the inspiration for doing this documentary and I hope you like it. Me and Hannah finished it just in time, so thanks. I hope you enjoy it."

Lights go down, the movie starts. The soundtrack is Han playing his guitar — the same melody that the shaman had been playing on his flute; he finally got it.

The movie is a strange mixture of random interviews, some with still shots, some moving, strange foggy scenes, scenes where you only see the trees passing overhead, shots of the spring, lot's of shots of the spring; everything is edited more or less randomly. Shots of Han at the spring preaching like John the Baptist. You see shots of him narrating the story. At these scenes his friends laugh and make fun of him because of his endearing sincerity.

The video ends, lights go on and everybody is clapping and yelling and hugging. There has been some beer drinking. In a chorus they acclaim Han and his outstanding contribution to modern cinema.

"Whoop! Whoop! Whoop!" Omar leads the cheers, Hailey jumps up and down.

Hannah stands nearby but apart. Chrissie is by her side. Han laughs, and moves in their direction. He's feeling the vibe.

"Cool party."

"Hi Han, Han." replies Hannah.

"We did it."

"You did it."

"Looks to me like you both did it." says Chrissie. She wears a hilarious expression on her face. Laughter pours out of all three of them until they finally stop, gasping for breath.

No one speaks for a moment although they are standing in close proximity to each other. It's as if they have completely forgotten who they are and for what purpose they have gathered there. Someone is playing a drum.

Finally Han breaks the spell and looks around at the gathering, at all his tribal mates gathered in the backyard.   "Wow." he says with understated conviction.

"We did it." said Hannah.

"Somebody did it." said Christine.   The laughter bursts forth anew as she composes her most curious facial expression yet.

"The scene with Hailey was inspired," says Omar who has moved into position next to them. "Storytelling with the rabbit."

Han hugs him, "Yeah mon, your kid."

"Han, Han, I like your party." says Hailey who has just appeared at his knee.

"Thank you Princess. It is a good party."

"I'm a princess?" says Hailey and runs off to rejoin her new friend that she has just discovered, another four year old playing in the grass underneath the big Pecan tree.

There is the sound of thunder far off in the northern sky.

"Ohhhh." say Han and Hannah and Christine and Omar in unison. Laughter arises anew. The campfire is going, the energy is flowing, the pow wow is rolling.   The drumbeat grows stronger, emanating from someone dressed like an ancient shaman, sitting close to the fire.

Bibliography

Chapter One City

Andrews, Anthony P. *First Cities.* Norton & Company, 1995
Kotkin, Joel. *The City: A Global History.* Modern Library Chronicles, 2005
Graeber, David. Wengrow, David, *The Dawn of Everything.* Farrar, Straus and Giroux, 2021

Chapter Three The Little People

Thomas, Lewis. *The Lives of a Cell: Notes of a Biology Watcher.* Viking Press, 1974
Enders, Giulia, *Gut. The Inside Story of Our Body's Most Underrated Organ.* Greystone, 2015
Gershon M. D. Michael D. *The Second Brain: A Groundbreaking New Understanding of Nervous Disorders of the Stomach and Intestine.* Harper Perennial, 1999
Mayer M. D. Emeran. *The Mind-Gut Connection, How the Hidden Conversation Within Our Bodies Impacts Our Mood, Our Choices, and Our Overall Health,* Harper Wave. 2016
Blaser M. D. Martin J. *Missing Microbes, How the Overuse of Antibiotics is Fueling Our Modern Plagues.* Picador, 2014
Rosenberg, Stanley. *Accessing the Healing*

Power of the Vagus Nerve: Self-Help Exercises for Anxiety, Depression, Trauma, and Autism. North Atlantic Books, 2017)

Chapter Five Symbiosis

Margulis, Lynn. *Symbiotic Planet.* Basic Books, 1998

Falkowski, Paul G. *Life's Engines, How Microbes Made Earth Habitable.* Princeton University Press, 2015

Musser, George. *Spooky Action at a Distance, The Phenomenon that Reimagines Space and Time — and What it Means for Black Holes, the Big Bang, and Theories of Everything.* Scientific American, 2015

Wholleben, Peter. *The Hidden Life of Trees: What They Feel, How They Communicate—Discoveries from A Secret World.* Greystone Books, 2016

Greene, Brian. *The Elegant Universe, Superstrings, Hidden Dimensions, and the Quest for the Ultimate Theory.* W.W. Norton and Company, 2003

Bohm, David. *Wholeness and the Implicate Order.* Routledge Classics, 1980

Kauffman, Stuart A. *Reinventing the Sacred, a New Vision of Science, Reason and Religion.* Basic Books, 2010

Odenwald, Sten. *Cosmology, Everything You Need to Know to Master the Subject — in One Book!* Arcturus, 2019

Gould, Roy R. *Universe in Creation, a New Understanding of theBig Bang and the Emergence of Life.* Harvard University Press, 2018

Krauss, Lawrence M. *A Universe From Nothing, Why There is Something Rather Than Nothing.* Simon & Schuster 2012

Benson, Michael. *Far Out, A Space-Time Chronicle.* Harry N. Abrams, 2009

Hands, John. *Cosmosapiens, Human Evolution from the Origin of the Universe.* Harry N. Abrams, 2017

Osserman, Robert. *Poetry of the Universe, A Mathematical Exploration the Cosmos.* Anchor, 1996

Leeming, David. *A Dictionary of Creation Myths.* Oxford University Press, 1996

Galeano, Eduardo. *Genesis, Memory of Fire.* W.W. Norton and Company, 1985

Chapter Seven Communicating with the Gods

Harari, Yuval Noah. *Sapiens, A Brief History of Mankind.* Harper Collins, 2015

Von Petzinger, Genevieve. *The First Signs, Unlocking the Mysteries of the World's Oldest Symbols.* Atria Books, 2016

Erickson, Jon. *A History of Life on Earth, Understanding Our Planet's Past.* Facts On File, Incorporated, 1995

Pfieffer, John E. *The Creative Explosion, an Inquiry into the Origins of Art and Religion.* Harper & Row, 1982

Leeming, David. *A Dictionary of Creation Myths.* Oxford University Press, 1996

Campbell, Joseph. *Primitive Mythology, the Masks of God.* Penguin Books, 1976

Campbell, Joseph. *The Hero with a Thousand Faces.* Princeton University Press, 1949

Pollard, Elizabeth. *Worlds Together Worlds*

Apart Vol. One Beginnings Through the 15th Century. W. W. Norton and Company, 2015

Stokes, William Lee. *Essentials of Earth History, An Introduction to Historical Geology, 3rd Edition.* Prentice Hall, 1973

Garlake, Peter. *Early Art and Architecture of Africa.* Oxford University Press, 2002

James, E. O. *Prehistoric Religion.* Barnes and Noble, Inc. 1957

Meredith, Martin. *Born in Africa, The Quest for the Origins of Human Life.* Simon & Schuster, 2011

Haviland, William A. *Anthropology, The Human Challenge,* 14th Edition. Wadsworth, 2014

Chapter Nine   The Ancient Book of Magic Secrets

Boyd, Carolyn E. *The White Shaman Mural, An Enduring Creation Narrative in the Rock Art of the Lower Pecos.* University of Texas Press, 2016

Shafer, Harry J. *Ancient Texans, Rock Art & Lifeways Along the Lower Pecos.* Texas Monthly Press, 1986

Zintgraff, Jim. *Pecos River Rock Art, A Photographic Essay.* Sandy McPherson Publishing Company, 1991

Kirkland, Forrest. *The Rock Art of Texas Indians.* University of Texas Press, 1967

Macrae, James Burr Harrison. *Pecos River Style Rock Art, A Prehistoric Iconography.* Texas A&M University Press, 2018

Coe, Michael D. *Mexico, From the Olmecs to the Aztecs.* Thames & Hudson, 1994

Chapter Eleven Gilgamesh

Mitchell, Stephen. *Gilgamesh, A New English Version.* Free Press, 2004
Gardner, John. *Gilgamesh.* Knopf, 1984
George, Andrew. *The Epic of Gilgamesh.* Penguin Classics, 2003
Bryson, Bernarda. *Gilgamesh; Man's First Story.* Holt, Rinehart & Winston, 1967
Damrosch, David. *The Buried Book: The Loss and Rediscovery of the Great Epic of Gilgamesh.* Henry Holt and Co. 2007